The Lost World

Of the

Wends

Lee-Anne Marie Kling

With thanks to the members of the Flinders U3A Writers' Groups: Thursday—Glenys, Audrey, Denise, Elfie, Joyce, Joy, Heinz, Ted and Rosemarie. And Wednesday—Alison, Anneke, Jim, Heather, and Sue.

And a special thanks to my mother, Marie for her many hours listening to the stories I read to her.

Wends Lost
Eastern Europe, 1848

The Prussian War raged, and a village of Wends, left their homeland, with plans to set sail for Australia. From the Eastern edge of Prussia, they journeyed by river on a barge destined for Hamburg's port, where they hoped to catch a cheap fare in the cargo-hold of a ship destined for the Promised Great South Land.

These villagers never made their Australian destination. No one ever noticed, nor missed them. The neighbouring villagers assumed they had arrived in the Great Southern Land, and considered them so far away, and too distant to maintain contact. In Adelaide, also, the city for which they headed, the inhabitants were blissfully unaware of their existence. Migrating Prussians had taken their place in the over-flowing cargo-hold and were sailing across the Indian Ocean to Australia.

On this barge, headed by a man, Boris Roach, the Wends sang hymns of praise to God for their liberation from religious persecution, and the war. They looked to the promise of prosperity and freedom to worship their heavenly Father according to the Word of God. Their hope that their children and their descendants may thrive in their faith in the Promised Land of South Australia.

Lost in the Desert

Central Australia, July 2016

For once in her life, Amie abandoned her iPad and peered around the Land Cruiser door. The Mission stirred up in a frenzy of people, milling, gawking, and pacing across the red sand. She raced through the metal gate and noted a television crew focused on a small huddle by the church in the historic village. She paused and stared. In the middle of the flurry, a pale woman shook. Her hair was tousled like a bird's nest. A man with greying hair, draped his arm around her shoulder. He also was shaking. She recognised them as "neighbours" from the caravan park in Alice Springs.

'Dad, what's going on?'

'Come along, inside. This is nothing to do with us.' Dad barged through the gate and guided Amie to the house.

A helicopter hammered above them. Amie could see Dad's mouth move but did not hear the words. 'Pardon? What did you say?'

Dad's face turned crimson, he opened and shut his mouth through his black beard and waved his arms around.

'What? I can't hear you!'

As the helicopter noise faded into the distance, Dad snapped, 'Where's Adam?'

'Adam? Adam?' Amie jumped up and ran through the house opening every door. Her search unsuccessful, she returned to the living room. 'I thought he came in. Where is he?'

'No, he didn't come in.'

'He *was* in the Land Cruiser.' Amie became worried. 'We didn't leave him in Alice Springs, did we?'

Dad pushed aside a tattered curtain and looked through the dust in the window. 'No, I don't think so. We would've noticed if Adam wasn't there.' Sirens wailed. A megaphone blaring with distorted words echoed over the compound. 'Mmm! Typical Adam! It's just like at Uluru. He's lost again!'

'Shall I go out and see if he's out there?'

'No, it's alright. You don't want to get caught up in all that. I'm sure Adam'll be alright. He'll come in when he's ready.' Dad tapped the keys in his pocket.

Pots and pans clattered in the kitchen signaling the presence of their host and family friend, Walter Wenke. He sang out, 'Dinner's ready in half an hour. Don't mind the excitement—just another lost tourist.' Plastic rustled as the balding Walter ferreted for food. 'Tourists! Can't trust 'em! Well, at least it's some excitement for the locals. We've had half a dozen offers to track already.'

Amie slipped outside and into the fray. On the edge of the crowd, she detected Adam's bleached mop of hair glowing in contrast to the charcoal faces.

As she approached the majestic red gum tree where Adam was, an Indigenous man appeared out of the dusk. He muttered to Adam. The man's fingers stroked the beard on his chin. Adam mimicked him stroking his own imaginary stubble.

'They want me to go tracking for the lost fella. Must be careful. There's a bad spirit out there. An evil spirit. He kills people. Or takes people away. I don't wanna go to faraway spirit land. I wanna stay here.' The man had a slight German accent, which surprised Amie.

The whites of the man's eyes gleamed reflecting the halo of Adam's hair. Spotlights shone on a policeman taking notes and nodding while the couple shook their heads. Amie hugged her bare arms. The sun crept below the clear horizon. The cold began to seep in. Goosebumps made her skin feel rough as she rubbed her forearms. She stamped her feet, sifting the cool sand between her thongs and toes.

'Hey, Adam, what's going on?'

'You know that boy you were friendly with at the caravan park back in Alice—' Adam smirked and stifled a giggle, 'he's got himself lost in the desert. Stupid tourists, they have no idea.'

'You mean Joseph?' Amie's heart pounded. 'He's just a friend. Anyway, it's no laughing matter.' She'd first noticed Joseph at Emily Gap when his old man was harassing him to get out of the motor home and Joseph refused. They then got in an argument about his dreadlocks and how embarrassing he was to the family. Amie had thought then, Joseph's father just made the situation worse by criticizing his son's hair style. Then to her amazement, Joseph and his family's motor home was next to theirs at the caravan park.

'Evil spirit got him. They won't find him. D' boy's not here.' The man waved a hand past his curls. Kamikaze beetles darted at the blonde highlights in the man's hair and bounced off.

Adam sniggered.

Amie slapped her younger brother. 'Told you, inappropriate. What's wrong with you?'

'Amie's in love,' Adam said in a sing-song voice while rubbing the welt on his cheek.

'Shut up!' Amie snapped. 'Dad's looking for you. Let's go!'

Adam waved to his new-found friend and followed Amie to the house. 'Maybe that lost guy Joseph could eat bugs if he's hungry.'

'Stop it, Adam Fleischer.'

Inside Dad was deep in conversation with his teacher friend, Walter. Walter Wenke had joined the education department in his forties after the Global Financial Crisis in 2008 had blown apart his career as a physicist. He hoped to join the Fleischer family as they journeyed out "West".

Walter and Dad had come to an agreement; Walter supplied the accommodation at the Mission, and Dad would supply the means of travel way out west to his favourite mountain and spring in that area. Amie and Adam's Dad, Arthur, had taught in the Mission many years ago, and the Indigenous owners of the land treated him like family. Before all this chaos with the lost tourist, Arthur Fleischer had arranged guides for the family in exchange for a few favours.

The aroma of roast chicken wafted through the pastel-green kitchen and over the polished pine table. Walter and Dad discussed the excitement gripping the small town.

'Lost. The boy is lost, out there on the way out West,' Walter said.

'How did they get out there?' Dad asked. 'I thought you need a permit.'

'Yeah, well, they're scientists. Mr. Smith is a geologist and commissioned to survey the unusual rock formations in the area out West, and some minerals found there. His wife's a botanist. She's interested in the rare plants found in the area.'

Amie interrupted. 'What about their son?'

'He wandered off while his parents were busy and got lost.'

'You can say that again,' her father said and then wagged a finger at her. 'Now, Amie, don't you go off and get lost.'

Amie glanced up at the ceiling. 'I won't. Anyway, that's the sort of thing Adam does.'

Adam squealed. 'I don't!'

'And now we're going to have trouble getting a guide. They'll be all busy looking for the boy and there'll be no one left for us,' Dad muttered.

'Oh, no! What a pity. I was really looking forward to going out there. Well, no use fretting. Let's talk about something different.' Walter turned to Adam. 'Have you heard of the Wends, Adam?'

Amie rolled her eyes. *Here we go, Walter's other great passion, family history.*

Adam looked up from his mobile phone with which he'd been discreetly playing under the table. Amie gave Adam a knowing smile and murmured, 'Here we go.' The siblings mused how the resident family historian Walter would do it this time—especially since he'd been out of circulation in this remote part of the world for six months. Still, by the size of the satellite dish on top of his home, Walter had internet.

The chair creaked. Dad rose and paced toward the oven. 'I'll just check how the chicken's going.'

'Bet the boy was taken by evil spirits,' Adam said, 'that's what Nathan told me.'

'Who?' Dad wrestled with the roast tray between the floral mittens he was wearing and an oven door that insisted to snap shut on his arm.

'He's my new friend. Nathan told me there's a ghost hanging around the old town, a boy about twelve.'

'Ah, little boy lost!' Walter launched into his dissertation. 'It reminds me of this Wend village. They were heading for Australia and vanished off the face of the earth.'

The Fleischer family exchanged glances, as Walter prattled on. Tonight, they would have Wend for dinner and dream of lost Wends before heading out West. *Better than quantum physics,* Amie thought. She liked a bit of history. And if they couldn't get a guide, she wouldn't mind a few Wend tales as they sat around the house or wandered the dirt roads around town. *Although some Dreamtime stories or tales of the pioneer missionaries would be nice for variety.* Truth be known, Amie was not keen on "roughin' it" way out West. After all, already she had to endure virtual starvation at Kings Canyon because the meat in the cool box went off. *Trust Dad!*

'Perhaps we might find the lost lad,' Dad said. 'We could offer to go out West and help search.'

Amie poured lime cordial into her glass. 'Who knows, we might even find some Wends, Walter.'

Mr. Wenke tightened his lips. 'I don't think so.' He then stood up, emptied the scraps into the rubbish bag. 'I'll take these for the compost,' he said, and left the kitchen. The laundry door banged. It banged again as Walter returned; his mission to save the earth, accomplished.

Amie and Adam took a stroll while their elders discussed physics, wormholes, and of course Wends. Outside the bright lights from the film crew were being dismantled and the crowd of drama-hungry onlookers had disbanded. The search teams had been dispatched, leaving the expanse beyond the cyclone fence dark and still. Joseph's parents stood trembling by the crumbling wall of the cemetery. Careful not to invade their not-so-private trauma, Amie and Adam crossed the road and continued their walk of the town.

Ghosts in the Precinct

Still, in The Mission, Central Australia, July 2016

Brumbies grazed amongst the gum trees beside the dry riverbed. Amie wanted a closer look at the horses. Walter had informed them that the locals bought the horses from a ranch near Alice Springs. They used the horses for racing. But mostly the horses roamed wild and free around the township.

A mangy creature, half-dingo half-greyhound, trotted beside them. The dog glanced at the brother and sister from time to time, his eyes protruding from bony eye-sockets.

'He wants something to eat,' Adam said.

'I guess that's why he's following us. You can see his rib-cage.'

'Poor thing.'

They walked on. The road seemed to take them on a lap of the outback town. They passed an unused gym with the equipment all rusty, a school with a state-of-the-art playground, and an empty arena of a basketball stadium.

'It's so quiet,' Amie whispered. 'Where is everyone?'

'Dunno.' Adam shrugged. 'Guess they're at home recovering from all the excitement. Not every day someone goes missing.'

'I overheard the policeman say a busload of German tourists got lost.'

'No, really?'

Amie chuckled. 'Imagine being stuck on a bus with a busload of German tourists.'

'Dad's worst nightmare.'

'No one to laugh at his lame jokes.'

'Yeah.'

Both sniggered as they turned another corner. The cemetery lay to their right, and to their left the Historic Precinct.

Amie stopped laughing. 'Funny how it is we have a boy lost in the desert, and Germans in a bus gone missing.'

'Maybe they've been abducted by aliens who have a fetish for boys and Europeans,' Adam said.

'Then, why didn't they take Walter Wenke?'

'Don't be silly, he may have a German name, but he's as Australian as you 'n me,' Adam puffed. 'If there's one thing I've learnt from Walter's long-winded historical lectures, it's that our ancestors emigrated from eastern Europe generations ago, in the mid-Nineteenth Century, to escape religious persecution. So, they have lived in Australia for over one hundred and fifty years, so I reckon that makes us Australian. Doesn't it?'

Amie gazed at the unsealed road of this town which she thought needed some "tender loving care" and remarked, 'Not as Australian as the original owners.'

'S'pose not.' Adam caught Amie's elbow and steered her away from the cemetery. 'So, Amie, do you reckon ghosts exist?'

Amie watched the dog disappear into the Precinct. 'Don't be stupid, of course not.'

'Nathan, you know the "Indig" guy I was talking to, he reckoned he'd seen one in the Precinct.'

'Sure.'

'Reckoned it hung around the morgue.'

'Really? That's creepy.'

'Hey, why don't we have a look.'

'Nah, I'm tired.' A knot had congealed in Amie's stomach as she thought about Joseph. Such a brief encounter. Yet she knew him. The reality of him lost in the wilderness was sinking in. She hoped he was alright. Tall, athletic form and blonde. Poor guy, his parents hovered over him—helicopter parents—making sure he was safe and didn't do anything that would corrupt him. And he was seventeen! How did he manage to escape their watchful gaze? God! He complained to her he'd never even had a mobile phone. What kind of parents were they? Perhaps he ran away from them.

Adam scampered over to the Precinct gate. 'Come on, Amie.'

'You can't go in there.'

'Why? Who's going to stop us?'

'The ghost,' Amie joked.

'Come on, there's nothing else to do around here since Dad took our laptops and mobile phones.'

'He wouldn't have if you hadn't been so annoying, Adam.' Amie stomped after him. She didn't want her brother getting lost again—not after the sand hills near Uluru—even if he annoyed the hell out of her.

'You started it.'

'Me?' Amie raised her voice. 'You're the one who makes all those demented noises when you played *Mario Kart* on the drive here.'

'I'm allowed to.'

'You were ruining my movie.'

Adam leant on the gate and faced her. 'And if Dad knew you were watching "Seriously Cracked-up" ...'

'Nothing wrong with that—although I think he would have a definite issue with your download, *illegal download*, of "Killer Kings".

'But...but...it's historical fantasy—War of the Roses—even Walter Wenke would like that.' Adam coughed. 'From a German, or should I say, Slavic perspective.'

Amie folded her arms across her barely discernible breasts. 'You're fifteen—not appropriate viewing for you Adam.'

'But—I like the dwarf...'

'Anyway, it's—you shouldn't—and if you go in there,' she pointed over the gate swinging free in the breeze, 'you could get into serious trouble.'

'Why not?' Adam pushed the gate. 'I'm game if you are.' He ran towards the historic church.

Amie hissed. 'Get back here!'

Adam shouted. 'But I want to see the ghost.' His small frame blurred in the darkness.

'You're trespassing.'

Amie bolted past the open gate. She was trespassing too, now. She chased Adam's retreating figure. 'There's no such thing as ghosts.'

She heard footsteps near the whitewashed walls of the church. She followed the footsteps and the yellow hair that shimmered in the moonless night. 'Adam, this is not funny. Come back now!'

No answer.

Footsteps crunched on the gravel. 'This is not a joke, Adam. Where are you?'

A cold rush of air barged past her. Hairs pricked up on the back of Amie's neck.

'Adam?' Amie called. She traced her fingertips along the rough wall of the church as she worked her way to the rear. 'Adam? Where are you?'

She thought she saw him by the little building behind the church. Was that construction a toilet block? Or did she hear someone, Walter perhaps. Was that building the morgue?

The pale stick figure drifted towards that little building and vanished into it.

The wind howled.

'Adam! Get out of there!'

Amie quickened her steps towards the building.

'Boo!'

Adam appeared in front of her. Amie screamed.

Adam laughed. 'Got you!'

Amie grabbed her brother by the arms and shook him. 'You idiot!'

Adam kept laughing. 'You should've seen your face. Like you'd seen a ghost.'

A low moan. Amie clutched Adam and stared at him. Her brother's eyes widened.

'What's that?' Adam asked, his voice cracking.

Another moan, longer, more agitated.

'It's the wind,' Amie replied. 'I hope.'

'It sounds human.'

A high-pitched wail. Amie and Adam froze.

'No, it doesn't,' Amie breathed.

Adam twisted his neck to look at the morgue. 'C-could b-be—'

A long low moan.

'It's coming from the morgue,' Adam said.

'Run!'

Adrenalin coursed through Amie. She galloped towards the gate. She pulled Adam behind her. In their frenzy the gate eluded them.

'Where is it?' Amie panicked.

'Jump the fence,' Adam said. He glanced behind and hesitated.

'Come on!' Amie yanked his arm.

They flew over the barrier, raced like the brumbies (wild horses) to Walter's house, and bolted through the door.

Their father and his friend reclined on their respective rockers in the lounge room sipping fortified tawny out of mini souvenir tin cups.

'What's the matter with you?' Dad asked.

Walter bared his wine-stained teeth in a sneer. 'You look like you've seen a ghost.'

'Nothing,' Adam panted. 'Just racing.'

Mr. Wenke raised a hairy eyebrow. 'Really?'

Amie did not like the leering expression he gave her. She nudged Adam. 'Yeah, actually, we've been taking a tour of the town.'

'Oh, I see,' Walter said. 'I hope you haven't been anywhere you shouldn't have gone.'

'No,' Amie replied. She ushered Adam out of view and into the kitchen. 'Walter's creeping me out.' To the men, she called out, 'We're going to bed. Good night.'

Dad called back, 'Good idea, early start tomorrow. We're going way out West.'

'And I'll be joining you,' Walter Wenke added.

Amie shuddered.

Adam thumped the wall softly. 'Great! Physics and history lesson! Just what I needed.'

'Thought you liked history.'

'Not the kind that Mister Wenke teaches.'

Amie gave Adam a hug. 'I'm with you there, brother.' She pecked him on the cheek. 'Good night, sleep tight and don't let the bed bugs bite.' Then she trotted to her designated bedroom at the end of the hallway.

'Or anyone else for that matter,' Adam muttered as he glanced at the lounge room. He then wiped his cheek as he entered the bathroom to brush his teeth and have a shower. He had touched something slimy on the door of the morgue and his fingers stank like fresh blood.

Potato Wars

World of the Wends, Luthertal—the Other Side of the Galaxy

Jane suspended her potato peeling and looked out the window to the dam. Alpine mountains cast shadows over the valley where the men were digging up potatoes. One minute she remembered singing hymns on a barge floating down the Elbe, the next, they were in ready-made community houses and she was peeling potatoes for the midday dinner. Jane frowned as she tore slivers of skin off the potato. She peered through the hoary window, into the dazzling light, searching. Herr Boris Roach had assured them they had reached the Promised Land—Australia. Now that they were here, settled, and with questions…he turned cruel; more like the rulers they'd fled than the friendly man he'd been. Questions? Herr Boris Roach forbade questions.

Jane yawned, then sighed and began chopping. Her vision blurred, and the knife shaved the top of her thumb. She put the injured digit to her mouth and paused. She checked her thumb. Ah—no blood. With a bread and butter knife, Jane slathered the potato quarters with butter. She stopped. Studying the empty path winding down from the mountain, she pulled at her fringe. Stray wisps escaped from her scalp and she watched them fall through her fingers. One hair laced itself over the tray and onto a greasy quarter demanding to be roasted. She extracted it and placed the tray in the wood oven.

Lunchtime and the men returned from farming to gather in the communal dining hall. Hans, Jane's husband and village bürgermeister (mayor) gave God thanks and sat down to the roast beef and vegetables.

Jane looked directly at him. 'Hans, what is going on?'

'What do you mean?' Hans spoke through a mouthful of meat.

'All this! It just doesn't make sense.'

'Looks normal to me.'

'But it's not right.'

'You should be grateful for the land God has given us.'

'Papa, the sky's so purple,' Friedrich, their son of twelve, said. He rubbed his nose and gazed out the window at the end of the rough timber table.

Hans leaned forward and peered out the window. 'Purple? It looks blue to me.' He sat back down on the bench. 'Anyway, this is Australia, there's bound to be a few differences.'

'But it's so hot!' Wilma, his five-year-old daughter fanned herself with the prayer book.

'I don't understand, dear. They never said it would be so hot.' Jane hid her mouth from the fellow diners. 'I've had to dispense with all the petticoats, or I'd faint from the heat.'

Hans threw back his melon-shaped head in mock horror. 'Oh, dear! That is terrible! What would people think?'

'Mama!' Wilma screamed. 'There's a cockroach in my prayer book!'

Jane Biar flicked the bug out of her daughter's book and continued her conversation. 'Speaking of people, where are the others? I mean, not us, but the settlers? The people from England? And the Indians? I'm sure the promoters that came to our village said there were a few Indians about.'

'We are pioneers, dear. Don't you remember what Herr Roach told us?'

'No.'

'Oh, well, what more can I say.'

'Papa, I've finished. Can I excuse the table?' Their daughter pushed the bench and eased herself from the table.

Papa pointed at the plate. 'No, Wilma, you sit there till those carrots and potatoes are all eaten. You want to grow big and strong.'

'Eat up. How will you sleep tonight if you don't eat all your food? Remember last night?' Jane said, then gathered the knives and forks together.

'I hate vegetables!' Wilma said. 'And I hate this country. Anyway, the goblins and ogres were real! And I really did see the world from far above the sky where it's all black.'

'Wilma, you talk a lot of nonsense!' Jane whisked the plates into a pile, scraping the bones onto the top plate. She dusted the crumbs into her palm and turned to her husband. 'So, here we are. In the middle of nowhere. And Herr Roach? Where's he? What are we supposed to do?'

'Why don't we hike up the mountains and explore them.' Friedrich jumped up from the dinner table. 'This is boring, I want adventure.'

One look from Papa and he sat down.

'It's so hot, I want to swim in the lake.' Wilma pushed the plate of vegetables away. 'I don't want my vegetables. I'm all full up.'

'Wilma, eat your food! There's a good girl.' Jane rubbed her calloused knuckles on her pinafore. 'You don't want to end up like the girl who did not eat her soup. You already look too skinny and fading away. I worry about you, Wilma.'

'We could hike to the mountains, have a swim in the lake on the way, and Wilma could have her vegetables for the picnic at the top,' Friedrich said.

Hans motioned him to sit down. 'This is not the time to be thinking of picnics on top of mountains. God has given us more important work to do.' He stood and drew in breath. 'We will do what the Lord has asked us to do, now that we are on the outermost parts of the Earth.'

Everyone in the hall turned to listen to Hans. 'We will find the natives in this land and we will preach to them.'

Cheers and "Amen" rose from the four corners of the refectory. But one lonely voice said, 'And we will clean up all the cockroaches.'

'Thank you Dr. Zwar," another man said, 'but, remember also the cockroaches, they're ruining my bread baking.'

Just what the baker would say, thought Jane.

'All we need is borax,' Dr. Zwar said.

'Then, the cockroaches will all crawl away und die,' the baker replied while twirling his drooping moustache.

'You, Zwar can deal with the cockroaches and save mens' bodies while I help you save souls,' Hans said. While the men in the room laughed, he nodded and bowed, then leaned over his daughter. 'Eat up, Wilma. You are not leaving the table until the plate is empty.'

Wilma pouted and poked at her roast potato. 'I bet the natives don't have to eat all their vegetables.'

With her head propped up by the palm of her hand, Jane kept vigil over Wilma's eating. She sighed. 'Eat up Wilma, or you will be having roast potato, peas, carrots for breakfast, you will.'

'But mama! I don't like vegetables; the cockroaches have been on them.'

Frau Biar poked through her daughter's carrots and peas. 'I don't see any cockroaches.'

Wilma frowned. 'They're not on them now.'

'So, you can eat them up, then,' Jane said, 'or no pudding this evening for you, and you *will* have vegetables for breakfast.

The Tainted Potatoes

Way Out West of The Mission, Central Australia

Amie sulked. Perched in a cave, and hungry, she struggled to see through her tears of want. At lunchtime, she wanted a biscuit, but "Father", she called Dad that when he made these unreasonable Wendish rules, had said "no". "Father" had banished bush biscuits to rations as if the Fleisher Central Australian safari were suffering a food crisis. Amie picked up a couple of stray white flakes. She flicked the flakes over the cliff and watched them waft into the canyon. This little mountain she'd climbed had this depressed land in the middle. Much like a cake that's flopped, she thought.

One flake stuck to her finger. Amie pointed her tongue at it and lifted it into her mouth. She savoured the taste—a hint of sweetness—like the paper around a desert nougat. *Bush tucker!*

Her Dad and Walter's wish had been granted. *Pity!* The community, desperate to find the lost young man, Joseph, accepted Dad's offer to help in the search. So, in the company of several indigenous trackers, the Fleischer family plus Walter Wenke, set out for the wilderness, way out west of The Mission.

The night before when they had arrived at The Spring, her Dad discovered petrol had leaked from the jerry can and the fumes had seeped into the potato sack. It had been a rough ride on an invisible track that only the Indigenous (or "Indig" as the locals called them) guides could trace. No spud was spared, and worse was that during the commotion in The Mission, the dogs had raided the supply of roast beef from the tucker box. Amie was sure she knew which dog; the mangy one that followed her and Adam around.

Their father persisted in baking the potatoes for their dinner that night, and then being Sunday, he preached a sermon on gratitude and he expected his flock to eat the food put before them. One by one the potatoes disappeared from the plates. However, they did not enter into his *lambs'* mouths. Adam, her brother, dumped his behind a spinifex bush. Amie hid hers under the kangaroo skin blanket. She suspected Dad's friend, Walter passed his to Nathan, one of the guides. Nathan, Adam's new friend, tossed the potato to Adam. Then, while Father had his back turned, Adam acted his age of fifteen, and threw his second unwanted potato at Amie. It hit her square in the mouth. *Ouch!*

Amie complained, 'Ugh! This potato is foul!'

Dad dug into his food. 'Eat up, Amie. Be grateful!' He wore mashed potato and gravy on his black beard.

Walter shoveled the potato into his mouth. 'Compliments to Master Chef Fleischer.'

A missile of potato flew past the said Master Chef Fleischer. 'Hey! What are you doing?' He glared at Adam.

'Dad, these potatoes are disgusting!' Amie defended her younger brother. 'We could all be poisoned eating these.' She stood up, marched to the rubbish bag and tipped her dinner into it.

'So be it, then. But you'll be sorry.'

Amie remembered her father's words and thumped the cave wall. 'How dare Dad starve his children! How dare he try and poison us! It's not fair!'

Her challenge this trip was being the one female amongst men. Mum had stayed home in Adelaide to look after the cats. From her cave and respite from the heat, Amie gazed over the valley.

The rest of the party were so preoccupied searching for Joseph, no one noticed her slip out of camp and out of sight up the gorge, over The Spring and into the hidden valley. She had to get away. She wanted to explore this weird and fascinating place where few people ventured.

'Anyway, I'm looking for Joseph Smith, too,' she told a passing rock wallaby. It stopped to rest on its haunches, glanced at Amie, and then bounded down towards the dry creek bed.

The mountain looked like it had sunk from the top so that like in a Western it had the veneer of being high and mighty as much as a stumpy Central Australian mountain could be high, but behind the façade, the one-time plateau had worn away over millions of years into a pound. She crouched in her hollow, focused on the narrow end of the gully from where she had come. Sobbing, she wished she had eaten those potatoes.

She buried her face and dark locks in her arms and sniffled some more. *Why him? Why did he have to get lost?* She wiped the red dust from her arm with her tears and grumbled to the ground, 'I bet the Wends never went without. Stupid Walter Wenke and his Wends. Get a life, Walter!'

A gust of wind whirred past her. 'Yohelaihedo!' It carried in its breath.

Startled Amie looked up. The last remnants of a "whirly whirly", a mini tornado escaped into the expanse of the valley. A soft breeze followed. As Amie stretched, wind flowed behind her, from the cave. It surged through her, and she marveled at her glowing skin. She held out her hand which pulsated with a soft red light exposing her veins. *What the—? Am I hallucinating?*

Amie turned and peered into the cave. The light faded and all went dark.

Amie shrugged. She assumed she's been resting too long and had fallen asleep. She sighed and decided to nap a few more minutes before heading back to camp at the base of this small mountain.

She swooned and drifted into daydream. There was something about this virgin timeless land that invited dreams. This land was untouched, and anything seemed possible.

***

The scene before her blurred. A village appeared; a cluster of mud-brick houses surrounding a church with a high steeple stuck in the middle. The worn desert hills had gone, replaced by snow-capped mountains. The tune of the old hymn "Rock of Ages" sang in distant enclaves.

Amie blinked several times and waggled her head from side to side.

The spinifex stalks swayed, and the golden landscape radiated with heat.

A head topped with honey-coloured hair matted like a bird's nest bobbed in the mirage of bushes down in the middle of the valley. *I'm not alone,* Amie thought.

Bang!

A flock of white cockatoos flew up screeching.

Amie shielded her eyes from the glare. *Probably just one of the Indig guides hunting.*

The guy with the matted hair sank into the valley and disappeared. Clumps of spinifex and the occasional native pine were once again the only inhabitants in this pound.

Camp to Nowhere

Same place, same "station" in Central Australia, same time...

Amie heard whistling in the bushes. *Must be Adam, only he has that annoying sound.* She stood, then marched, hunting for her brother. The wind flurried through the scrub with a hint of roast potato on its breath. In anticipation of kangaroo, cooked in its juices, she commenced the descent from her cave. That morning the Indigenous guides had returned from hunting at dawn, with a big red kangaroo slung on a rod carried between them. The campfire was stoked and when the coals were a mixture of white ash and glowing red, Dad had dug a hole and the complete carcass was placed inside, then covered with white-hot coals and left to cook for several hours.

Amie increased her pace. She picked her path past all the familiar landmarks. Navigating the stony creek bed on the north side of the sunken valley, she scrambled downwards. Nimble as a mountain goat, she negotiated the rocks in the dry creek. Before long, she had passed the pipe leading from the subterranean rock springs and reached the cattle trough. There she paused to splash the cool water from the trough over her face and shoulders.

Scanning the grove of gum trees, she expected the aroma of kangaroo roast to greet her. There was none. Cattle scarpered upon her approach. Dust lingered in her nostrils. She could hear a bull grunting at the edge of the clearing.

'Dad!'

No answer.

'Adam!'

Nothing! Not even an annoying whistle.

'Walter?' Now she was getting desperate.

There were no swags, no campfires, no four-wheel-drive vehicle, and no footprints. Amie tramped to a neighbouring dry waterhole. She assumed she'd gone to the wrong place. A herd of brumbies startled, and then thundered into the scrub.

Amie shrugged and stared at the hoof-print embedded mud. 'Must've shifted to the waterhole.'

Dragging her feet, she headed east to the permanent waterhole. After trekking up and over the first ridge, she followed the line of gum trees to the crevice in the hills. She skidded on a scree of stones. Undeterred, she scrambled over the narrow ridge to the next gully. Prickle bushes had made themselves at home in this crack in the hills. Amie hopped to the adjoining gap which promised to widen. However, as she wound her way up, the space between the red walls of rock became narrower. She rounded a bend, and a spider the size of a small bird eyeballed her from a web that spanned the width of the passage.

She hoisted herself up the rocky cliff and climbed to the ridge on the hilltop. Thirsty, she fished in her backpack for the water bottle. Her fingers touched a sticky apple core and jerked to another part of the bag. She latched onto a soft warm bottle and extracted it. Tipping back her head, she put it to her mouth, closed her eyes and grimaced. A white paste oozed from its lid. After spitting, she planted the sunblock on a boulder and tipped the contents of the pack onto the dry grass. The apple core rolled down the cliff-face. A windcheater, her dusty diary, a pen, and cosmetic bag glowed in the sunlight. The valley dipped and rose with long shadows cast over half of it. At the far end of the elevated land, was the cave. The last time, she remembered, the flask was in the cave. She sighed and stuffed the useless contents into her bag.

'Well, I'm not going to trek all the way back there,' she said.

After climbing to the top, she began to lumber along the crest of the hill. She promised herself five more minutes, then five more after that. Hope of the waterhole tucked around the next corner, lured her along the ridge. Every so often, when she rested, she imagined that she could hear water trickling. A few steps more and she was certain that she could hear laughing.

They must be there! She quickened her pace. There was a splash. She ran.

A large crack of a gunshot echoed from a distant slope. Hope. Amie paused to take in some deep breaths and savoured the gully of promise. She tottered towards the edge of the hillside. Side-stepping down, loose rocks crumbled under her feet and shattered in the valley below. Crab-like Amie descended. She zigzagged along the hill face but refused to look down. The slope disappeared a few feet in front of her. More stones gave way and clattered down the cliff. Amie skidded in the same direction. A ghost gum whizzed past her. Amie threw out her arms and hung onto the knotty root. Pulling herself up onto the root as a seat, she glanced down. The last of the rocks scampered and hopped over a six-metre drop and plopped into the waterhole below.

Amie wiped a drop of perspiration from her cheek. 'Well, at least I found it.' She scanned the surrounding countryside for a route to lead her to her goal and sighed again. Following the sound of a faint trickle, she ascended and traversed the crest around until she discovered a stream feeding the waterhole. She cupped her hands, dipped them in the bubbling stream and then slurped up the water before wetting her face.

Flicking droplets over her body, she peered down through the ferns into the treacherous unknown. *Do I take the long way? It would be safer. Nah, live life fearlessly.*

After mounting the mossy rocks, she brandished her pack before her and hacked a path through the gully of prickle bushes. Spinifex needles bit at her shins. Slippery stones threatened to turn her ankles. The water gushed laughing louder and louder.

'Maybe I'll jump.' She sliced a curtain of ferns with a stick. Ten meters below, the waterhole sparkled through the shade of thirsty native pine trees. 'I've jumped from jetties higher than this.' She slipped on a wet patch and thudded onto her bottom. 'Ugh, maybe not. There must be another way.'

Too late! Amie's foot slid from under her. Pebbles cascaded, showering into the pool. Amie screamed. Falling. The rock wall, branches, and leaves shot upwards. The wall of water whacked her back and caved in over her. Icy water shot into her mouth and nostrils stinging her sinuses. She blew air from her lungs. Opening her eyes, she watched the bubbles blob to the surface far above. She flapped her arms and pushed towards the filtered green light.

Prospecting

Meanwhile... from the mountains near Luthertal,
World of the Wends—Other side of the Galaxy...

Friedrich hiked up the steep valley. The higher he ascended the mountain, the drier and more faded the landscape became. The blue grass turned into brown-red rocks, golden grasses and those irritating prickly bushes. The sky had changed colour to royal blue.

He approached a cave. The sand near the cave sparkled and winked at Friedrich. He knelt and examined the glitter. His fingers played with a gem of translucent crystal. He turned it round in his hand and added the treasure to his pocket.

After entering the cave, Friedrich wriggled between a narrow split in the rocky wall. The inside of this mountain hummed, and a soft red glow guided him onwards. This twelve-year-old Wend boy sidestepped slimy surfaces, weaved through a labyrinth of stalactites and stalagmites, and then following a light that widened into an opening on what he presumed was the other side of the mountain. Shielding his eyes from the harsh sunlight, he shuffled toward the cave's opening, caught his foot on something solid, and stumbled. A bag, with straps like a knap-sack was the offending item that tripped him. Friedrich squatted and studied the sack. Glancing around to check for its owner and finding no one, he slung the sack over his shoulder, stepped out into brilliant sunshine and blue skies, and continued to walk down to the bottom of the valley and then into a narrow gully.

Friedrich looked back at the hill behind him and took note of the cave from which he had come. That was his landmark. He whistled and skipped. 'No English language lesson today! No more silly Englishmen! No Herr Roach. Ha! Ha! Ha!' He sang the tune of an old hymn, "Rock of Ages". Seemed appropriate considering his surroundings. He did not feel guilty at all. No one would notice, especially Roach.

As a precaution, that morning at breakfast, when Wilma had been presented with her left-over potatoes to eat, and his mutti was busy with the washing up, he had offered to take the potatoes as a trade-off. His sister had willingly agreed. She promised to tell the teacher that he was helping on the farm that day.

Friedrich dug into his pocket and pulled out the roast potato. It had gone soft and leathery. Friedrich bit through its skin and enjoyed the powdery substance of cooked potato that melted in his mouth. He stared at the rise on the far side of the valley and tried to figure out in his twelve-year-old mind why rain did not fall on this part of the land.

Thirsty, the boy trotted along a dry creek bed in search of water. The harsh solar rays beat down burning the nape of his neck. His tongue stuck to the roof of his mouth, especially since he'd eaten such a dry potato, and needed something to wash it down. He hunted for any object that offered relief from the sun. Then, he remembered the sack on his back. Spotting a pure white tree nestled in a small outcrop of rocks, he scrambled to its sanctuary of shade and perched himself on a flat boulder.

Sucking in the dry air, he tugged at the mouth of the bag that seemed locked by teeth. The tiny black teeth clung like a rabid dog with lock-jaw and refused to open. He could hear water sloshing, but where? He lifted the bag above his head and gazed at its underside. The sack seemed heavy. There must be water there, somewhere. He lowered the sack, and, as he did, he saw it. Shiny and shaped like a log. Was that the water vessel? Tucked in the side of the sack? He drew from the pocket; the flask wrapped in a thick blue cotton and unscrewed the lid. The boy sniffed the opening. The water smelt fresh, so Friedrich tipped the spout to his mouth and with long slow gulps the water slid down his throat. As the bottle emptied, Friedrich welcomed the remaining drops which dribbled down his neck and under his white cotton shirt. He gasped with satisfaction and wiped his mouth with his sleeve.

Revived, he fiddled with the mouth of the bag. He remembered Herr Roach wore trousers with a similar device. "A fly", Herr Roach called it, his beady eyes glinting. He remembered Herr Roach behind the barn pulling at a tag at the top of his fly. Friedrich shuddered. He didn't want to go there again, not even in his mind. He'd been curious. So what if he'd just happened to be passing when he assumed Herr Roach had decided to "water" the geraniums near the barn? That's what men do. But that day, when

Herr Roach had undone his fly to water the geraniums, he had seen that Herr Roach was not exactly human.

Friedrich shook his head. What did Herr Roach do with all those legs? What? He'd counted an extra two right there, wriggling out from his pants.

He located the tag at one end of the teeth and pulled. I hope there's no legs jiggling about inside this sack, he thought. With a gentle ripping sound, the bag opened, and Friedrich peered inside. 'Das ist gut!' he muttered. There was a torch, matches in small a box, and another box similar to Herr Roach's magic box only smaller. Friedrich pressed the button to see if the box would light up the white tree trunk with English words, but all it did was go "click" and flash in his face, blinding him for a moment.

As the green spotted blindness wore off, he heard another click and something cold and hard on his ear. 'Stealing is verboten.' A voice spelt out in measured words.

Friedrich turned from bag-rummaging and faced the foreign voice. The barrel of a narrow and light-looking rifle was an inch from his face. He raised his hand to the barrel and moved it to one side. 'Es tut...bitte,' he said, his eyes pleading for mercy.

'So, who are you?' Now the foe was speaking English and Friedrich had no idea what he was saying. He wished he'd paid more attention to English lessons.

'Ich weise nicht.' Friedrich raised his hands above his head and retreated from the offending bag and its owner.

His opponent laughed and placed the rifle on the ground. 'Du weise nicht? Spreche sie Deutsch?' He squatted, and rested his hand in his messy blonde hair and chuckled. He spoke in words similar to Friedrich's tongue, but with a very strange accent. 'You don't know? You don't know who you are? You're a funny one! What a jolly joker! Wise guy! Are you from one of those queer sects that set themselves up in the mountains and then with cyanide kill themselves? Are you? You look like one. Dressed like that.'

'I er I don't understand.' Friedrich peered at this fellow who must work an awful lot of time out in the sun as his face was tanned. 'If—if you are Australian, why do you speak the language of the Kingdom of Prussia? Have I not left that land? Am I not in Australia?'

The stranger picked up some red earth and sifted it through his fingers. 'Well, yes, you are in Australia.' He shrugged. 'We are in the *Centre* of Australia. Both lost, right in the middle of it. Think about that!' The young man reclined against the white trunk and placed his hands behind his knotted locks. He wore what seemed to Friedrich to be only under garments, his grey under-garment bearing a red heart with a white cross. He paused, gazing at Friedrich. 'What I don't understand, is why you keep on about Prussia. Do you mean Russia, where the Communist come from? Because Prussia has not existed for over a hundred years.'

Friedrich kicked the rock. 'Well, to tell the truth, I—I'm a Wend—a Sorb, you know.' He gestured with his hand self-consciously. He had a habit of feeling intimidated and inferior to all who were not Wend. And this fellow had the ruddy complexion of someone from Bavaria. *Or was he a real Australian? The earlier settlers his Papa was on about? Did he have to preach the gospel to this young man, who was, he could see looked about seventeen years of age?*

The older lad returned a blank expression. 'Wend? What is Wend? Never heard of them. Are they some religious kooky sect?'

'No! No! We're just a people on the edge of the empire—We're quite normal. We came to Australia for a better life. That's all. We're not kooky, whatever that means. We're a good people, really.' If this fellow has not heard of the Wends, Friedrich was not going to enlighten him. He was eager to impress. He wanted no trouble. He had seen his family go through enough hardship back in the homeland because of their religious beliefs, so he wasn't that keen on spreading the gospel.

The young man smiled. With a wave, he beckoned Friedrich to come closer. 'You're okay. I was just testing. You never know what strange characters you come across in these parts. Come, I know this great waterhole. We can swim there. Let's go!'

'I would love to. But I don't have my swimming trunks.'

'Don't worry about bathers. There's no girls around.'

Friedrich hesitated.

'Underpants would be fine, then.'

Friedrich relaxed. 'Well, then, what are we waiting for?' He raced after his newfound friend.

***

Friedrich and his friend dozed on a slab of rock. The afternoon had ebbed away in bomb dives, swimming races, pot shots at lizards with his friend's rifle, and more bomb dives. They lay there soaking the warmth as the sun's sting had begun to subside. Friedrich admired the older lad's swimming trunks. They were made of a material unfamiliar to him. He assumed they were

Australian. Unlike his heavy hemp trousers, the fabric was fine and stretchy, and dried rapidly in the sun.

Friedrich basked in the mellow late afternoon. 'This is much more fun than boring English lessons.'

Cold interrupted the drying rays. Friedrich opened his eyes. There was a shadow cast over his body.

Village of the Wends

Friedrich sat up and rubbed his eyes.

This thin silhouette raged at him. 'So, there you are!'

'Aber—aber,' he stammered.

'You idiot! Why did you desert me like that! I've been looking for you for hours!' The skinny girl stomped her feet on the stone, emphasizing her incomprehensible babble with a splat.

'Ich—ich—'

'What? Are you thick or something?' Her arm swooped over his head. 'I got myself half-drowned because of you!'

Friedrich's hands clung to his head and he cowered. 'Es tut—es tut.' Through his fingers, he could see the dark-haired girl bellowing at him and her face turning as red as beetroot. Her skinny arms flailed around her.

'Hello! Do you hear me? Adam? Are you there? Look, you moron! Stop ignoring me! I've had it with you!'

Friedrich scuttled backwards. He fumbled for his shirt. He hunted for the support of his friend. He patted the damp boulder, his hand shaking in the vacant space where his friend once was.

This skinny girl lunged towards him. Friedrich ducked and shivered. He hugged his knees while his teeth chattered. 'Please—do—not—hurt—me. I—do—not —understand—English.'

Amie wiped her eyes and blinked. 'Oh, I'm sorry. Oh, woops! Oh, my goodness! Gee, I'm sorry! I thought you were my brother.' She blinked again. 'I fell into the water and I don't know, everything's blurry.' She squinted. 'You're not Joseph, he had dreadlocks—oh, unless you had a haircut.'

'I-don't-understand.'

'He speaks German only, Amie.' Joseph, dreadlocks in place as she remembered, appeared by a river gum. 'He doesn't understand English. You'll have to use that German you learnt at school.'

She stared at Joseph and then said, 'So here you are.' She twisted a damp curl around her finger and sniffed. Shading the sinking sun from her eyes, she studied the two. 'So, I have to speak German, do I? I can do that. Easy!' She scratched her forehead and extended a hand to Friedrich and in halting German said, 'Guten Abend. Ich heisse Amie. Und Sie?' (Good evening. My name is Amie. What is yours?)

Friedrich glanced over at his friend before accepting the hand that greeted him. The friend nodded. 'Friedrich Biar.' His fingers touched hers and slipped away.

Amie nodded at Joseph. 'Was that okay?'

Joseph shrugged.

'Hey, come on! He understood me and answered. My German is not *that* bad. Besides, I got an "A" for it in the trial exams.'

'It's textbook, and Friedrich's isn't. But I guess we'll get by, what with my experience enduring a year in Germany with my mum and dad...'

'What? Germany? Or your mum and dad?'

'What do you think?'

'I thought so,' Amie said. 'Talk about helicopter parents.'

'You're not kidding—my father's a control freak.'

'So, you ran away?' Amie stepped from one boulder to the next towards Joseph. 'Everybody is looking for you.'

'Everybody?'

'Yes. They all are. We have helicopters, police, and all the television crews.'

'Are they?'

'Yes, even the indigenous trackers are looking for you.'

He shook his matted hair. 'Typical! Just like my parents to over-react.'

'But you're missing!'

'So? I don't care.' Joseph picked up a stone and then skimmed it across the waterhole.

'But they're your parents.'

'You don't know my parents.'

'Well, I saw them and they were very upset.'

'They'll get over it. They'll have more room in that stupid van, now.'

'You mean, that you left them on purpose?'

'Yeah, didn't I make that clear?' Joseph skimmed another pebble making it go plop, plop, plop over the surface.

'I thought you were kidding,' Amie said. 'Well, that's not very nice of you.' Amie yanked leaves from an overhanging branch and flicked them at Joseph.

Joseph grimaced. 'You don't know what it was like. With them. Drive and hike. Hike and drive. And Dad made me wear these dumb yellow skivvies. So I wouldn't get lost. It's not like the Swiss Alps, you know. Blind Freddy could find his way round this desert.'

'Hey!' Friedrich threw a stick at Joseph. 'I am not blind.'

Joseph fended off the projectile and spoke in German. 'Sorry, friend. I forgot you speak a little English.' He shrugged. 'Anyway, I'm free now. I can do what I like. Besides, my parents are embarrassing and cramp my style. You heard Dad go on about my hair at Emily Gap. That's only the half of it. In Alice Springs I decided to move creatively, you know, do some Parkour, and Dad just couldn't help himself telling me off. Told me I was a danger to myself and others. As if I don't know what I'm doing.'

'Park—what?'

'Parkour. The art of creative movement from one point to another.' In one fluid action, Joseph bounded from one bounder to the next and then with a somersault plunged into the waterhole.

Amie looked on. 'Right.' She could see Joseph's father's point if Joseph performed such feats down Todd Mall leaping over rails and stationary locals.

'I must get home now, my father and mother are waiting,' Friedrich said in his native tongue. He scrambled to be with the older two. 'We go through the cave.'

His father would be so angry if he was late. Angry like "donner und blitzen". Friedrich gazed at the setting sun. He had to hurry. This was not his land—not the land where his Wend villagers had settled. The hues of pink and purple with hints of sunrays played on the pond, making diamonds of droplets in the waterfall. 'We must go.' He beckoned Amie and Joseph to follow him.

As twilight encroached, they trailed him over the ridge and into the hidden valley, and up the side. At the cave, Friedrich waited for the two in strange attire to catch up.

'Come!' He gestured. 'Come and see my home.'

Joseph tipped his head and spoke in what these new friends called "German". 'Why not? It'll be an adventure.' He was quite fluent using his words.

'Are you sure we should?' Amie asked with a frown on her oval face. Her language sounded stilted, unsure.

Joseph nudged Amie to crawl into the cave. 'Where's your sense of adventure, Amie?'

Joseph and Friedrich followed.

A thin red ray quivered at the far end of the cave. Amie stopped just short of it.

'Go through,' Friedrich urged.

Amie wrung her hands. 'I don't know.'

'Where's your sense of adventure?' Joseph challenged.

'But, we might get lost.'

'It's alright, I go in and out from my world to your world all the time,' Friedrich said. 'Sometimes I use the outhouse underneath, sometimes the cave in the mountains. You can always come back.'

His two new friends looked at him.

'It is safe,' Friedrich said.

'Alright,' Amie took and deep breath, 'I will try.' She stepped forward through the light.

***

In no time at all, Friedrich led Amie and Joseph down the hillside by the goat path to his village, Luthertal. Dark had enveloped them. Feeble gas lights from the village sped them onwards.

'We're here.' Friedrich galloped down the grassy slope and raced to the end of the gravel road where a hall was decorated with lamps.

At the steps leading to the entrance of the wooden structure, Amie inhaled. 'That smells like roast something. Oh, my tummy is grumbling! I could eat a horse!'

'Be careful what you wish for, Amie,' Joseph said, 'might be just that.'

'What?'

'Roast horse, had it in a beer house in Cologne.'

'Yuk!'

Joseph nudged her. 'Rather tasty, actually.'

Friedrich ushered his friends into the dining hall. The congregation stopped supping and in unison turned. His father rose like a monolith from the midst and glared.

Friedrich took a deep breath and said, 'Papa, these are my new friends from Australia, the real Australia.'

Dinner With the Wends

Luthertal, World of the Wends, Other side of the Galaxy

The big man's lips thinned. 'Friedrich August Biar, you are late!' He pointed a sausage-thick finger in his son's direction. 'Go to my study and wait for me there.'

Staring at the ground, the boy shuffled out the hall and into the darkness. Amie and Joseph watched him go. Then they glanced at each other.

'I hope we haven't got him in trouble,' Amie muttered.

'He'll be fine,' Joseph said and then chewed his lip.

'I'm not so sure. Did you see how angry his dad looked?'

'If it was my dad, I'd be worried.'

'I don't know.' Amie stood on tiptoe to see through the window and catch sight of Friedrich as he ambled down the road to his home and the consequence that awaited him in his father's office.

The man worked his generous girth around the benches and diners, arms outstretched. 'Welcome!' He grasped Joseph's arm with both hands and shook. 'Welcome to our humble village.' His hand engulfed Amie's fingers, then squeezed and with a flick released them. 'My name is Hans Biar. I am the burgermeister, here.' He turned and gestured them to follow. 'Come, there is plenty left over. Have some dinner. You must meet Frau Biar.'

'What about Friedrich?' Amie asked as they side-stepped through the dining room. 'Poor Friedrich, he'd be hungry.

'Shush! Be quiet!' Joseph touched his finger to his lips. 'You'll get us into trouble!'

'But he's—'

'Shush!'

Amie chewed a nail and examined where the large man called Hans Biar was taking them. At the head of the narrow and crowded room, a lady rose, tall and thin, as the man was wide. She bowed her head which was shrouded in a brown scarf.

'This is Frau Biar.' The man put his arm around her waist. 'Let me introduce, now who did you say you were?'

Joseph bowed. 'Joseph Smith.'

'Amie Fleisher, pleased to meet you.' Amie thrust her hand between the men and crockery. Frau Biar hesitated, before accepting the gesture.

Herr Biar indicated space on the wooden bench. 'Please, sit down.'

Amie sat beside a petite girl who appeared to be a miniature replica of Frau Biar. She couldn't help but feel conspicuous in shorts and tee-shirt, while surrounded by women covered neck to toe in modest dress, and frilly caps covering their hair. These women seemed to frown at her, their eyes narrowing disapprovingly as if she were some sort of brazen hussy. And the men in their long-sleeved shirts and trousers held up with braces, blushed and tried not to stare at Amie. Joseph who sat opposite her appeared almost naked, if not delicious, his muscular arms bulging out of his sleeveless tee-shirt.

China basins of pumpkin soup with fresh baked bread appeared, delivered by a rotund woman in black. The visitors gulped and slurped. Amie went one step further and dunked her bread.

When Joseph raised an eyebrow at Amie's boldness, she threw a piece of bread at him.

Joseph caught the chunk of bread and popped it in his mouth.

'Just as bad,' Amie joked in English.

'So where did you say you were from?' Hans wiped his mouth and waited for Joseph to finish his mouthful of bread.

Amie didn't wait for Joseph to answer. 'We're, I mean, I'm from Adelaide.'

'Adelaide? Hmm!' Hans stroked his beard. 'And, you? Young man? Are you from Adelaide too?'

Joseph covered his mouth and made a muffled sound.

'Yes, I think.' Amie could not help speaking for him. 'He got lost in the bush and we had everyone looking for him. Even the aborigines.'

Joseph blushed. 'I'm from the Adelaide Hills, just outside of Adelaide. And I'm *not* lost.'

'Lost, you say? Mmmm!' Herr Biar folded his napkin and placed it on the table. 'So, where exactly were you before you became lost?'

'I'm not lost. I'm on adventure. We both are.'

'Where were you when you started this—adventure?'

Amie replied, 'Central Australia, of course.'

'Out West of the MacDonnell Ranges to be exact, where only the aborigines live. In the middle of the desert.' Joseph took another chunk of bread and popped it in his mouth.

'Why would they want to know that?' Amie said under her breath to Joseph.

'I don't know. But perhaps they want more detail than just— Central Australia. It's a big place. And Germans like detail.'

'Yeah, whatever.'

'I mean, they must know that they are in Central Australia, or there is something wrong with them.' Joseph scanned the room. 'Or, maybe there is.'

Amie frowned at him. 'What's that s'posed to mean?'

'Oh, well, you know, just a…' Joseph grinned, then raised his camera and aimed it at a puzzled Wilma.

'What, do you think you are doing?' Amie whispered.

'Just a snap,' Joseph replied and pressed the camera's button. 'Proof.'

'Yeah, right,' Amie snorted. 'Better be careful, or you might be lynched for witchcraft; what with flashing that technology around.'

Joseph tucked the silver box back in his back pocket. 'It's a camera. They had cameras in the nineteenth century.'

'Did they? Not like that,' Amie said. 'Google it, you'll see.'

'How?'

'Now, now, no need for a lovers' quarrel,' Frau Biar said. She then whisked up the dishes and ferried them to the kitchen.

Herr Biar leant back in his ornately carved Grandfather's chair at the head of the table and placed his fingers in his vest pocket. His thumbs stuck out as if pleased with themselves. 'Well, well, that's settled then, is it not? I think we have answered all of the Frau's questions. Indeed we are in Australia. And not that far from Adelaide, are we not?'

'Not exactly—Adelaide's—'Amie started, but the burghermeister had turned from her and was whispering to his wife. '—one thousand, five hundred…' Amie concluded into the air.

'Right, early start tomorrow,' Herr Biar said to his wife and then turned back to Amie and Joseph. 'Joseph, you will be with the doctor, Doctor Zwar. I will do the introductions. He has a nice home not far from here, with lots of rooms, just for visitors. And Amie, you will be with us—you can share a bed with Wilma, here. I think it will be good for her.'

Amie glanced about her and at Frau Biar. The Frau should protest at the arrangement, but she didn't. With a sense of obligation, Amie and Joseph filed out of the dining hall behind Burghermeister Biar. At the door before parting, Amie caught Joseph by the arm. 'First light tomorrow, we're out of here.'

'I don't know.'

'All right for you getting a room all to yourself in the doctor's house, but I have to sleep next to a little girl. So annoying!'

'You got any other suggestions?' Joseph's eyes lit up. 'Perhaps you could get the doctor to put you up too. It would be nice to have you close by.'

'Get lost!'

'Already am, so?'

'LOL!' Amie gave Joseph a gentle nudge. 'Don't you want see your family again? Don't you want to go home?'

'No, not particularly. Told you, you don't know my family.'

'Yeah, but, can't be more crazy than these guys. I mean, talk about Dark Ages. They're loonies.'

'Better than my mum and dad.'

'Impossible—besides, there are no computers, mobile phones. I can't live without my mobile phone.'

'You'll survive, you'll see. It'll be a new experience for you.' Joseph patted his back pocket. 'Anyway, I have my digital camera, if you get techno-lonely.'

Amie sighed. 'I'll be fine.'

Frau Biar ushered Amie over to the Biar home. Once Herr Biar had delivered Joseph to Doctor Zwar's, Herr and Frau Biar, Wilma and Amie crowded into the living area of the tiny brick home. Frau Biar swept dust off the mud-packed floor while Herr Biar showed Amie up a narrow flight of steps to Wilma's room. From the hallway, she noticed Friedrich in a small room lined with books. He riveted his eyes to the floor and did not see her.

A little later on, Amie poked her head out the door. Herr Biar was pacing towards the study, belt strap cradled in his palms. Amie gasped and then hid under the quilt and covered her ears with the feather stuffed pillow.

After the third thwack, a tiny voice beside her said in German, 'He was a naughty boy, you know. He did play truant. He made

Herr Roach very upset. Made him throw his machine hard across the room, he did. It broke into pieces. I guess he won't be playing his magic slate anymore, will he?'

'I guess not,' Amie replied as she tried to block out the sobs from down the hallway.

'Herr Roach taught us English,' Wilma said. 'Do you speak English?'

Amie blocked her ears from the muffled sniffs that seeped from the room next door. 'Yes, I do. But it's time for sleep,' Amie whispered and then she rolled away from her companion.

'Herr Roach, you know, he is mean,' Wilma said.

'Is he?' Under the soft soothing feather down quilt, Amie's mind spun, as she plotted her escape.

Wilma had the final word. 'I don't like Herr Roach.'

Missing

Central Australia

Arthur Fleischer clumped into camp. 'Amie, we're home.'

The sun hovered just above the horizon, its rays bathing everything in its path in orange hues. A cool breeze eddied through the clearing picking up the red dirt.

Fleischer paced the campsite glancing left and right, up and down. No Amie. After a fruitless search for the lad Joseph Smith, not much older than Amie, a chilling thought crept up on Fleischer. 'Not Amie too,' he murmured. He cleared his throat. 'Nah, don't be silly, she wouldn't've gone far.'

Adam straggled into camp and looked around. 'Where's Amie?'

'Dunno.'

'Probably gone to the waterhole and got stuck there with the white bull trapping her. Remember the white bull we saw, Dad?'

'Oh, could be.'

'I bet she went skinny-dipping and got trapped by the bull and a dingo ate up all her clothes.' Adam sniggered.

'Don't be silly. She's probably just forgotten the time. I'm damn cross with her. She promised to mind the camp while we were out searching.'

'Yeah, well, she'll turn up.' Adam picked up Amie's mobile phone snug in its "Hello Kitty" pouch. 'I mean, she's left her phone here. She can't be far if she's left her phone behind.' A smile spread across his face. 'Cool, I've always wanted to check out her phone.'

Adam jumped into the four-wheel drive and fiddled with his sister's phone.

Walter Wenke strode into the clearing. 'What? You haven't started dinner yet, Fleischer? I'm famished.' Then glancing around the campsite, he added, 'I thought we're having roo. Where's the roo?'

'Is that all you can think about? Food?' Fleischer gazed at The Range, its ridges now glowing pink, and without looking at the coal-pit, he muttered, 'Still cooking in the coals, I guess. And, anyway, you seen Amie in your travels? She's not here.'

'Her bad luck if she misses out on tea, I say,' Wenke replied. 'You should get something together before it gets dark.'

Their indigenous guide, appeared. He had stolen into their presence without making a sound.

'Ah, Nathan, you gotta stop doing that,' Fleischer said.

'You wan' me to knock?' Nathan picked up a shovel. 'What? Dinner still in oven?' He then drifted over to a campfire and shovelled out the blackened kangaroo carcass from the coals. The aroma of cooked meat filled the air. 'Dinner. Well done. I go get more wood for the fire tonight.'

Nathan then vanished into the bush in search of fuel for the fire.

'Cool! Roo!' Adam came out of rover-hiding to inspect the effigy, stiff and black. 'Wait till Amie sees it. She'll be grossed out. Wicked!'

'Yeah, if she doesn't take her time getting back.' Fleischer paced back and forth across the campsite as if he were walking on coals. 'Where could she have gone?'

'I'll go to the waterhole. I'm sure she's there.' Adam galloped towards the gully where the waterhole was situated. As he ran, the sun, a flattened shiny disc, slipped below the horizon.

Fleischer called after him. 'Wait, Adam.'

Adam stopped and looked back. 'What?'

'Let Walter go with you. I don't want you getting lost.'

Walter rubbed his hands together and then loped after Adam.

They disappeared over the crest of the hill, and Fleischer busied himself with tidying up the campsite. He moved billy cans and fry pans from one side of the fire place to the other. Then he moved them back. He shovelled stones from the clearing. He rearranged the luggage in the back of the rover. He did anything to keep busy. He had a bad feeling that he just couldn't tidy away.

Nathan returned from gathering wood. After placing the sticks on the coals, he gazed at the tracks criss-crossing the clearing. 'Where they go?' he asked.

'To the waterhole.' Fleischer pointed towards the gorges in The Range.

'Why go there?'

'Amie's there.'

'No, she's not.'

'What do you mean?'

Nathan placed his hands behind his back and like an emu searching for food, he stalked the sandy ground. He pointed at some twigs. 'She go this way. She go to The Spring.'

'That doesn't make sense,' Fleischer said. 'She'd be back by now. What's there at The Spring?'

Nathan studied the gorge in the grey light of twilight. 'She climb over into the Hidden Valley.'

'How do you know that?'

'I jus' do.'

Fleischer ran to the four-wheel drive. He grabbed a torch and then offered it to Nathan. 'Can you find her? Can you go looking for her and find her?'

Nathan ignored the torch. He tipped his head back and seemed to sniff the icy breeze of the coming night. ''s too late—she's gone.'

Fleischer shone the torch up the gully. 'Don't be ridiculous. She's only been missing a few minutes—hours. She can't be gone too far.' He said this to allay his growing sense of alarm.

Arthur Fleischer stormed from the camp. He swished the torchlight from side to side. He had to do something to will his daughter back.

Nathan turned and began building up the fire.

Fleischer stumped back into camp and stood over Nathan. 'Well, aren't you coming?'

Nathan looked up at Fleischer. 'She's not here, Arthur.' He then crouched down and blew at the coals igniting the fire.

'Oh, don't give me excuses.'

Nathan rested on his haunches. 'She's okay, Arthur. She's in other world. Safe for now. Don' worry spirit people look after her.'

'I don't believe you, she's not dead.'

'She's no' dead. She wi' boy,' Nathan said. 'She'll come back.'

Fleischer scanned the first stars blinking in the sky. 'Yeah, right, I think you're making it all up. Well, I'm going to find her.' He shone the torch up the gorge and then paced out of the campsite.

Nathan called behind him. 'She come home unless the bad man stop her. That Walter, you watch him. Him bad man.'

Arthur Fleischer shook his head as he tramped up the gorge. 'Not here—another world—spirit people. Chewing too much "pitcherie" if you ask me.' He scrambled over boulders and climbed higher. He yelled over and over. 'Amie? Amie? Are you there? Amie? Where are you?'

The man called Walter heard Fleischer's desperate cries. He and the bratty boy stood by the waterhole. The pool was dark, still and devoid of any sign of Amie.

He massaged his hands and entertained a perverse pleasure being alone with the boy. *So young. So innocent...*

'What do you want more than anything, my boy?' he asked. *So impressionable.*

'Right now, I want to find my sister.'

'Well, for that we'll need to wade across the pool and climb up that cliff.'

'But it's dark and the water's cold.'

'You want to find your sister, don't you?'

'I'll get my clothes wet and get hypothermia.'

He touched the boy's back. 'Take your clothes off then.'

Adam shoved him. 'No way, you pervert.'

He held up his hands. 'Fine then, you don't want to find your sister.' *Not so easy after all.*

At that moment, Nathan materialised beside the rocky bank near a ghost gum.

This particular Walter hunched over and scowled. 'What's he doing here?'

Adam scrambled up to Nathan. 'She's not here.'

Nathan, the whites of his eyes glowing, glared at Walter. 'Com'on Adam, you come ba' to camp. We have kangaroo for dinner.'

'I'll keep on searching,' the man called Walter muttered as he slunk into the bushes.

Adam, his Dad and Nathan chewed their kangaroo meat in silence. Nathan promised roo for breakfast...tomorrow for lunch...and dinner...and the next day. So much kangaroo meat, that his dad stored chunks of it in the cooler attached to the four-wheel drive. A battery-generator kept the cooler running as well as lighting up the campsite at night.

'I'll keep it on;' Dad glanced at the light and then said, his voice wobbling, 'a light to guide Amie home.'

Walter's anticipated return hadn't eventuated. Adam was glad. The guy grew creepier by the day. He couldn't figure out why Dad had invited him on this trip. He couldn't stand the man. He had these beady eyes that followed you everywhere. Adam reckoned he saw him early that morning and he looked like a zombie. True. Adam knew the Indig guide, Nathan didn't like him. He'd heard Nathan call Walter a "cockroach". But try telling Dad? Dad just wouldn't listen.

Adam gulped down the last of his kangaroo meal. He looked up. The Milky Way spilt out across the velvet sky. Still no Amie. *Where's my sister?* Adam sighed.

'Come on, Adam, time for bed,' Dad said.

'But I can't—not when I'm worried for my sister.'

'Your sister's fine. She's probably sheltering in a cave. We'll find her in the morning.'

'But I don't want to go to sleep. What if a dingo's in the cave 'n got her?' Adam looked at Nathan. 'Do you have any idea what's happened to her?'

Nathan stared at the fire. The billy hissed and spluttered signalling the water had boiled, ready to make tea.

'Come on, mate,' Dad said. 'It'll be alright in the morning.'

'But she'll starve. She might die of cold. Poor Amie.'

'She's alright. Keeping away fro' cockroach man. She's alrigh', okay,' Nathan said.

Adam took this to mean Amie had purposely run away to avoid any unwanted attention from the wanton Walter. 'Okay,' he said, 'but I'm sleeping by the fire tonight.'

Nathan stretched out on his swag by his personal fire. 'You sleep Indig style tonight.'

'If I can sleep, what with Amie lost too,' Adam mumbled.

***

Walter Wenke crept into camp in the wee hours of the morning.

Nathan heard him buzz around the camp. He opened one eye and saw him hover above the boy and his father huddled by the fire.

The guide leant up on one elbow. 'You back then.'

Walter jolted. He shuffled over to Nathan. 'You don't miss a trick.'

'I see everything you do.'

'What'cha going to do? Do your woo-woo magic?'

Nathan chuckled.

'I'm not afraid of you. I could wipe you off the face of this planet right here, right now. And no one would ever know.' Walter shimmered oily and black. 'Tell 'em you gone walk about.'

'Go on then.'

Walter raised his hand. He pointed his finger. It hummed and glowed hot red. While the Fleischer father and son stared through tear-filled eyes at the flames, he was no longer Walter Wenke, but Boris, master of the galaxy. Boris' finger turned white. Electricity arced over the knuckles of his hand. He was pleased to rid his world of minor irritations like Nathan.

Boris aimed.

Boris looked, left, right, up and down. 'Hey, where did he go?' The space Nathan occupied was vacant.

The need to annihilate seemed pointless.

Boris with his charged-up weapon eyed the backs of the catatonic Fleischer pair. Fresh meat. Given, he was hungry. But he had superior plans for those two...

'Damn!' Boris snorted and then zapped Nathan's campfire into a plume of smoke and flames.

Cockroaches

World of the Wends

The rooster crowed. Amie yawned and stretched her hand slapping against Wilma's pillow. 'Oops! Sorry,' Amie mumbled. Wilma did not stir; she slept like the proverbial babe.

Amie peered at the window.

The rooster crowed again.

Amie eased her way out from under the doona, and then tottered over to the window. The landscape was cloaked in shades of violet, the black blocks of village buildings barely discernible against the nightscape. Standing at the window so long she shivered, Amie studied the stars, trying to make sense of them. Stars sparkled through a cloud shaped like the hand of God. She thought it must be a cloud. *Why do the stars all look so different?* She examined the clusters but couldn't make sense of any constellations. None seemed familiar. 'Must be I'm tired or perhaps dreaming,' she murmured.

The rooster crowed yet again.

'Oh, go on, you! It's the middle of the night,' Amie said. She returned to her bed and crept under the quilt.

The rooster continued to herald the dawn. Cockle-doodle-doo! Cockle-doodle-doo. Amie lay awake. Cockle-doodle-doo. Cockle-doodle-screech! Squawk! Squawk! Screech!

'Don't tell me—foxes.' Amie turned over and tried to steal a few more hours' sleep. But sleep eluded her.

The hens clucked. The rooster squawked. A gate squeaked and then clunked. Then the noise of chooks in the chook yard sounded like a party with a cacophony of squawking, clucking, cockle-doodling and footsteps scrunching.

Amie heard a thud. Shrieks and the sound of wings flapping followed.

Must save the poor rooster. Wearing only her nightdress that Frau Biar had lent her, she raced out of the bedroom. She stumbled in the darkened living area as she made her way to the door. The squawking spurred her on. She fumbled for the knob. No knob. She groped at a long metal thing—a latch. She worked the latch, tugging it, pulling at it, wiggling and waggling trying to open the door.

A long raspy shriek hit the airwaves.

Amie finally hoisted the latch out of its cradle and the door sprang open.

By the light of the "hand of God" cloud, that hadn't moved, Amie galloped to the chook yard.

Herr Biar and his son Friedrich paced the pen. Herr Biar carried an axe.

'It's over there,' Friedrich said. With hands outstretched, he ran to the corner of the hen house.

The chooks whooped and bocked in protest. Something feathery skittered out into the yard with Friedrich in hot pursuit. Herr Biar joined the chase. Round and round the pen they ran. Tracking their frantic laps made Amie dizzy.

Amie mused. *What were they doing chasing some small feathery animal, probably the rooster? Did his crowing tick them off that much, they get up in the middle of the night to kill the poor bird?*

Rays of a torch lit up the scene. 'Wicked! A headless chook!' a voice said behind her.

Amie glanced over her shoulder. Joseph stood there grinning like the Cheshire cat. 'What do you mean, headless?' she asked.

'Look.'

Leading the father and son on a merry chase, a rooster's body. Blood spurted out of the open neck. Hens pecked at the detached head. They looked like they were enjoying a feast.

Meanwhile, Biar and his son cornered the headless creature. Father made a grab for it, but it ducked out of his reach. Friedrich hurled himself on the rooster's body, but with a life of its own, it slipped from his tackle.

Friedrich rose to standing and dusted poultry poop off his shirt and trousers. 'That beast is not normal. It has eyes on its body, I swear.'

'Why do you think we kill it?' his Papa said.

Biar darted left, his son right, again trying to trap the unruly body. But the ball of feathers and muscle darted in between them.

'It's got a life of its own,' Joseph said.

'It's one very angry body,' Amie said. 'It didn't like them chopping its head off. Why did they do it?'

Joseph leaned close to Amie and whispered, 'I heard Herr Biar talking to his Frau last night at dinner. Apparently, the cock has been fathering defective stock.'

'Stock? What do you mean? Mutant chickens?'

'Yes, not surprisingly, knowing this place. Look around. Look up at the sky. How could the chickens come out normal?'

'You mean I'm not imagining the stars being all different?' Joseph swayed his head.

The headless rooster slowed. Friedrich pounced on it and commenced plucking out the feathers.

'But why would the rooster be all munged up, I mean, his offspring?' Amie asked.

Joseph shrugged. 'Dunno. But I bet Boris's behind all this.'

'Boris? Who's Boris?'

'You don't want to know—but I guess you'll have to, one of these days.'

Herr Biar held the carcass by its feet, the blood dripping onto the floor of the pen. He approached the spectators. 'The rooster was evil. What is this place, Australia?'

'This place is not Australia, Herr Biar.' Joseph leaned on the fence pole. 'This place is not even our world.'

The first touches of dawn reflected pink on the mountain peaks. Herr Biar studied the sky, now a lighter shade of purple. 'Nein, I thought as much. I should believe my wife.' He nodded. 'We've been tricked by the devil.'

Friedrich ambled up behind his father. 'I told you, Papa. I told you that Herr Roach, was bad. I had a bad feeling about him. Didn't I tell you, Papa? He gave us that rooster and it was bad too.'

'So, what did the chickens look like?' Amie was curious.

'Chickens? No, no chickens,' Biar said. 'When the eggs hatched, giant cockroaches come out of them.'

'Urgh! Gross!' Amie fixed her attention on the rooster body. Blood fell with a plop to the dusty floor. Then it seemed to crawl away. One blob scuttled over her foot. 'Yew! The blood's moving!' Another blob rolled towards her. She jumped. 'It's alive.'

Joseph stomped. 'No, Amie, it's not blood, they're cockroaches.'

Herr Biar and Friedrich glanced around their feet and screamed. The chicken yard floor was alive and heaving with cockroaches. In the morning light, Amie witnessed millions of them swarming like a plague over the pen and into the paddock. Biar and Friedrich jogged on the spot as black beads streamed up their legs. Hens flapped and squawked as the critters hung onto their wings and feet.

'Get them off me!' Amie slapped at her limbs, and face. Some critters flew in her hair. She swiped at her locks trying in vain to untangle these unwanted hair pieces.

'Quick, the dam!' Herr Biar pushed through the gate and led the way to the body of water.

Amie, Joseph and Friedrich staggered after Biar. Amie wiped her eyes of the roaches that wanted to lodge there. As she swiped at them, they dislodged and flew away.

'Are you sure the water's safe, Papa?' Friedrich asked.

'Either we die from the cockroaches, or risk whatever's in the water,' Biar replied and then waded into the water. He washed the roaches off as he went deeper.

Joseph plunged in. A ring of roaches swirled around him. He sank under the water's surface and bobbed up a few metres from the floating bugs.

Amie jumped in. She sprang straight up. 'It's cold.'

Friedrich stood on the shore. He flicked bugs from his face and arms.

'What are you waiting for? Jump in. It's fine,' Joseph said.

'I don't like the cold.' Friedrich continued to flick. He looked like he had a nervous tick.

'Get in, son. It's the only way to get rid of the cockroaches.'

Friedrich, still twitching, dipped one foot in the water, and then the other foot. He shivered. A cockroach crept over the corner of his mouth, and then made for his nostril. Friedrich blew. But the critter held on. The boy waggled his head and wiped his nose. As the creature slid off his face, Friedrich grimaced. Then he closed his eyes tight and pushed his way into the water. With one dunk, the roaches floated off Friedrich.

Friedrich asked through chattering teeth, 'How long do we stay in the water?'

'Until it is safe, son,' Biar said.

The four gazed to shore. In the salmon toned morning light, the beach from where they had come was black and writhing.

'Could be some time,' Joseph said.

'Great, and I was hoping to be back by lunchtime.' Amie brushed a sluggish roach from her arm. 'You do realise although we've escaped the cockroaches for the time being, we may not've escaped the effects of hypothermia.'

'What's that?' asked Friedrich.

'Dying of cold.'

'We cannot do that,' Herr Biar said, 'we'll swim around the lake and then walk back to the house.'

'But the cockroaches, won't they have invaded the house?' Amie asked. 'And what about your hens? Won't the cockroaches kill them?'

'Not if Frau Biar has anything to do with them,' Herr Biar said.

Friedrich added, 'She'll be swatting them with her big broom.' He began paddling to the far shore.

'Come on, we better help Frau Biar and Wilma,' Joseph said.

Following Friedrich's lead, Amie, Herr Biar and Joseph swam to the far shore.

When Herr Biar, his son, Amie and Joseph dragged their dripping bodies back to the house, Frau Biar was on the front porch sweeping the last of the cockroach carcases into a pile on the garden path.

'Ooh! Someone's been naughty! Very naughty!' Wilma said.

Frau Biar stopped her sweeping and placed her hands on her hips. 'Who left the door open?'

'Oops, sorry!' said Amie.

'You weren't to know,' Frau Biar said. 'At least they were only kleine ones this time. I doused them mit vinegar. They don't seem to like vinegar.'

'And all out of a dead rooster.'

Frau Biar sighed. 'What did you do this time to upset Herr Roach?'

Herr Biar shrugged. 'Ich weiss nicht,'

Friedrich shrugged and then avoiding eye contact with anyone, crept towards the door. He looked like he was guilty—of something...

'Oh, no, you can't go in,' Wilma said, 'the floor ist wet. And the chickens are upstairs—safe.'

'But I'm wet and cold. I need to dry by the fire.' Friedrich trembled.

Amie hugged her wet waist and she shivered. 'We can't stand here, Frau Biar. We'll die of cold.'

'I know that,' Frau said. 'Here, we will make a bonfire in the garden. We will burn the cockroaches and dry you all at the same time.'

'Sounds good to me,' said the father. 'Und, I'll douse the yard and by the lake with oil and then burn off to rid our land of cockroaches.'

'Great! A bonfire! It'll be like New Year's!' Friedrich cheered.

'Careful you don't start a wildfire,' Frau Biar warned.

'We have to do something.' Herr Biar shrugged. 'I'll be careful, I promise.'

'You better,' Jane Biar said, then struck a match on the slate step and lit the fire.

'But cockroaches—'

Joseph nudged Amie. 'Don't—'

The Biar family gathered sticks and piled them on the mound of roaches. Meanwhile Amie hung back and argued with Joseph.

'Why can't I talk?' she whispered in English. Amie had visions of the family, Joseph and her, dying from the stench of cooked cockroach.

'They already think you have a big mouth. You're a girl, remember?'

'So?'

'You're in the world of the Wends, and the Wends are from the olden times, the nineteenth century—what now is Eastern Germany. In those times girls never spoke up.'

'Well that's a stupid idea,' Amie muttered. 'What did women do? Stay barefoot and pregnant?'

Joseph chucked a stick into the flames. 'More or less.'

'So much for women's liberation.'

'Not for another hundred years.'

'Maybe they should think about some changes—I mean, if Dad here had listened to his wife, maybe they wouldn't be in this mess—on another planet being conned by this cockroach Boris character and bullied by him.'

'Perhaps.'

They stepped up to the growing fire and spread their hands over the flames.

Frau Biar scurried into the house, and then emerged carrying blankets. Amie, Joseph, Herr Biar and Friedrich, under the cover of their blankets, peeled off their damp clothes. Then, wrapped in their blankets they began to thaw by the bonfire. Friedrich snuggled up to his father and soon both sat curled against each other, and dozing.

A second sun shimmered on the horizon and the morning buzzed with heat.

Amie turned to Joseph. 'This place is crazy. We're not staying.'

'I don't know. I quite like the place. The Wends grow on you.'

Amie rolled her eyes. 'Suit yourself. But I'm not hanging around to see what this Boris guy's going to get up to. Anyway, my Dad's going to be stressed out 'cos I'm missing.'

Helicopters

Central Australia

Arthur Fleischer watched the helicopters from Glen Helen circle the sacred mountain. They looked like dragonflies flitting and flying over the range.

He'd radioed on the CB late the previous night and Glen Helen had dispatched the helicopters at the first hint of dawn. Two police officers from the Mission had arrived and Arthur had gone through the motions of statements and likely scenarios with them. A couple of Indigenous trackers from the local station promised to help Nathan search, but by mid-morning, they still hadn't arrived.

Arthur Fleischer had not slept. Nor had he eaten. Although, he pretended to do both. He didn't want his son worrying. He witnessed Walter creeping into camp at goodness knows what hour. He witnessed the altercation between Walter and Nathan. *Good grief, that guy's a complete embarrassment!* Arthur was ashamed to call him a friend. *What a slime ball! And racist.* He'd threatened to kill Nathan. *So different from when they taught together down south. And how did Nathan just vanish? There one second...gone the next. What's with that?*

Nathan appeared at dawn with the first streaks of light. Briefly. Then he wandered off following Amie's tracks.

Fleischer tapped his pocket. Keys still there. At least that's some security in a very insecure situation. He pulled out his mobile phone, unlocked it, and peered at the screen. No bars, none whatsoever. This place, so isolated, forsaken, even by the Telstra network. 'Damn!' he sighed. 'I can't even call home to tell Carol what's happening.' Then thought, *I suppose it's for the best, don't want her worrying.*

Walter sidled up to Adam and side by side, they ate their cornflakes. Walter seemed not to have a care in the known universe. Fleischer didn't like the way Walter sat just a little too close to Adam—*He's just a little too friendly.* How did this guy get to teach anywhere? *Definitely something suspect...what if Walter had something to do with Amie's disappearance?*

Arthur strode up to Walter. 'Time to get moving. You need to start searching for her.'

Walter rose. 'But of course, I'll check out the waterhole and beyond, shall I?'

Fleischer nodded.

'Dad?' Adam chipped in. 'What about me?'

Fleischer waved at the first fly of the morning. 'You're staying here with me. We're minding the camp, in case Amie returns.'

Walter hung around like one of those pesky flies that stick to a person.

'I said, 'Go!'' Arthur snapped. 'Adam stays with me, today.'

'Naw, but...can't I help the police trackers?' his son asked.

'No!' Arthur replied. He then turned to that pest of a man. 'Go Walter! You join the police trackers.'

Walter shrugged. 'Are you sure you'll be okay?'

'We'll be fine.'

Walter marched off in the direction of the waterhole. He appeared to boldly go where the two Northern Territory policemen had gone half an hour before.

Adam slouched on an inflatable mattress by the fire and played Tetris on Amie's mobile phone. 'Something's seriously wrong, Amie would've never left her phone at camp and gone off,' he said.

Arthur paced the clearing. Every step, every minute, wore a groove in his heart eroding hope.

Boris, as Walter, climbed the first ridge leading to the waterhole. Not a policeman nor an Indigenous tracker to be seen. He spoke to the air and a couple of accompanying flies, 'Now, where did that Nathan get to?'

He stopped and surveyed the landscape. The sacred mountain's cliffs jutted like teeth above the nearby ranges. The atmosphere shimmered in the moist heat. Thunder clouds built up like steam in the west, and tiny flies formed a permanent halo around Boris.

Boris morphed out of his Walter appearance, and unfurled his wings. He used his surround vision of multiple eyes to check no one was watching. He twitched his antennae scanning for human life just out of sight and helicopters above. Nothing—so far so good. Wouldn't want them seeing a giant cockroach flying through the air.

The thought of bumping into a helicopter tempted him. He resisted the urge to amuse his deviate self. Must not raise suspicion. He had plans for this part of the world. Plans to get a foothold to rule the whole planet.

Boris rubbed his abdomen. *Mmm! Seven billion humans to enslave, to dominate, to eat...*He rose into the air, his wings whirring much like the helicopter's. *Now how's that Wend community of mine? They make such agreeable slaves.* He laughed.

Then he stopped laughing. *Where did that Nathan get to?* His wings whizzed faster. *I hope he hasn't found my cave.*

Boris zoomed above the mountain, and then into the pound. Gum trees, rocks and scrub blurred as he darted to the cave. When he arrived, he flitted to the entrance and then peered in.

Boris sighed. The cave was empty.

He looked out. Just over the precipice, he detected a dark man bobbing up and down through the scrub. *Just in time.* Boris chuckled. *He'll take at least an half an hour to get here.*

He scuttled in and through the portal. Mountains dressed in mauve and silver welcomed him. 'Can't have any unwelcome visitors coming through,' he said.

Boris turned. He charged up his weapon-hand and then shot a steady laser beam at the ceiling. Rocks broke and tumbled down, followed by thick clumps of soil. 'Can't have them digging.' He aimed his laser hand at the soil. He held the heat of the laser on the soil for a few minutes until it hardened to stone. 'There, that'll stop them.' Boris cackled. 'I still have the other portal, and they'll never find that.' He then massaged his stomach. 'I wonder how the real Walter Wenke is going? I do like them when they're prepared and marinated just so. Although, they must be fresh.'

***

Nathan traced Amie's trail—a broken twig here, a dislodged stone there, some shoe prints in the dusty soil, and a bucket hat.

Nathan mused. 'The boy's been this way.'

He hiked up to the Spring and then further, up over the lip of the mountain and into the pound. He followed the path to the cave.

At the entrance, he examined animal tracks. *Hmm, unusual,* he thought. *Never seen tracks like these. Like big cockroach.* In around the cave, more tracks—Amie's and another person's, a male.

He crawled into the cave sniffing out the tracks as he progressed. The tracks and Amie's and Joseph's footprints stopped at a pile of large rocks.

Nathan studied the boulders. He lifted the sand at their base and sniffed it. 'Hmm, fresh,' he said. 'Is she trapped?' He leaned against the rocks and called, 'Hello? Anyone there? Amie? Are you there?'

The cave remained cold and silent.

Nathan pushed the rocks. He tugged at the rocks. He tried to grip them but they slipped in his hands. The boulders were wedged in the cave.

Maybe they're deeper in the cave. Perhaps they're trapped there, Nathan thought.

He crawled out of the cave and began to saunter back to camp. He'd tell the others of his find. He was positive Amie and the lad Joseph were still alive.

The Cave of Escape

World of the Wends

Frau Biar insisted Amie wear a modest wool-knit tunic and blouse with puffy sleeves—colour scheme, monochrome grey and white. So, for an hour while Frau Biar baked biscuits and swept the kitchen floor, again, Amie perspired and itched in her woollen attire.

Then the Biar family vacated the house to attend to their various chores. Frau Biar had picked up her wooden bucket and headed for the barn to milk the cows. Herr Biar, with a hoe over his shoulder, tramped over to the field to nurture his barley crops. And the "kinder" Friedrich and Wilma tucked their slates and books under their arms and dragged their feet down the hill to the church hall, which, during weekdays, became the school.

Once they had all gone, Amie and Joseph were alone in the house.

Amie pointed at Joseph who was dressed in trousers held up by braces over a white shirt. 'Ha! You look like one of those Puritan—Amish types from the nineteenth Century.'

'Yeah, so? We're with sort of Puritans from the nineteenth century, so I fit right in with the fashion now.'

'Pff! As for me, I don't care about fashion. Not when it itches. It's coming off—*now*.'

Amie scurried upstairs to the girl's room, pulled off the dress and then wriggled into her jeans and t-shirt again.

She climbed down and then commenced pacing the floor. 'Phew! That feels better. I thought I was going to die from heat exhaustion. Now what are we going to do?'

'You're making me nervous,' Joseph said. 'You look like you're busting to go to the toilet. If you have to go—go.'

'But Joe, I want to *go*—not to the loo—I want us to go back to Earth. And I want you to come with me.'

'Aw, I dunno, can't we wait a bit?' Joseph helped himself to the plate piled high with home-made biscuits. 'Mmm, we don't get bikkies like these on Earth.'

'Take some with you. We're going, alright?'

'But we're having roast tonight.'

'What? Roast chook stuffed with roach? Or is it roach duck? With roach potatoes.'

'Oh, come on, they wouldn't.' Joseph munched on his biscuit. 'I've never had a roach—I mean roast before. And what they had last night was absolutely divine.'

'You've never had a roast?'

'My parents are Vegan,' Joseph said his mouth full of biscuit. 'You don't know what it's like growing up without meat, or milk, or eggs.' He swallowed. 'This place is heaven.'

'Except for Boris and the plague of cockroaches.' Amie marched to the door. 'Come on! Let's make a run for it before they return. When we get back to Earth, I'll have you round for Sunday lunch at my nanna's. We have a roast every Sunday. Promise.'

Joseph gazed at the blackened wood stove, cooking implements hanging by hooks from rafters in the ceiling, and the cedar crucifix adorning the mantelpiece. 'But I like it here,' he said.

'We don't belong here. We don't want to wear out our welcome.'

'Shouldn't we say, "thank you" before we leave?'

'We'll write them a note—how's your German? Mine's hopeless.'

'Reasonable—we spent a year in Germany with relatives.'

Amie poked around the living area, sticking her nose into shelves, pulling out tins and replacing them. 'Paper and pen—you see any of those about?'

'Maybe we're not meant to go—maybe we're meant to stay awhile and help them,' Joseph said. He picked up another biscuit and took a bite.

'Yeah, like helping yourself to all their cookies.' Amie couldn't resist thinking that Herr Biar's weight-problem might be more with the constant supply of honey biscuits rather than Boris and his merry band of cockroaches. 'You'll end up looking like Herr Biar if you keep eating them.'

'Amie, that's not a nice thing to say.'

'It's true.'

'Anyway, I'm helping him eat less biscuits.' Joseph examined another cookie before popping it in his mouth.

'I'm going.' Amie marched to the door. She stopped and turned. 'Oh, come on Joe, come with me. Your parents are worried too.'

Joseph didn't move. 'But I really like this place. I dig the simple lifestyle. And the food tastes so good.'

'Look, Joe, we don't have much time. We want to make the cave before the suns set. Besides you know you'd miss television, your computer, and mobile phone.'

'I don't think so. I really like the slow pace and getting back to nature.'

'But, don't you want to know how Breaking Bad ends?'

'Breaking what?'

'Oh, never mind. Anyway, wait till they ask you to pull your weight and work.' Amie strode back to Joseph and tugged his sleeve. 'Come on. If you really have the urge to come back—do. You know where the cave is.'

Joseph grabbed a couple of biscuits and shoved them in his pocket. 'What about the note?'

Amie hauled open the door and then raced out.

***

Amie and Joseph fought the glare of the afternoon suns as they trekked along the saddle. High on the mountain range, the heat of the two suns was tempered by the breeze. Orange-coloured mushrooms dotted the alpine landscape. Every so often low cloud drifted over, blotting out the scenery.

Amie skipped along with a sense of hope and amazement. *Wow! An alien planet! What adventure!* 'Wait 'ntil I tell Adam, my brother.'

'He won't believe you.'

Amie halted. 'What's your problem? We're on an adventure and all you can do is think of the negative?' His attitude, now that she considered it, especially the pessimism, annoyed her. 'Look, Joseph, we're nearly at the cave—and they *will* believe us. I'll take some photos.' She patted her pockets. 'Oh, crud—I left my phone behind.'

Joseph swayed his head. 'Typical,' said in such a way as to underlie the subtext "female".

His chauvinism also peeved Amie. 'And where's your phone or camera?'

He patted his back pocket, then thrust each hand in each side pocket of his baggy trousers and pulled out the lining. 'Crud! I don't have either. I think I left it at Dr. Zwar's—with my clothes.'

'Snap!' she said.

They marched forward in silence. Amie stewed how she never had any success with the opposite sex. Arm's length—they always treated her at arm's length. She recalled the time at youth church—*why is it the boys always overlook and ignore me?*

Amie glanced back at Joseph. Fine looking fellow—but—even with no female competition—he kept his distance.

She shoved her hands in her pockets and continued stewing.

Their steps quickened as they heard the thunder of a waterfall. Still it seemed like ages before they reached the river at the top of the plateau. Amie marvelled how the plains were washed in a soft shade of mauve.

Amie beat her way through the stumpy shrubs, blue with white-cotton flowers that stuck to her t-shirt. She stopped and gazed at the river. The icy air stung the skin of her bare arms and she shivered. Tonnes of mint-green water surged over the lip of the falls. The water was too deep, too forceful to negotiate a crossing.

'Now what?' Joseph just had to be negative.

Amie sighed. 'We'll walk up the hill a bit. Maybe we can find a crossing further up.' She stepped onto a rock by the water's edge, crouched down, and then cupped some rushing water in her hands.

'What are you doing?' Joseph yelled.

'Going to drink some water. What does it look like?'

'But you might get some alien germs in your stomach.'

Amie twisted around and locked eyes with Joseph. 'Oh, shut up! I've had enough of your negativity to last me a lifetime. I drank this water yesterday. Do I look dead yet?'

'Well, I for one, am not drinking that water.'

'Eat your biscuit, then.' Amie scooped up some more water and slurped it. She stood and then stomped along the riverbank. *Won't be asking for his phone number, or wanting him to be my friend on Facebook,* she thought. *No invitation to Nanna's neither.*

They hiked further up the hillside. The landscape levelled out into a network of creeks that crisscrossed the plateau.

Amie and Joseph hopped along the grassy tufts and rocks until they arrived at the river, where, at this altitude, had narrowed into a stream. Rocks plotted a path over it.

Joseph looked at the stones scattered across the water. 'They're too far apart; you'll never get across without falling into the water.'

'Give it a break, Joseph,' Amie said. *Talk about glass half-empty.* 'I thought you did that Parkour?'

Joseph cupped his hand to his ear. 'Huh? What?'

'Oh, never mind. Can't be too hard.' Amie rubbed her hands together, took several steps back, and then ran at the creek. She leapt and danced across the stream as if playing hopscotch.

When she reached the other side, she beckoned to Joseph. 'Come on. Bet'cha can't.'

'Bet'cha I can.' Not to be outdone by a girl, Joseph raced towards the stream and leapt onto the first rock. He wobbled and teetered, then balanced.

Amie watched him jump, wobble, teeter and balance on each rock.

'Come on, I thought you could leap between tall buildings in a single bound,' Amie said with a laugh.

'This is different.' Joseph rubbed his stomach. 'I shouldn't have had all those biscuits.'

'Lost your mojo.'

'Get lost!' Joseph placed his hands on his hips and shifted his feet on the rock. 'I'll show you.'

'What's the worst that can happen?' Amie said. 'You'll fall into the water, get wet, and get alien germs.'

'If you can do it, I can.' Joseph sprang to the bank.

A clod of mud slid under his foot. He began to reel backwards.

Amie caught his hand. But the force of gravity caused her to overbalance.

Joseph landed on his back in the bubbling brook and Amie fell on top of him.

'Whoops!' Amie giggled as she rolled off Joseph. 'Now you have girl germs too.'

Joseph pulled himself to standing and holding Amie's arm, he helped her to the shore.

They sat on the bank to catch their breath. Amie brushed lumps of mud and algae off her shins and knees. 'At least when we get back to Earth, it'll be boiling hot and we'll dry off really quickly.'

Joseph pulled a soggy mush from his pocket. 'I was saving these for when we crossed the river.'

'I guess you won't be eating them, now.' Amie pushed her shoulder against Joseph.

They laughed.

Amie paused; conscious there was no distance between them at that moment. Maybe she had him all wrong. She caught him gazing at her. Her heart skipped a beat. 'Sorry, I was mean to you before—you're alright, really.'

'It's okay,' Joseph touched her arm. 'Come on, we must get to the cave before dark.' He stood and reached out to her.

She grasped his hand, warm, enclosing hers. He pulled Amie up and his hold lingered, then he released her fingers.

Joseph paced towards the rise. 'I recognise that rise over there; the cave is just over there.'

Amie followed him.

The first sun had sunk behind the peaks causing faint shadows over the stony terrain. The second sun seemed more distant, cooler and the alpine air had a biting chill to it.

Amie and Joseph approached the cave. An amber light glowed in it.

'That's funny,' Joseph said. 'I don't remember there being any lights.'

'Perhaps you only see it when it's getting dark—there has to be some sort of energy that operates the portal.'

Joseph crept ahead, advancing up to the cave's entrance. Amie followed his lead.

The atmosphere was still, like in an ice cave. The glow grew more intense along with the sound of crackling like a fire.

Joseph stopped at the side of the cave. Amie caught up to him.

A shadow wiggled and jiggled on the red walls.

'What are you stopping for?' Amie nudged Joseph.

Joseph turned and put a finger to his mouth. 'Shhh!'

Someone cackled like a witch.

'We have company,' Joseph whispered.

'No need for all the secrecy, I know you're there,' the voice echoed in the cave.

Amie and Joseph froze. They looked at each other, eyes wide as if caught in a guilty tryst.

'Come on!' the voice urged. 'I was wondering when you two would get here. You know, they're all searching for you back home.' He sounded familiar. 'Pity you'll never get back there, now.'

The Power of Prayer

World of the Wends

Amie peeked into the cave.

Walter Wenke perched on a rock slab and warmed his hands over a campfire.

Amie said, 'Walter? What are you doing here?'

Joseph looked in and then hung back.

Amie gestured to Joseph. 'It's okay, it's just Walter, my Dad's friend.'

Joseph grabbed Amie's elbow and yanked her out of the cave.

'What are you doing?' Amie shook him off.

Joseph pushed her away from the cave and muttered, 'Since when does your friend Walter have wings?'

'What do you mean?'

Joseph continued to push her. 'Don't look back—run!'

They ran, stumbling down the slope. This time no rock hopping over the stream. They swam. Then they galloped down the hill.

To catch their breath, they huddled against a rocky outcrop.

Amie gasped for air and then said, 'So what you're saying, that wasn't Walter—but that Boris you're always on about.

Joseph gulped and nodded.

'Yeah, well, here's the thing, if he is, how come he hasn't chased us?'

A flutter of wings made them look up. 'You were saying?' a voice above them said. Walter Wenke's face loomed in the darkness above them. He squatted on the ledge, his wings vibrating in the wind, four arms resting on his ribbed chest, and antennae twitching above his eyebrows.

'I have a bad feeling about this,' Joseph murmured.

Amie locked eyes with the beast. 'Let me just get this straight, so you're not Walter, you're Boris. Does that mean my family was travelling with you all the time we've been in Central Australia?'

Boris laughed, a hacking cackle, the type that sounds like he was coughing up phlegm. 'Oh, I have enjoyed getting to know you, Amie, my dear...'

'Let me just clarify another fact, Boris,' Amie continued unfazed by Boris' sleazy comment. 'When you said at the cave, we'd never get back, does that mean you've done something to the portal—I assume it was a portal—that we went through?'

'How perceptive of you—I do like that in a female.' Boris glanced at Joseph. 'Don't you, my lad? Good breeding material for my foot-soldiers.'

Amie shuddered.

'Don't disgust me,' Joseph said.

Amie slapped Joseph. 'I disgust you?'

Joseph rubbed his cheek. 'No, not you—him!'

Amie eyeballed the creature. 'If you think I'm going to breed cockroaches, like those poor hens in the village, you have another thing coming.'

'Cockroaches? Who said anything about cockroaches? I breed humans—super humans—for my domination of Earth.'

'Give me a break, how corny. Then what are the Wends for?'

'Why, practise, of course,' Boris touched his chin with one spiny finger. 'They do make solid breeding stock. The females are so strong—and compliant. And there's so much meat on the men.'

Amie leaned back and studied Boris. 'You don't scare me. You're just a big fat corny cockroach. What're you going to do? Infiltrate the Earth with blonde Germans and eat the fat ones? Get a life! Can you believe this guy?'

'Oh, but, my dear, it's all true. I'm executing my plan at this very moment. Nothing can stop me. Mwa-ha-ha-ha!'

They watched Boris as he wrung his two pairs of hands and laughed.

Joseph tugged at Amie. 'Let's go.'

While Boris mused over his own delusion of grandeur, Amie and Joseph crept away, and slipped into the gully. Amie kept glancing back, certain Boris would haunt them, but the only thing Boris did was make his laughter ring through the hills and valley. He seemed, for the moment, caught in self-absorption, entranced by the glory of his own power.

***

Upon reaching the Biar cottage, they stowed inside. No locks on the doors.

Herr Biar and his Frau sat at the table by the light of a candle.

'You're back,' Herr Biar said.

'Sorry,' Joseph spoke in his fluent German. 'We were trying to return to our world...'

'To get help,' Amie said in her textbook German.

'And did you?'

Amie shook her head.

'We've been praying for you,' Herr Biar said.

'The evil one is active.'

'Boris?' Amie asked.

They nodded, a sombre expression on their faces.

'Oh, I wouldn't concern yourselves, with that stinky old cockroach,' Amie said.

Their eyes widened.

Herr Biar's voice rose an octave. 'You met him?'

'Yes, he's 'armless,' Amie said in English giggling at her own joke—more nerves than anything. Then she explained. 'I mean, he had four arms, two legs, and wings. But we got away from him, didn't we, Joseph?'

'You escaped?'

'Yes, he was too full of himself, that guy—we ran away while he admired his own what'sit.'

Herr Biar slapped the table. 'You got away?'

Frau Biar gazed at her husband. 'I told you, mein Herr, prayer works.' She then bunched up her apron and stood up. 'Right you two, you've had a long day—time now to schlaf—schlaf vol!' She ushered Amie and Joseph up the stairs. 'You, Amie sleep with Wilma tonight, and Joseph, you may sleep in Friedrich's room. I'll bring you hot chocolate and cookies shortly.'

***

Joseph had to do what nature requested. With candle in hand, he padded down to the end of the garden at the back of the house to the little outhouse, the dunny.

He steeled himself against the lingering smell of raw sewerage, and settled his bottom on the wooden bench over the hole.

No toilet paper, he observed. No newspaper, either. Now what? 'Damn, how am I going to wipe?' he muttered. 'Awkward!'

He pondered how he'd solve this issue. The sound of leaves fluttering in a wooden vat caught his attention. *Leaves.* 'Ahh!'

As he wiped with the leaves, the fluttering sound turned into a buzz, then a whizzing sound.

Joseph pulled up his pants and held his breath—not from the smell, but the sound which was quite loud by this time.

'Now, young man, let's see if I find you here,' a man's voice said.

Joseph recognised that voice. *O-oh, this is not good!* Fear like an Antarctic blast, paralysed him. He perched on the bench. The rustling was the other side of the outhouse door—an unlocked door—the Wends didn't believe in loo locks—apparently.

Then he came to his senses. He puffed out the candle-flame. He slid to the floor, and lay flat. At least he could pretend the dunny was unoccupied. Maybe the fruity scents would put Boris off.

'Now, I bet my little man is in here...' Boris said.

Maybe not...

He heard scuffling.

Joseph counted the seconds until Boris ended his life or began hundreds of others in his breeding programme. Probes. Would there be probes?

His fingers touched a handle in the floor.

He pulled.

A wooden flap moved.

The door cracked open.

He lifted the flap and scrambled down the ladder. The flap slammed shut.

He entered a room bathed in smoky light. In one corner was a box with a screen and knobs and switches down one side. A red laser light pulsated on the far side. Piled on the other side, the stinky pile, steaming and fermenting for the Biar's garden.

Joseph recoiled from the earthy stench and stepped over to the beam.

The trapdoor creaked.

Joseph searched for a shadow in a corner to hide. He charged through the light. The place blacked out. In the inky darkness, he groped for a wall. His hand ran over a slab—hard like concrete. The air was cold and still. He was reminded of the solitary confinement cells for convicts in Port Arthur, Tasmania. His mother refused to enter the cell. She said it spooked her, as if the ghosts of the tormented convicts lingered there. An odour hung in the atmosphere of this room; a pungent, unforgettable smell. Joseph gagged. He remembered that smell, having lived on a farm in the Adelaide Hills: the odour of dead animals.

Then, out of the darkness, a moan, a low anguished groan like a ghost or a demented alien. Joseph imagined all sorts of creatures grew in the darkness, they multiplied like demons in hell.

Joseph turned and darted across the red line of light, and back into the cellar. He returned just in time to see Boris' backside disappear up the ladder through the trapdoor.

'Phew! That was close!' Joseph wiped his forehead damp with sweat.

As the trapdoor clicked shut, Joseph stepped back and cowered in the moaning blackness for a few moments. He took several deep breaths, and regretted doing so. He couldn't decide which was worse, the pong of excrement, or death. Both made him gag. He then stepped over the red beam again and into the warm but unwelcoming air of human waste.

'I hope Boris hasn't locked the trapdoor,' he mumbled as he climbed the ladder.

Joseph reached the top rung and pushed. As the trapdoor lifted, he sighed. 'That's a relief.' He peeped up into the outhouse. Beams from the Hand of God nebula filtered through the cracks in the wooden structure. All was quiet.

He heard thumping in the garden.

Joseph scrambled up and shoved the bucket of leaves against the door. *Better than nothing. Or was it?*

Thud! Thud! Thud!

Joseph curled himself in a ball and huddled in a corner. Below him, moaning echoed. The door thudded and knocked over the bucket. *Can't be Boris, he'd let himself in.*

Bang! Bang! Bang! *Perhaps it's one of the Biars.* Joseph opened his mouth to speak. Then imagined Boris lurking there the other side of the outhouse door. Silently, he shifted to the door and sat, pushing against it.

***

Amie had snuggled into her bed she shared with Wilma. She had sipped her hot cup of cocoa, and had enjoyed the chocolatey taste of "Mutti Liebe".

'I love cocoa,' Wilma said. 'It's made with Mother's Love'.

Amie nodded and tipped the cup to her mouth ready to take another sip. A lumpy bit of cocoa floated on the surface. Amie slurped it into her mouth and swirled it with her tongue. Nothing like chocolate bits.

But the "bits" seemed to wriggle like they had legs. *What the?* Amie gulped. She gagged. The lump seemed to claw at her tonsils. She coughed...and coughed...and coughed.

'What's wrong?' Wilma asked.

The lump slithered down Amie's throat into her stomach.

Amie wheezed. 'I think I swallowed a spider...' It jiggled inside her like some giant bug. A sickening feeling sloshed in the pit of her stomach. *Not a cockroach—not just any cockroach—a Boris-roach...Oh, no, I hope it's not going to grow and breed in my stomach.*

Amie jumped up and out of bed. 'I've got to get it out.' She snatched the cup and then tossed the remaining cocoa out the window. Then she scrambled down the stairs and forgetting to take a candle, bolted to the outhouse.

Amie, head down, hands stretched in front of her, charged at the outhouse door. It didn't budge.

She rammed it again. This door was tough. Must be wedged tight. Or someone was in there sitting up against it. She butted against it using the side of her body. No movement.

'Look mate, I'm not letting you in, wait your turn,' a voice distinctly Joseph's said. Well, not distinctly, obvious, as the voice spoke English.

Amie stopped door bashing and replied in English. 'Oh, sorry,' she paced, 'Can you hurry? I need to vomit.'

'Use the garden.'

'You don't understand—I swallowed a cockroach—one of those Boris ones—I need to get it out—now!' Amie banged on the door.

'Shhh!'

'I don't want it growing and bursting out of my chest. I need to barf it out before it takes over my body,' Amie said. 'I can feel it crawling in my stomach.'

'Chuck in the garden, if you're that desperate.'

'No, it has to be flushed down.'

'No flush here,' Joseph said. 'It's a long drop.'

'Oh.' Amie pictured the contents of a sewerage pit. 'Never mind, that'll do the job.'

'If it's a bug, I doubt it, and if it's a Boris one, definitely not.'

'But better stuck in a deep hole than getting into chickens. Come on! Let me in!'

'You'll regret it.' Joseph opened the door and gestured for her to enter.

The pong overwhelmed Amie, the fruity atmosphere causing her eyes to water. 'Phew! Was that you?'

'No, it's a long drop—probably only gets emptied once a week, if you're lucky.'

'Aw!' Amie waved her hand. 'I can't believe anything, even a cockroach could survive in that. It's gross!'

'We'll see about that.' Joseph shifted to the side of the small room.

Amie glared at him. 'Well, aren't you going to leave?'

Joseph shook his head.

She could just see his profile by the light of the nebula.

'Why?' she asked.

'Shhh!'

'What do you—'

He clapped a hand over her mouth. 'Quiet, hear that?'

Joseph pulled her out of the doorway and to the side. Amie obliged, staying still and silent, against him. His heartbeat against her spine, fast.

They heard a quick succession of clicking sounds.

Joseph pushed the door slowly until it shut. Then he pushed himself against the door.

Amie crouched by the door and peered through a crack. 'What's out there?' she whispered.

'Boris.'

'Boris? But this'll be the first place he looks.'

'Not necessarily.'

A wave of nausea hit Amie. 'I think I'm going to be sick.'

'If you have to, try and be quiet about it—I don't want to attract his attention.'

Amie bent over the hole in the wooden slats and heaved. The lump along with cocoa and water, and other stuff with the consistency of peas and carrots she didn't recall eating, hurled into the stinky abyss and made a distinctive plop way down below.

'I said, "be quiet".' Joseph sounded like he spoke between his teeth.

'I'm sorry.' Amie wiped her mouth with her sleeve. 'Any water?' She smacked her lips together, the acidic taste making her grimace.

'What do you think?'

Something whirred near the door.

They stopped in their poses like stations of the cross. The whirr faded.

They heard knocking. 'Oh, Herr and Frau Biar, Boris here, just wondered if I could have a word.'

'It's late, make it quick,' Herr Biar snapped.

'Pardon the lateness of my visit, but—you haven't seen two young people—a young female, and a young male, have you?'

'We have no young male or female here apart from our children.'

'Oh, but, I beg to differ—now come, tell the truth, or I'll take drastic action and you don't want me to take drastic action, Herr Biar.'

Amie touched the door.

Joseph placed his hand on hers and shook his head.

Amie looked at him in the dim light. 'But I don't want them hurt.'

'They'll be fine—he's bluffing,' Joseph whispered. 'He doesn't know we're here.'

'How?'

'Tell you later. Now shush.'

Amie peered through the crack.

Candlelight flickered as the men ambled in the garden. Boris hunted high and low, his laser torchlight shone into bushes and up trees.

At the back of the house, Boris bowed to Herr Biar, who then went inside closing the cottage door. After making a final sweep of the yard, Boris marched around the side of the house, to the front, and then out of sight.

'Amazing,' Amie said. 'He didn't even give the toilet a second look.'

'Must've been satisfied by the first,' Joseph snorted in a brief laugh.

'But how did he not see you?'

'This.' Joseph crouched and then traced the floor. He tugged at something and opened the trapdoor a little. Pink light filtered through the crack.

'What is it? Some sort of cellar?'

Joseph nodded.

'So, you hid there?'

'Yes, sort of.'

'What's the light?'

Joseph shrugged. 'Glow worms? A buried spaceship? I don't know.'

'And Boris went down, looked, and didn't see you?'

'No.'

'We'll have to investigate further.'

Amie moved to climb in.

Joseph held up his hand. 'No, not yet.'

'Why? Maybe it's a ship or perhaps another portal—we must find out.'

'No, we have to be careful.'

'But why?'

'It's creepy down there. I wasn't alone. There was something down there. I could feel its presence.'

Moaning echoed from below. Sounds of agony filled the little toilet. Amie and Joseph looked at each other, eyes wide with terror.

Joseph slammed the trapdoor shut.

Amie stood, then stepped and stumbled over the bucket. Her knees crunched on dry leaves. She grabbed the bucket and flung it behind her. It clattered on the bench. Joseph crashed open the door. Leaves whirled in their faces.

The two teenagers scrambled out and raced to the house. Reaching the back porch, Joseph looked around and then tapped on the window. The door opened and Herr Biar appeared. He glanced over them and out into the night. 'Hurry,' he said, 'before Boris catches you.'

Wake and Walkabout

Central Australia

Walter groaned. His head throbbed as though a giant cockroach had clobbered him. Then he remembered. A giant cockroach had clobbered him over the head.

He jerked and wriggled on the slab. Someone had bound his feet and hands with ropes. Probably the giant cockroach.

He writhed on the slab. He rubbed the rope on the stone.

The rope held fast.

Walter squirmed. Why was it so dark?

He teetered on the edge. He wriggled some more to keep balance. He teetered some more. Wriggling, squirming, it made no difference.

He crashed to the floor, the impact stunning him.

He woke. A thread of light shimmered.

Walter heard breathing. Feet scuffled on the dirt floor.

A human form shifted into the light, blocking it. Then black again.

Pain racked Walter's body in waves, and he moaned.

***

Morning: Arthur spoke to his wife on the CB Radio.

'Carol—dear, I have some—um—bad news.'

'Oh, no, it's one of the children.'

'Well, um, yes.'

'What's happened?'

'Amie, she's missing.'

'Oh God!' Carol paused. The radio crackled.

A tear trickled down Arthur's cheek.

'Where?' Carol asked. 'When? How long?'

'Out West—near The Spring. She's been missing since yesterday—I mean, two nights.'

'Two nights? But it's so cold. She could've got hypothermia.' Carol raised her voice. 'And you didn't think to call me earlier?'

'We didn't want to worry you—if it was just overnight...' Arthur's voice trailed off. He was in deep—doo doo—burying his whole being in it.

'Right. I'm flying straight up,' Carol said. 'I'll be at The Mission this afternoon, if I can. Tomorrow at the latest. Okay?'

'Yes, dear.' Arthur trembled as he replaced the receiver. Amie's absence was all the more real now he'd told his wife. He stared at Adam bunched up in the front seat of their Land Cruiser. Adam played his mobile phone game, so dealing with the crisis by losing himself in the digital world.

Arthur Fleischer sighed. *If only it was that simple.* However, he knew he must stay focussed on the here and now—the real world, missing Amie.

Fleisher scanned the horizon. Even at eight in the morning the atmosphere shimmered with heat and a haze of flies.

By the way, what's happened to Walter Wenke? Arthur wondered. He hadn't seen him this morning. *Hadn't seen him most of the day before, come to think of it.* He last recalled Walter had gone "searching" after breakfast yesterday and that was the last he saw him. Not that he missed Walter—*That bloke has become just a little too slimy. I don't like the way he sidles up to Adam—just a little too close,* he thought.

Never-the-less, Arthur asked Dan Hooper the policeman. 'You haven't seen Mr. Wenke have you?'

Officer Hooper shook his head.

'That's another one we have to look for, a third lost person.'

'Hmmm,' Hooper said. 'This place is becoming the Bermuda Triangle of Central Australia. How can three people just vanish?'

Fleischer nodded.

'Not to mention the busload of tourists,' Hooper mumbled.

'What?'

'Er, nothing, nothing to be alarmed about. Happens all the time—break-downs, going off the beaten track—that sort of thing.'

'Oh.' Fleischer looked around the campsite. No Nathan. 'Where's the tracker?'

'You mean there's a fourth?' Dan said, then shrugged. 'No worries. With him, it's probably just walkabout, or he's been tracking through the night. They have a different sense of time.'

Fleischer raised one eyebrow. 'Really?'

'You don't think they look at their watches and say to themselves, 'Oh, dear, we're late, we've been out all night, we better get back now,' do you?'

'So, you're not worried about Nathan, then.'

Hooper chuckled. 'Why should I be? He'll be right. I know Nathan, he's the sort that doesn't give up.'

'I hope so.'

Hooper placed his hand on Fleischer's arm. 'You need to get some rest, Arthur. You've been up all night.'

'I can't, I've gotta do something.' He tore away from the officer and then marched up the gorge ripping plants in his way left and right. 'She has to be here—somewhere—she can't've just vanished.'

'Let the experts…' Hooper followed and called after him.

Arthur staggered up the slope and then slumped under a ghost gum. He sat on a stone, his face in his hands, and his whole body shaking.

Dan Hooper put his hand on Arthur's shoulder and guided him back to camp.

***

Nathan stepped into camp.

Food—anything—toast, porridge, or even dull, colourless and boring semolina, and a cup of billy tea—just the thought tantalized his tastebuds.

Dan Hooper and Arthur Fleischer cut through the eucalypt saplings and entered the campsite. Fleischer raced over to the four-wheel drive to check on his son who looked like he'd been playing games on his mobile phone all night.

'What took you so long?' Dan asked.

'Been tracking all night. Found nothin''

Dan gave Nathan a soft punch to the arm. 'Some tracker you are.'

'What?' Nathan rubbed his arm. He knew Dan. He knew he was joking. 'Whad about you sitting on your backside all night?'

'Aw, I've been holding Daddy's hand,' Dan whispered. 'Do you know how challenging that has been?'

'Don't get too close.' Nathan laughed. He then looked down. 'I tracked 'em to a cave. Two lots of footprints. One boy. One girl. But in cave, no boy, and no girl there.'

'Great! Just what we need.' Dan kicked the sand. 'Look, mate, we have to give it a rest. The helicopter's still out there, we have the guys up from Alice still searching. But we need to take these guys,' he pointed at the father and son, 'back to The Mission. The wife, Carol Fleischer's coming up.'

'But, boss, I'm close. I feel their spirits in the cave.'

'No use without their bodies.'

'They're still alive. They're in the world where the sun always shines.'

'Sounds like heaven.'

'No, not heaven. There's a cockroach man there. We need to find and save them before the cockroach man get them.'

Dan Hooper rolled his eyes. 'Is this another one of your stories?'

'No, it's real.'

'Is this the same cockroach man who you say took the bus load of tourists away to the land of flying insects?'

'Yes, Dan.'

'This cockroach man seems to be quite busy lately.'

'He is, Dan.'

'So, if this cockroach man has taken the boy and the girl, what do you think he'll do with them?'

'He'll breed them, Dan.'

'I see.' Dan scratched his chin. 'And the tourists?'

'Breed some, and eat some, Dan.'

'So, I'm looking for a cockroach, Nathan.'

'Well, not exactly.'

'What do you mean? What does this cockroach man look like?'

'You're not going to like it.'

'Try me.'

'You won't believe me, Dan.'

Hooper beckoned. 'Go on, I'm curious.'

Nathan stared at his feet. He raised his hand above his head. 'This tall. Him little bit fat. Round face. Brown curly hair. Check shirt, glasses, navy shorts and long white socks.'

'Do we know this person, Nathan?'

Nathan nodded.

Dan shook his head. 'No, not...'

'Walter, Dan.'

'Walter Wenke?'

Nathan nodded again.

'Well, that takes the biscuit.'

'Last I saw him, he had wings.'

'You're winding me up,' Hooper nudged the fire with his boot. 'I don't believe ya.'

'Told ya, ya wouldn't. But it's true.' Nathan picked up a bowl, then the packet of cornflakes. As he shook the cereal into his bowl, he said, 'And he tried to kill me. He's a bad cockroach man, Dan.'

'I don't believe you,' Dan said. He turned and trudged over Mr. Fleischer and son.

Nathan munched on his cornflakes. *Why do I bother? You tell'em truth and they don't believe you. The cave was blocked. But there's another way. Cockroach man must have another way close to home. Might check out old morgue...strange goings on around that place lately...*

***

The trek returning to The Mission in Dan's patrol car began in silence. The traverse along the wheel-ruts towards The Pass seemed endless.

Dan concentrated negotiating the rough track. He bumped his deluxe four-wheel-drive along at twenty kilometres an hour.

Nathan waved a hand at the direction of the track, sometimes hidden by overgrown bushes and lack of use.

Dan's thoughts began to meander like the trail. *He seems to spot the bush tracks fine. Why can't he find the lad and the girl? Surely, they hadn't strayed that far. Could he be right? Had they been abducted by aliens? Filleted cows. Nah, too much like science fiction. Has to be a logical explanation. Wasn't one for the cows, though. Irrelevant. That was Switzerland. This is Australia. Haven't seen any strange phenomena concerning cattle in this country. There was that dingo in the Precinct...How did all those cockroaches get in its stomach?* Dan nodded. *Maybe Nathan has a point.*

Dan glanced at Nathan. His head rested on the window. Every so often it bounced against the pane as the vehicle rolled over a rock. Nathan's eyes remained shut.

Poor chap, he needs his sleep. I guess I'll have to find the track on my own. He glanced behind. Father and son, heads bent towards each other, eyes closed. Phone hung loosely in the boy's hand and the father was snoring. Dan gripped the steering wheel and squinted at the lines in the sand.

In the west thunderclouds plumed, their underbellies pregnant with moisture ready to burst and storm.

As he struck the The Loop, Arthur woke and plopped a comment. 'I feel a bit bad leaving Walter behind.'

'He'll be alright,' Dan said. 'He can come back in your car with the search crew.'

'Yeah, I s'pose.'

Nathan woke and looked out the front windscreen.

'Probably better this way, Dad.' Adam yawned. 'Nathan and him don't get along.'

'Hmmm. I noticed that.' Fleischer wrung his hands.

'He's creepy,' Nathan muttered. 'You keep your children away from that beast.'

Arthur cleared his throat. 'You've known Wenke a while, Officer, how does he come across to you?'

Dan swerved avoiding a mound of cow carcass. He also narrowly missed a wedge-tailed eagle, so bloated from gorging on the carcass, it ambled across the road unable to take off. 'How do you mean?'

'He means kiddies,' Nathan said.

'Oh, that's a pretty serious allegation.'

'No, I mean people. He's been acting kind a weird,' Arthur said. 'And he threatened Nathan the other night. Said he'd shoot him. I mean, that's not the Walter Wenke I knew from teaching down south. He's changed since he came up here.'

Dan massaged his temple. All this new information about Walter Wenke was giving him a headache. He'd seen Wenke teaching the kids at the school. They liked him. The little tackers always ran after him when they saw him around the place. His impression of Wenke—a walking encyclopaedia, distinctive in his checked shirt, long white socks and navy shorts, his specialty family history, and a gentle demeanour.

Dan tried to imagine Wenke holding a rifle and threatening to shoot. He tried to visualise him morphing into a cockroach. Nah! Ridiculous! Besides, Walter was the kind of man who, if he saw a cockroach on his kitchen floor, preferred to catch it in a jar and place it outside in the garden.

Dan gasped. *I guess Walter Wenke wouldn't be the first white man to come to the Centre with good intentions and baggage.* Dan shivered. *Maybe not good intentions. Maybe not a man at all…*

'Yeah, well,' Dan said, 'the Centre does things to people. We're at the coal face—we're it. We see things here that you city people're insulated from. We're all there is, you see. If there's a car accident, we're it. A break in. We're it. You get the picture?' *If there's paranormal activity...Am I it? "It" all started with the strangely dissected cows in Switzerland...*Dan sighed. But he wasn't going to share his other cap—investigating extraordinary events over the past few months—the busload of missing tourists, a cockroach plague and reports of strange lights over the Meteorite Range. And the ghost or whatever it was haunting the Precinct. Only last week, a local girl reported a red glow coming from the old morgue, and someone's dog died full of cockroaches. *Did Walter Wenke have something to do with these strange events? He'd arrived six months ago when all these odd things started to happen.*

'Do you think Walter Wenke did it?' Adam echoed Dan's thoughts.

'What makes you come to that conclusion?' Dan asked.

'Well, when I was at the waterhole—he was like—like—weird—um—like the witch in Hansel and Gretel.' Adam bounced up and down in his seat. 'He looked at me like he was going to eat me.'

The hairs on the back of Dan's neck stood to attention. *How did he miss Wenke?* Then a more disturbing thought. *Nathan's right. The Indig have been mumbling about it for months. The Min-min Man.* He'd dismissed it as local folklore—a myth. *Maybe Nathan's not making it up. Did aliens really exist? Was Walter Wenke an alien in disguise?*

'If it wasn't for Nathan,' Adam continued, 'that man would've, I don't know.'

Dan glanced at Nathan. 'Sorry mate—about not believing you this morning. We'll look into it.'

'What?' Fleischer asked.

'We're doing what we can to find Amie and the lad. We've another line of enquiry.' He hoped they would find them in time.

'We'll not stop until we find 'em two,' Nathan said.

'Thanks,' Arthur said.

In his rear-view mirror, Dan noticed Adam had resumed his game on the mobile phone. Just like his son—a son he'd barely seen in his fourteen years. The job and divorce had robbed him of his son just as the desert had robbed Arthur of his daughter and the Swiss couple their son. How ironic, these people had tried their best for their children to get out there, off the computer, see the world—and how does fate repay them? The wilderness snatches them away...or the cockroach man did.

***

Boris gazed at the human form that wailed and squirmed on the ground.

'Like a worm,' he mused. Just like a little fat worm. That's what these earth creatures reminded him of—what, with no shell, and all soft and fleshy. He held his rumbling abdomen. 'Not yet,' he spoke to his stomach as if it were a sentient being.

Boris needed more Wenke cells to take on that particular man's shape. If he ate the poor chap, which for Boris was a very tempting proposition, he'd have to be plain old Boris the Bytrode, and that wouldn't do at all.

Boris patted his tummy. 'All in good time.'

He crawled over to Walter and jabbed his neck with his needle finger.

Walter Wenke went limp. His moaning stopped.

The cockroach extended his proboscis and vacuumed it along his arm. 'Hmmm, tastes so sweet. I do love the taste of fat humans.'

Boris then positioned Walter against the corner sitting him up. 'Now don't go waking up on me, you hear?' He injected more anaesthetic into his victim's jugular vein. 'There, that should keep you out of trouble for a couple of days.'

The Bytrode cockroach studied the human. He looked pale. His face had thinned slightly. Boris rolled his eyes. 'Well, I suppose I better feed you.' His proboscis emerged from his mouth like a hungry snake in search of adventure. It forced its way into Walter's mouth, down his throat and into his stomach where it pumped regurgitated chicken and fresh tender Wend. He'd snatched the baby that very morning. Someone had to pay for hiding the young man and the girl.

Boris then stood on his hind legs and waited. The cells took effect, morphing him into human—into Walter Wenke.

He dressed himself in the jeans and checked shirt he'd stored in his shell. Then, unlocking the door, he stepped out into the Precinct.

The setting sun peeped through a break in the storm clouds, drenching the gum trees and historic church in blood-red hues.

Boris looked left and right. After he bolted and locked the morgue, he strode through the open gate and to Walter's house. He entered through the back. The door was never locked.

The policeman, Fleischer and his wife sat at the table in the dining area. The brilliant sunset shone through the window shrouding in scarlet Adam who sat by it. Brumbies flashed past the window as they galloped along the road; a sight missed by Adam who kept on playing his phone game.

'Well, there you all are.' Boris announced his arrival.

The three adults snapped their attention to him. Speechless and pale.

They knew something. And Boris didn't like the something they might know.

In the distance, thunder rumbled.

Sunday Worship

World of the Wends

Clang! Clang! Clang!
Amie bolted upright.
Clang! Clang! Clang!
Amie nudged Wilma. 'What is it?'

Wilma stretched and yawned as if she had all the time in her lost world.

Amie grabbed her upper arms and shook her. 'Wilma! What is it?'

The sound of clanging echoed from downstairs.

Wilma shrugged Amie's hands off her and then stretched and yawned again. From outside came the ominous sound. *Bong! Bong! Bong!*

Amie yelled. 'Wilma! Wake up! Was is that clanging and bonging?'

Wilma blinked. 'Church. It's the Lord's Day. We must go to church.'

'Church? We're going to church?'

Frau Biar burst into the room. She hammered a saucepan with a wooden spoon.

Amie huddled under the quilt and covered her ears.

Frau Biar roared. 'Hurry!' She ripped the quilt off the girls. 'You're late! Naughty girls! We're late for church? Hurry!' Wilma's mutti swatted the spoon at Amie and Wilma.

Avoiding the spoon, the girls scrambled from the bed. Wilma flung on her black frock and frilly white cap.

Picking up a larger version of black dress hanging from the back of a chair, Frau Biar flung it at Amie. 'Quick!'

In fear of the wooden-spoon-wielding Mother Wend, Amie peeled off her nightclothes and then slid into the dress.

Frau Biar, satisfied with their prompt cooperation, descended the stairs. Amie and Wilma straightened their black attire and followed.

The mother of the house mumbled something about the men leaving ages ago, and then stormed out the door, leaving the girls lagging behind.

'Sure we're not going to a funeral?' Amie asked Wilma.

Wilma frowned.

Amie was sure Walter Wenke said the Wends wore colourful clothing. She mused. *But what if Walter's Boris? What can I believe?*

'Why is everyone dressed in black?' Amie asked again. 'It's like someone has died.'

Wilma bit her lip and still looked confused.

'Why all the black dresses?' Amie pointed at another family straggling up the path to the church entrance.

'It's our Sunday dresses.'

'Sunday dresses? What's with the little nanny cap?'

'The bonnet? We must wear a head covering for church. It is in the Bible. It is one of the commandments,' Wilma said with big eyes.

'The bonnet? Thou shalt wear a bonnet in the church? Never heard that one.'

They caught up with Frau Biar who tapped her foot at the church gate. 'It's in the Bible. Women must submit to men and wives must submit to their husbands. The hat is a sign of submission.'

Amie looked up to see a cast-iron bell slung between two tree trunks either side of the gate. *So that's the bell responsible for the bonging.*

Frau Biar grabbed Amie's arm. 'Hurry! We're late!' She dragged her to the church door. There she stopped, dusted and shook her dress like a duck settling its feathers, and then walked in.

Amie and Wilma trailed after her, entering the sanctuary. Pairs of eyes tracked their every move—especially Amie's.

Amie halted, overcome with a combination of embarrassment and self-consciousness. She tiptoed down the centre aisle. She glanced up at the dark rafters, down at the mud packed floor, and sideways at the plain glass windows—anywhere but at the people.

Amie had to look at them eventually to find a pew. She spotted Joseph who had an empty space beside him and made a beeline for him. As she reached him, he held up his hand.

'Why?' she asked, then moved to sit by him.

'No,' he whispered. 'Men sit this side. Ladies over there.'

Amie gazed at the pews on the other side. Fifty pairs of eyes watched her, making her face burn as the heat of embarrassment cascaded from the top of her head down her face and neck. She murmured, 'Oops,' and then sidled into the nearest pew on the women's side.

Standing before altar, Herr Biar lead the service. He signalled for the congregation to rise and sing the first hymn. Amie recognised the tune, "A Mighty Fortress is Our God".

The service progressed rather slowly. Amie bumbled through the liturgy and hymns, trying to make sense of the Latin "Kyrie Eleisons", Hebrew "Hallelujahs" and "Amens" and Apostles' Creed chanted in German. She sat when she should be standing, and stood up when she should stay sitting, and sat when everyone else knelt—like some female version of Mr. Bean entering the church service for the first time. She consoled herself. *I guess this is the first time I've participated in a Wendish service.*

Herr Biar prepared to give the sermon. His generous frame filled the pulpit and he pursed his lips as he presided over the people. Amie expected Herr Biar to roar and thunder damnation on the congregation, but his face softened and in a gentle voice, he extended his sympathies to the couple who just last night, lost their infant.

From that moment on, Biar's sermon on false prophets and how to pick them was lost on Amie. During the ten-minute address, Amie craned her neck to glimpse the poor couple. She thought she picked them out—husband on the men's side, his head bowed, and his wife on the other, a friend patting her hunched back. Every so often, the bereaved mother convulsed in a wave of weeping.

Amie kept straining to see the woman. She pondered. *What would it be like to lose a baby? Did Boris have anything to do with her loss?* She became aware of the lady next to her glaring—at her. Her cheeks burning again, she straightened her spine, and lifted her eyes to Herr Biar who had just finalised his sermon with "Amen".

After several more embarrassing moments where Amie added to her already long list of religious *faux pas*, she staggered out into the brilliant light of two suns.

***

'Well done, Amie!' Joseph said from behind her.

Startled, Amie turned. 'What?'

'You've given this sour-faced bunch more entertainment than they've had in years.'

'Me? Oh, don't be ridiculous. I made a fool of myself.'

'Yeah, I know. It takes some getting used to. My family never go near a church, except for weddings and funerals.' Joseph tapped her elbow. 'Come, let's get out of here for a while. Let's walk by the river before lunch.'

Amie smiled. 'I'd like that.'

They strolled to the riverbank side by side. The river sparkled in the light, the ripples like diamonds. The sky was a pale mauve. A soft breeze fanned them.

'Aren't you worried about Boris catching us?' Amie asked.

'Didn't you hear Herr Biar? Boris seems to be gone for now. Usually Boris conducts the church service and tells the people what to do.'

'Boris? But he's evil.'

'We know that. The Biars know that. But the other villagers— apparently don't.'

'So that's why Herr Biar gave a sermon about false teachers, then.'

'Yeah.' Joseph nodded. 'Last night Herr Biar and I stayed up and had this long talk. He knows Boris is evil but he's having a hard time convincing the villagers they've been had.'

'What? Even with the cockroach plague and chooks filled with critters?'

'Yep. Like they don't want to lose face. I guess they've invested their whole lives and all their savings into Boris' promises. They're not going to admit they've made a huge mistake—even if the obvious is staring them in the face.'

'But it's only going to get worse if they don't accept the truth.' Amie stopped. She picked up a stone and then skipped it across the water. 'I mean, how much are they going to put up with?'

'Heaps, apparently.' Joseph tossed a pebble into the water. 'Herr Biar said the Wends used to be such a colourful and cheerful people—now look at them—dressed like they're going to a funeral and walking around all gloomy like they're going to be zapped by lightning. That's what Boris has done. He controls them and they fear for their lives.'

They stared at the waves gently lapping the shore.

'What a spoil-sport,' Amie said.

'And the worst of it—you know the baby? Herr Biar is sure Boris did that. He reckons when they were still in Silesia, babies didn't vanish at all. But now, here, it's happening all the time.'

'I knew it. I reckon he eats them.' Amie hurled a stone into the water and watched the ripples spread from one bank towards the other side—like evil. She trembled. The sense of fear and loss overwhelmed her. She sniffed.

Joseph folded his arms around her and kissed her forehead. 'We'll stop this Boris. I'm going to get the creep. I promise.'

'How?'

'I don't know, I'll think of something.' He held her tight. 'You and me together, we'll help save the Wends.' His lips touched her forehead again. 'Come, we better get back to the Biar's. I'm starving.'

Amie and Joseph returned to the Biar home. Amie tingled all over. She was sure if she looked in the mirror, her image would be glowing. She swooned. *He's into me. Wow! He's into me.*

The aroma of roast chicken greeted them as they entered the home. Wilma, a smirk spread from cheek to cheek also greeted them. 'Here come the love-birds,' she sang.

Frau Biar also had a wide smile. However, she pretended to chastise her daughter. 'Wilma don't say such things. You'll put a hex on it all.'

Herr Biar rang a bell as he entered the home. With his face unreadable like a mask, he clomped into the living room. 'Right, you two, up you go, into the attic. Find some nice trunks to hide in.'

'Why?' Amie asked.

'What? What for?' Joseph said.

Herr Biar didn't miss a beat. 'Our false teacher is back. You must hide.' He ushered them up the stairs, then the ladder and into the attic.

Joseph climbed into one trunk. Amie, unable to find a box in a hurry, covered herself in a pile of rags sitting in front of Joseph's trunk.

Amie could hear Boris as he thundered through the home. He sounded like he was ransacking it. 'Where are they?' he shouted.

'I know nothing,' Herr Biar replied.

'Why do you have six places set?'

'We have visitors coming.'

The stairs creaked.

Boris' footsteps grew louder. 'I know you're hiding them.'

'Where? It's such a small home.'

Crash! Thump! Bump!

'I can smell them.'

'No, that's the roast you smell.'

'Don't get cheeky with me.' Pause. 'Now, what's up here?'

Click! Click! Click! Creee—k!

'Oh, you don't want to go up there, Mr. Roach, it's just filled with junk.'

'But, I do, Herr Biar. You'd be amazed at what junk may hide. Or would you?'

The beams groaned under Boris' and Herr Biar's weight as they entered the attic. The creaks and groans grew louder.

Amie peeked through the clothes pile. Boris poked his torch in corners. Over cobwebs. Under boxes. Closer. Closer.

Amie held her breath. Boris stank. Like crushed cockroach. She willed the creep to avoid her rag collection.

Something grabbed her collarbone.

She gasped.

A hand wrapped over her mouth. 'Shhh!' Joseph whispered.

Where did he come from? She couldn't ask aloud. For one thing, his hand stuck over her mouth. For another, they had to be quiet with Boris hunting in the attic.

Then she noticed Joseph's other hand. It had a life of its own and wandered across her breast and the fingers undid the top two buttons of her shirt.

She wanted to ask, *What are you doing?* But it was as though she was in the dentist's chair, with dental stuff filling her mouth and the dentist asking a string of questions.

As his fingers meandered over her skin, she wanted to push them off, but any movement would attract Boris.

The fabric mound filled with light. 'Hmmm, I wonder what's underneath this assortment of cloth?' Boris said.

A sheet fluttered away from above Amie.

Joseph circled his arms around her.

Amie stiffened.

Boris shone his torch on them. 'Well, well, well...What do we have here?'

Roast Cockroach

Amie pulled away from Joseph, and then fastened her buttons. Joseph gasped, 'Oh, how embarrassing! We've been sprung.'

Amie glanced back at Joseph. He pulled on a shirt.

'I see,' Boris said.

'I'm so sorry, Herr Biar,' Joseph continued, 'we—we just couldn't help ourselves—and—and we know how you folks from the nineteenth century feel about—um—um—that stuff...'

Amie caught on. 'Especially on Sunday...I don't know what came over us.'

Herr Biar blushed. 'I'm glad we caught you two just in time. You do realise that it is a sin what you do—and on the Lord's Day—and you will have to confess it in front of the church.'

Boris glanced from Herr Biar to the "compromised" couple. 'A sin? A little bit of hanky panky in the attic? A sin?'

'Yes, it's against God's law. The ten commandments.'

'A sin? A sin? Well, I'll be...Next you'll be telling me drinking wine is a sin.'

'That also is.'

Boris stared at Amie and Joseph.

'They sinned,' Herr Biar said. 'They must confess. We must get the villagers together and hold a special service of confession.' He winked at the pair.

'Oh, that's taking things a bit too far—and remember, I'm the authority around here. No, I don't believe you. They were hiding—you, Herr Biar were hiding them all this time. You—will—pay.'

Boris drew his hand as a gun. Light flashed. Blinding them. The lamp beside Amie disintegrated.

Amie and Joseph like statues in shock, gazed at the shattered particles sprinkling down to the floor.

'Next will be you, unless you do as I say,' Boris barked. 'Now, you—move it—out!'

Boris forced them to the manhole. They climbed down the ladder.

'Sorry for embarrassing you,' Joseph whispered to Amie. 'I didn't know that stuff about sin'n standing in front of the church and confessing.'

'How are we going to get out of that?' Amie asked.

'We can't—we have to go along with it.'

'Quiet, you two!' Boris prodded Joseph. He pushed them into the dining room and slammed them down into chairs at the table. 'Now that I know who the real visitors for Sunday lunch are, we'll have the roast Frau Biar has prepared. Oh, and I thought, some extra garnish and my own unique stuffing for you all to enjoy.'

'I don't like the sound of that,' Joseph muttered to Amie.

Friedrich set an extra place for the "honourable" Herr Roach.

The seven sat around the dining table in silence. The roast steamed in the centre. Candles either side guarded the meal. Thunder rumbled over the hills and mountains. Lightning flashed.

Boris nursed his ray-gun hand and then he placed it beside his knife; a reminder in case any member of the group chose not to cooperate, Joseph assumed.

'Oh, I'm going to enjoy this,' Boris purred. 'Thank you, Herr and Frau Biar, for inviting me. I do apologise for not being at the service this morning. I had a little business to take care of.' With an evil twinkle in his eye, he glanced at Amie. 'How was the service?'

Amie gulped.

'Boring,' Friedrich said in a sing-song voice.

Frau Biar and Herr Biar tightened their mouths. They frowned at Friedrich and shook their heads.

Wilma piped up. 'Joseph and Amie are in love.'

'I know,' Boris looked at Herr Biar. 'Well, aren't you going to do the honours? Cut up the chicken. I'm sure you're all dying for the roast.'

A black bug crawled out of the chook's orifice. Everyone watched as it meandered across the tablecloth.

Boris drummed the table. 'Come on! I'm hungry!'

Herr Biar sighed. He sharpened his knife and sliced off some chicken breast.

'No! No! A proper cut! Cut the chicken open!' Boris rose and stood over Herr Biar.

Herr Biar jabbed the knife in the centre and flayed the roast.

Cockroaches teamed from the cavity and over the plates, cutlery and vegetables.

Joseph flicked them as they sauntered over his plate. Amie shook them off her dress.

'Come on! Cut the meat up Biar!' Boris raised his voice. 'We want to eat.'

Herr Biar served portions onto the plates. Boris helped. He scooped up the black stuffing and slopped a spoonful on every plate. The stuffing reeked of a rancid stench that filled the room.

'Now, the vegetables,' Boris said. 'Frau serve the vegetables. We must have our vegetables.'

Frau Biar lifted with fork and knife, the roast potatoes garnished with cockroach entrails and plopped them on the plates. Then she added the steamed peas and carrots mixed with bugs.

Six stunned people studied their portions of festering food, not daring to touch it. Boris presided over the group. He grinned from ear to ear, imitating the Cheshire cat from "Alice in Wonderland", as he poured lumpy gravy over the chicken on each plate.

'Go on, eat up,' he urged. 'Oh, and by the way, Amie and Joseph, I have your families—just where I want them.'

Joseph tracked a couple of roaches tumbling in the gravy.

'My, what a fine young man Adam is.' Boris leered. 'Make good breeding, he would. Did I mention your mother's coming up to join the search, Amie? I've got my eye on her. She's a rare bird.'

Boris cackled.

Joseph glanced at Amie. A tear rolled down her nose.

Boris turned his attention to Joseph. 'What's the deal with your folks? Skin and bone.' He curled his lip. 'They'll need fattening up. Some fresh meat'll do—then I can make a nice meal out of them.'

Boris leaned back in his chair and patted his stomach. 'Of course, if—you—cooperate…I might reconsider plans—for them—and if you're really good, I might even let them go.'

Boris gestured. 'Come on, eat!'

Joseph played with the meat and vegetables on his plate. 'Where are they?'

'I said, EAT!'

Joseph skewered some white meat.

'What part of cooperate don't you understand? Do you think I'm not serious? One false move and say "ta-ta" to your parents. Do you want that?'

Joseph shook his head.

'Then, eat.'

'But I'm vegetarian.'

'A likely excuse. Eat! Or your parents die.'

Joseph lifted the fork to his mouth and nibbled a corner of chicken breast.

Boris thumped the table. The cockroaches crawling over it bounced. 'Eat! The rest of you!'

All the others wiped as many bugs as they could off their plates and then put food into their mouths. They chewed in silence.

Joseph took another bite. The meat stuck to the roof of his mouth.

Boris grinned. 'That's better.' Then his smile vanished. He pouted. 'No, it isn't! You're all neglecting my stuffing.'

'But it looks like cockroach vomit,' Friedrich said.

His father and mother glanced at each other. Then while Boris turned his head away from them, Herr Biar caught his son's eye, and tilted his head in the direction of the door.
Friedrich's eyes lighted up and he responded with a slight nod.

Boris switched his focus to them and roared. 'I don't care if it's got maggots! You eat it! All of you!'

Each one at the table except Boris, pushed a tiny portion through their lips and grimaced.

Boris rumbled as he laughed. His stomach jiggled up and down. 'Oh, I am enjoying this. How did you enjoy your mashed baby with cockroach? Rather special—fresh from last night.'

The colour in Frau Biar's face drained.

Herr Biar rushed from the table holding his mouth.

Joseph spat the portion he had not swallowed onto the plate.

Amie wiped the bitter bits into her napkin. 'We've gotta get out,' she murmured.

Friedrich pushed his plate away. 'I'm not eating anymore. Don't care what you say, Herr Cockroach.'

Wilma wailed. She turned white as a ghost. Clutching her stomach, she rose. Then she dropped to the floor, her body smacking against the floor like a sack of potatoes.

Rushing to her daughter, Frau Biar moaned, 'Oh, my baby!' and plucked Wilma into her arms. She glanced up at Boris. 'Look what you've done! You've made my baby sick.'

'I fail to see how, eating reconstituted baby, can make one ill. Pull yourself together, woman!' Boris pointed at Joseph. 'That's the one you should be worrying about. Bet my boots he made her sick. You behave yourself, me laddie, or the town's goin' to get to know what you've done—baby stealing and kiddie poisoning—oh, and there's your parents, remember?'

'You don't scare me, Mr. Roach,' Joseph said. He just couldn't fathom how the villagers would believe such a creepy, evil man.

Meanwhile, Frau Biar sat on the floor rocking her limp child and sobbing.

Milked

World of the Wends

Herr Biar stormed back into the kitchen.

A bolt of lightning zapped the rod on top of the outhouse and a fireball raced along the fence chasing him. Unfortunately, the bull didn't follow Herr Biar into the kitchen. He had opened the gate for George the bull but the "donner und blitzen" spooked the animal. The bull refused to budge.

'That was close!' Hans Biar panted. 'Like Martin Luther, I almost got zapped.'

'How can you joke at a time like this?' Jane Biar said. 'Our daughter is dying, Hans!'

Amie whispered, 'What's he joking about?'

Joseph kept his eyes fixed on Boris. 'Martin Luther, was a young lawyer when he was out in a field during a lightning storm. Terrified, he bargained with God...' Boris glared at him. 'Tell ya the rest later.'

Boris leaned back and rested his head in laced hands. 'Ah, Martin Luther, I remember him. I dropped in on him while he slept. He woke up and told me to go away. The cheek of the monk.' Smug. Very smug. He seemed to take the brooding weather and chaos in his stride as if he were born to exist in such an environment.

He's the devil incarnate, Hans thought.

'Look at our dear Wilma, Hans,' Jane screamed. 'What are we to do? Look at the *terrible* mess we're in.'

'No thanks to Boris here.'

'Oh, but that's not a nice thing to accuse your guest of,' Boris interjected. 'Then again, I did warn you, if you are naughty, you will pay.'

Hans said nothing. He glanced out the open door.

More flashes. More rumbles. He pulled a red spotted handkerchief from his pocket. *Worth a try.* He shook it, and then wiped his brow.

'Hans, aren't you going to do something?' Jane urged. 'Call the doctor—get help.'

Boris rolled off his chair. 'Let me have a look.' He scuttled to mother and child and then hovered over them.

'No!' Jane recoiled. 'Stay away.'

'If that's how you feel.' Boris stepped back to his place at the table and then pointed his gun-hand at Joseph, then at Amie and then at Friedrich. 'Don't you try anything. Understand?'

Herr Biar flicked the handkerchief again. *Come on, George!* He then blew his nose, loud making the sound of a trumpet.

Boris narrowed his eyes so that they looked beadier than ever. He pointed the gun at Hans. 'Move over by your son, Herr Biar. Don't want you making any smart moves.'

'Wouldn't think of it,' Hans said as he paced up to his son. He blew his nose again. The nose cloth fluttered in the breeze from his nose. 'Pardon me, must be the dust—hay fever.'

Another flash and on top of it, thunder cracked.

'I do like it when it storms—reminds me of home,' Boris sighed.

As he gazed out the open door, Hans held the handkerchief up to his mouth and whispered to Friedrich, 'Bell—now!'

Friedrich whipped the dinner bell up from the table and swung it in the air.

The room echoed with ringing.

Boris frowned. 'Now, why did you—?'

Snorting together with hooves thundering drowned out the bell and whatever Boris intended to say.

Hans picked up a chair, and at the same time waved his red rag. 'Go, George! Go!'

The sienna bulk charged through the door. With head down and horns thrust forward, George collected Boris. He pushed him to the wall. And pinned him there.

'You'll pay!' Boris screeched.

The bull butted Boris and gored the wall around him.

'I don't think George likes the sound of Boris' voice,' Hans said.

Hans helped Jane carry Wilma upstairs to her room. From the top of the stairs, he called out to his son. 'Oh, Friedrich, my son, it's milking time. You know what that means.'

'Yes, Papa.' Friedrich raced out the house.

Hans settled mother and child into bed. Wilma was unconscious but still breathing. Jane stroked her forehead. 'Good work, my man. But, did you have to wreck the kitchen?'

'I'll make you a better kitchen, my dear,' Hans answered.

Herr Biar tiptoed down the stairs to gauge the progress of his plan and assess the damage to the kitchen and dining area.

The bull in his enthusiasm to attack the smelly man Boris, had stuck his horns in the wooden wall. He'd pinned Boris there.

The young couple had slipped out.

Hans sighed. *Gut! They've escaped.* He hoped they'd muster up some help. He hoped his countrymen would hear their story and finally, after this morning's sermon, listen and come to their aid. He hoped and prayed God had heard his prayers and the folk would run this charlatan out of town.

The bull pawed the floor and groaned. He was stuck. But so was Boris—for now.

Hans grabbed his own gun and aimed it at Boris. 'So, Herr Roach, I think we have some negotiations to discuss.'

'Never!' Boris curled one side of his mouth. 'Besides, that gun won't work on me.'

Hans flipped the gun in his hand and examined it. 'Really? I'll give it a try all the same.'

'Good luck.'

Hans aimed the gun at Boris. 'Say your prayers cockroach.'

'I still have my hand-gun, you know,' Boris hissed. 'You can't stop me.'

'No harm in trying.' Hans tried to get a clear view of Boris but the bull was in the way. He placed the gun down, and then plucked up the bell and shook it. 'It's milking time.'

A whip cracked.

A gate creaked.

Cows mooed.

'Oh, I'm scared,' Boris mocked.

'Nothing more frightening than a herd of cows with their udders full, my friend.'

One by one, the cows barged into the house, baying, tramping, shoving and pushing.

Hans climbed the stairs. Boris was barely visible squashed against the wall in a room wall to wall with cows and one stuck bull. 'Try and wriggle your way out of this one, Boris.' He chuckled.

Hans checked on his wife and daughter.

Jane looked up and asked, 'What have you done, Hans? My kitchen!'

'I told you,' Hans said, 'you'll get a new one.'

Jane touched Wilma's head. 'It's hot. Get the doctor, now!'

Hans opened the shutters and gazed out the window. He detected Amie and Joseph running up the road. 'Help is on the way,' he said. *I hope.*

Meanwhile, after guiding and then releasing the milk-frenzied cows on Boris, Friedrich ducked into the outhouse.

He sat on the bench. His whole body was shaking.

Just a minute or two. Just to catch my breath. What am I to do? Friedrich prayed. 'Dear Lord, save us from Boris. I'm sorry all the times I was mean to Wilma because she told on me. Please don't let her die. Please let Amie and Joseph get the doctor to help. Amen.'

The Doctor

World of the Wends

Amie and Joseph raced up the road.

Drops of rain plopped on the dirt—with a splat it bubbled on the dust. Those random drops hurtled to the ground; a hit or miss affair, mostly missing Amie and Joseph.

'So how are we going to find the doctor?' Amie asked.

Joseph shrugged. 'Go to the biggest, fanciest house and look for the Merc...'

'All the houses look the same. And I don't think they've discovered cars yet.'

'Knock on a few doors, then. It's a village—everyone must know the doctor.'

They paced up a path lined with pansies.

Joseph knocked on the door.

'You talk,' Amie whispered. 'Your German's better than mine.'

Joseph glanced at Amie. 'Yours is okay—but, whatever. Patriarchal society 'n all that. So better if I speak.'

A lady with a withered face, and so stooped she probably only looked normal if she sat, opened the door. 'Yah?'

Joseph used his best German. 'I beg your pardon, but would you be so kind as to tell us where the doctor resides?'

The old lady grimaced and with an arthritic finger also bent double, pointed down the street. 'At the end of the road, on the corner. The one with the Merc—can't miss it.'

Amie and Joseph caught each other's eye.

'Did you say, 'Merc'? A car?' Joseph asked.

'Yah. Ze horseless carriage—he didn't want to be doctor—he vas our pastor. Aber Herr Roach insisted...persuaded him.'

'With the Merc.'

The woman nodded. 'No one likes it—it spooks the horses.'

A black cloud blotted out any light. The hills rang with the sound of thunder. Lightning flashed, layer upon layer, without a break.

Joseph bowed. '*Danke Schon.*'

Amie and Joseph then hunched over like the old woman and ran down the road. A fork of lightning hit the ground with a crack. The pair stopped and looked up—but only for a moment. Then they bolted to the corner.

Sure enough, there was the house, bigger than any of the other houses, rising three levels and mansion-like. Parked on the side, the Mercedes.

As they crouched under the eaves by the huge cedar door, Amie said, 'This storm gets any worse, and we'll have to drive the Merc.'

'I wonder if the doc knows how to drive it?' Joseph gazed at the silver chassis splattered with rain drops.

'You'd think Boris would give him driving lessons.'

'Not necessarily.'

Joseph knocked.

They waited.

Amie glanced up at the window under the slate roof. She watched for movement of the lace curtains. 'You'd think he'd have some servant to answer.'

'Sundays off, I'm guessing,' Joseph replied.

The rain thickened into a steady wash.

Another bolt hit the weathercock. Crash! Bang!

Joseph and Amie grabbed each other and held on.

'I really like you, Amie,' Joseph said. 'If anything happens to us, I want you to know that.'

'O-kay.' Amie wasn't expecting Joseph to declare his "like" of her, during a thunderstorm on an alien world. 'I like you too—but—um—I think we need to get help for Wilma before it's too late.'

'Yeah, yeah.' Joseph knocked again. 'Perhaps the doctor can't hear above the storm.'

'Why don't we go around the house and have a look through a window.'

'Right.'

They edged their way around the house. They hugged the mud-brick wall, squeezing between it and the garden bed and fruit trees.

When they reached a window, they stood on tiptoe and peered in.

'Do you see anything? Anyone?' Amie asked.

'Looks like the lounge room. There's an armchair. Is that hair? A hand?'

Amie scanned the room. Plush! Definitely plush. There, a mahogany bookcase overflowing with leather-bound books. In the middle of the Persian rug, a blackwood coffee table. A set of lounge chairs upholstered in royal blue velvet were arranged each side of the rug. Smoke spiralled from a silver ashtray.

'Fancy, very fancy wancy,' Amie remarked. 'I reckon there's someone about—they've been smoking a pipe.'

'A doctor? Smoking? Doesn't he know it's bad for his health?'

'Apparently not.'

They paused in silence. So did the thunder.

'Do you hear snoring, Amie?'

'I do.'

Two feet in black socks lifted to the coffee table. The snoring grew louder.

'Do you think he's asleep?' Joseph asked.

'Yes, I do.'

'Well, I'll be. What'll we do?'

'Break in and wake him up.'

'I don't know, he may not like it.'

'We haven't any choice.'

'But—'

'He's a doctor.' Amie prodded the window. 'It's his duty to wake up and help us.'

Joseph rubbed the window. 'How?'

'Window?' Amie pushed at a pane. 'Nah, it's—I don't know—it won't budge.'

'What then?'

'Back door—I bet the back door's unlocked. My mum said when she was little, they never locked the back door. Well, these folks come from a hundred and fifty years ago—I'm surprised they lock the front door! No harm in trying the back, but...'

'Whatever,' Joseph muttered and then led the way to the rear of the house.

By this time sheets of rain had replaced sheets of lightning and peels of thunder. Even so close to the house, the deluge dumped on them and soaked them.

Sure enough, the back door was unlocked.

Amie and Joseph crept in.

Joseph stopped in the hallway, examined the artwork and then nodded. 'These are originals.'

Amie studied the one nearest her; sunflowers in a jug in bold bright strokes. 'That looks familiar, where have I seen that before?'

'It's a van Gogh, an original van Gogh.'

'I see. Oh, look at this! I like this one. Two girls in a field...and the poppies.'

'Monet. Original.'

'Wow! You know your artwork.'

'You pick up these things when you don't have television or computers and stuff.'

'Amazing! And look at the gold fittings on the lamp—and the tapestry—how did this guy afford it all? It's like stepping into a rich man's mansion.'

'He's the doctor of the joint,' Joseph paused, 'although, didn't that grandma say he *was* the pastor?' He sucked the air through his teeth. 'He's been paid off—I wouldn't put it past that Boris. We better tread carefully. Come on, we haven't got much time.'

'He may not be much of a doctor, but...'

They entered the living room.

A stout man slumped in the leather armchair. In his hand, he held a tumbler of red liquid, probably port. His stomach rose and fell in his tweed suit, and he snored, buzzing like a chainsaw.

'He doesn't look like much of a doctor,' Amie said.

'He's the best they've got, I guess.' Joseph sighed. 'Excuse me, sir.'

The bald man continued to buzz. He smacked his lips and drooled down the side of his mouth.

Joseph tapped the wall while he cleared his throat. 'Excuse me, sir. We have an emergency.'

The doctor spluttered. 'What? Who?' He put his spectacles on and blinked. Amie mused he looked like "Toad" in *Wind in the Willows*.

'It's the Biar girl, she's gravely ill.' Joseph held out his hand. 'I am Joseph Smith, from Adelaide, South Australia, remember me? I stayed with you the other night. This is Amie Fleischer, from Adelaide also.'

The doctor sprang out of his chair and grasped Joseph's hand. 'Of course, Joseph. Good to see you again.' He grabbed Amie's hand with both of his. 'Amie from Adelaide, so glad to meet you. How can I help?' He then glanced around the room. 'I'm sorry, the servants. They have Sunday off.'

'It's Wilma Biar. She's very sick,' Joseph said.

Doctor Zwar flapped his arms and searched the room. 'My glasses, my glasses, where are my glasses?'

'You're wearing them, sir,' Amie said.

'So I am.' He fiddled with the pair on his face. 'How can I help?'

'You're the doctor, sir,' Joseph said.

'So I am.' Dr. Zwar whipped up his doctor's bag and then pelted past them and out the front door.

Amie and Joseph rushed after him. They collided into him as he stood on the porch.

'Donner und blitzen, it's raining!' the doc said.

'Yes, it is. But we need to hurry,' Amie said.

'But I'll get my suit wet. I might catch a chill and pneumonia,' the doctor said.

Joseph lifted his gaze to the Mercedes wasting in the rain. 'We could drive.'

'The useless carriage? I don't know how.'

'I think I do,' Joseph rubbed his hands together. 'Where's the keys?'

'In the carriage.'

Joseph looked at Amie and then raised an eyebrow. *So different from our world,* Amie thought. *You could never leave a Merc in the driveway—with keys.* 'Come on, let's get in and drive,' she said.

They hurried through the torrent. Each yanked at a door and then flew in.

Joseph sat, his hands in mid-air. 'Where's the steering wheel?'

Doctor Zwar tapped the wheel before him. 'You mean this?'

'Yes!'

Simultaneously, the doctor and Joseph leapt out of the car and ran around it. They jumped in soaked like drowned rats.

'Just my luck it'll have a flat battery,' Joseph said.

'Be positive,' Amie said.

'It's a Merc.' The doctor shrugged. 'Herr Roach assured me no problems.'

Joseph raised an eyebrow. 'If you've had it awhile and not driven it, it may not start. Fact.' He turned the ignition.

The engine roared to life.

'See?' Amie said.

'Told you, it's a Merc,' Doctor Zwar said.

Joseph engaged reverse and weaved down the driveway and through the gate, collecting it.

'How much experience have you got?' Amie asked.

'Be positive,' Joseph replied. 'Besides, it's raining cats and dogs.' He swung the car onto the road and after shifting the gears in quick succession, accelerated so fast, he fish-tailed all over the dirt road.

'Aghh! Careful' Amie screamed. 'We want to get there in one piece.'

'Be positive, Amie. I'm sure the Merc has all the safety features.' Joseph missed an oak tree by millimetres. 'I know what I'm doing.' He catapulted the car towards the Biar's home.

The doctor clutched the dashboard so tight his knuckles were white. 'It's a Merc!' he rasped.

Joseph sped down the road like it was a speedway. Within seconds, he jammed on the brakes and the car spun doing a donut (360) on the Biar's front lawn and crushing the border of roses.

'Quick,' Joseph said, 'we need to climb up to the second storey and through the window.'

'Why?' Dr Zwar asked.

'The cows are in the kitchen—oh, and a raging bull,' Amie said.

'The bull's trapped Herr Roach,' Joseph said.

Amie stared wide-eyed at Joseph. *He shouldn't've mentioned that cockroach.*

'I see.' The doctor nodded.

Amie gulped.

Dr. Zwar patted her arm. 'Yes, Amie from Adelaide, once we have helped Wilma, maybe you can help us.' He then scratched his head. 'But how are we going to get up there?'

'Maybe there's a ladder in the barn.' Joseph jumped out the car and ran over to the barn.

Amie and the doctor watched him disappear into the wooden shed. Rain washed over the windows, splashing as if buckets of water were being tossed over the vehicle.

Amie and the doctor watched through the blur as Joseph returned empty-handed. 'No ladder,' he said.

'We'll have to help each other climb the wall,' Amie said.

Joseph slumped into the driver's seat. 'How?'

'Drive the car right up to the house. We'll climb onto the car roof, and then I'll climb onto your shoulders.'

'And then what?' Joseph stared out the window at the stone wall. 'Don't tell me, Park-our.'

'Something like that.'

'What about the doc?'

'He'll have to go on your shoulders and then I'll help him up.'

Joseph glanced at the doctor whose face had turned an ashen colour from the rough ride. 'I don't know. He doesn't look that well.'

Amie didn't waste any time arguing with Joseph. She jumped out of the car and into the rain. Using the rough masonry to her advantage, she scaled the stone wall up to the window and then tapped.

Herr Biar opened the wooden shutter and then pulled her in. 'Where's the doctor?' he asked.

Amie leaned out the window and pointed at the Mercedes. Beside the car were the two men, one younger, one older, and both looking wet and miserable.

'Tell them to get up here,' Herr Biar said.

Wilma moaned.

'Hurry!' Frau Biar urged. 'She's burning up.' The mother mopped her daughter's forehead with a damp cloth.

'But we need help,' Amie said. 'I don't think the doctor has climbed a wall of a house before.'

'Aber, they can come through the kitchen—the cows have gone and so has Boris and the bull.'

Amie leaned out the window and called, 'Come through the kitchen, it's all clear.'

As Joseph and the doctor tore up the stairs, Amie reflected, *Boris gone. But where has he gone? And for how long?*

While Dr. Zwar examined Wilma with the contents of his bag and more superstition than medical knowledge, Amie, Joseph, Herr and Frau Biar stayed downstairs in the now wrecked kitchen and dining room. They stood as not one chair remained unscathed by the attack of cows which had udders full with milk. The group averted their gaze from the slush of cow pats and puddles, shielding their noses from the overpowering pong.

'Friedrich must've got them out of here, somehow,' Joseph murmured to Amie.

The doctor descended the stairs. He stared at mud-trampled floor and shook his head. 'Time will tell,' he said. 'Time will tell.'

Frau Biar wailed.

'Pray to God that she will survive,' Doctor Zwar said.

Frau Biar raised her voice. 'What do you think I've been doing?'

Herr Biar patted her hand. 'We'll pray harder.'

The doctor holding his leather bag and a grimace on his lips trudged through the stinky slurry to the door. The outside was a blur of rain.

'Shall I drive you?' Joseph offered.

Zwar scraped his boots on the grass. 'Nein, danke. I'll be fine.'

'Why wouldn't he accept your offer?' Amie whispered as the doctor disappeared into the watery glaze.

'I could teach him.' Joseph gazed out the window that faced the car.

Hardly knows how to drive himself, Amie thought.

Time like the rain drove onwards while all in the Biar home were still, suspended in delayed shock after their encounter with the evil of Boris.

The rain eased to a steady soaking. Amie watched the droplets plop from the roof of the house onto the roof of the car. Beyond the car, and the garden, cows grazed on the blue grass. Two suns like Siamese twins, glowed through the cloudy mist. If it wasn't for them and the strange colour of the grass, she could fool herself into believing this was Earth. After all, she remembered someone from somewhere telling her, that in certain parts of her world, blue grass did exist. But two suns? She'd never seen two suns on Earth.

The men groaned and then moved to shovel the mess left by the cows out of the kitchen-dining area. Frau Biar removed her boots and tip-toed in her socks upstairs to be with Wilma.

Minutes later, the mother appeared at the top of the stairs. 'She's sleeping peacefully, but she still has fever.' She glanced at each person in the warzone that was the dining room. 'Where's Friedrich? Why hasn't he come back? The storm has passed. Why is he not back?'

Rabbit-like

World of the Wends

'I'm sure he's fine,' Herr Biar said. 'He'll be checking on the cows after that nasty storm. And he'll be milking them. There are plenty of cows to milk all by himself. I think there was a pregnant one too—the shock may have sent her into calving.'

Herr Biar caught Joseph's eye and then jerked his head to the door. He then spoke again to Frau Biar. 'Jane, you go up to our dear Wilma and I'll go and see how Friedrich is.'

'We'll go and see if Friedrich needs any help,' Joseph tugged Amie. 'Come on, let's go.'

Joseph and Amie trailed after Herr Biar to the paddock. The cows seemed as calm as they did before, when Joseph had viewed them from the window just a few minutes ago. There were no pregnant females in distress.

Joseph, Amie and Herr Biar wandered along the fence. They scanned the cobalt coloured hills. After the storm, the pair of suns burnt through the clouds, bleaching the sky, and splashing the landscape in vivid hues—like a van Gogh painting.

'Not a bad place to live,' Amie remarked.

'If it weren't for that Boris creep,' Joseph said.

Herr Biar shaded his eyes. 'I can't see Friedrich.'

'Where's that cow Myrtle?' Amie asked.

'Who?' Herr Biar seemed distracted.

'The pregnant cow. Where is she?'

'Oh—her,' Herr Biar said with a chuckle. 'Actually, she doesn't exist—between you and me. Friedrich and I, since all this with

Boris, made her up—she only exists when we have Boris-business and we don't want to alarm the women-folk.'

'I see.' Joseph knew exactly what Herr Biar was getting at. Like when his father on the pretext of going to the local hotel to watch the football, told Joseph's mum he was going fishing. 'Maybe he's in the barn.'

They trooped over to the barn and poked around in the bales of straw. No Friedrich.

'Perhaps he's in the outhouse,' Amie said.

'Or under it,' Joseph added.

'What do you mean?' Herr Biar asked.

'He might be in the cellar underneath,' Amie said.

'What cellar?'

'The one with the glowing blue light,' Joseph said. 'Maybe he's hiding there.'

'Or gone to the other side,' Amie said.

Herr Biar scratched his forehead. 'What do you mean, other side?'

'Where we come from?'

'What? You think the outhouse can take us back home?' Joseph waved his arms around. 'I don't think so, Amie. It's more like where Boris has his office and a heap of nasty demons to keep the likes of us out. Or in.'

'Think about it,' Amie said. 'He's blocked off the cave so the likes of us can't get through—but that means he can't get through either. But somehow, he knows everything about our families. How do you think he knows? Besides, where is he? Hiding in some cave licking his wounds? No, he's gone back to Earth, to check on them. Don't you reckon?'

Joseph shrugged. 'I just assumed he flew back to the cave and rolled away all the rocks.'

'Well, I guess that's a possibility.'

'And have you considered he might've taken Friedrich?' Joseph kicked a stone.

'Stille!' Herr Biar whispered. 'Let's not alarm the Frau.'

Joseph turned and stomped from the barn.

Amie and Herr Biar scrambled to catch up to him.

'Hey, where are you going?' Amie called. 'What are you doing?'

Joseph mumbled. 'Arguing about it isn't going to get us anywhere.' He marched towards the outhouse and then entered it. Amie and Herr Biar were right behind him. 'S'pose it's closer—we'll try this first.'

Joseph was forced to admit Amie had a point. *Maybe—just maybe, Boris had taken Friedrich and was holding him captive in his den. Maybe, just maybe, the moans and groans he heard were the voices of other prisoners Boris held down there.* And he dreaded to concede there was a distinct possibility Amie was right—that the cellar was a conduit to other worlds, including Earth.

Joseph groped for the handle and then pulled open the trapdoor. It was dark down there.

Herr Biar looked on. 'We will need some light.'

'Hey! Yeah! Where's the light?' Amie said. 'The blue light.'

Herr Biar reached over Amie to a ledge. With his large hand he collected a candle and some matches. He struck the match against a grey stone by the door. Then, with his palm cupped around the flame, he lit the candle.

One by one, by candlelight, they climbed down the ladder.

The group huddled together and shuffled around the small room, more like a miner's dugout than a command centre of an alien creature. With the feeble glow, they averted their eyes and noses from the pungent sludge pile ripe for compost and scanned the dusty and broken bits of furniture that resembled remnants ready for rubbish collection rather than tools for interstellar warp-transportation.

Herr Biar picked up a hammer from a broken shelf. 'Oh, that's where it went. I've been looking for that for ages. How did it get down here?'

Joseph traced his hands over the dirt wall, now damp from the recent downpour. 'I don't understand—it's just nothing.'

'Maybe Boris has blocked this too,' Amie said.

'How? The wall's rock solid.' Joseph squatted and continued to examine the wall. 'I'm sorry—but I think we have established Friedrich isn't in here.'

'You're right.' Amie sighed. 'Boris must've gone to the cave in the mountains. And he's taken Friedrich with him.'

'This can't go on.' Herr Biar slumped on a bench. It collapsed under his weight. 'Just what I need!'

***

Herr Biar and Joseph arranged to climb the mountain to the cave while Amie stayed behind to support Frau Biar and Wilma.

'But can't I go with you?' Amie pleaded as the men filled their sacks with current buns, water, hooks and rope for climbing.

'Bitte! Bitte! Bitte!' then resorting to English, 'Pretty please!' Amie ran after them as the men trudged up the valley to the mountains. 'How will you get across the rapids?'

'We have to do this, Amie—and Frau Biar'll be suspicious if we don't go right now to find Friedrich,' Joseph said.

'But it'll soon be dark. You'll never reach the cave in time.'

Herr Biar marched on ahead, his fat legs powering on like pistons.

Amie cantered alongside Joseph. 'It should be me going with you—not him. He'll never make it up the hill—he's not fit.'

'Go back to the home, the women need you,' Joseph said.

'But what if you don't come back? What if Boris gets you? We need you here.'

Joseph placed his hands-on Amie's arms and drew her close to him. 'We'll be back. Promise.' He leant towards her and pressed his lips on hers. She trembled as he wrapped his arms around her and held her. Then he drew back and stroked her cheek. 'I must go now.'

Amie touched her mouth as the men hiked up the hill and disappeared into the valley. The sweet taste of Joseph lingered as she sauntered down the hill back to the Biar home.

***

The night dragged on. Neither Frau Biar nor Amie were hungry. They kept vigil over Wilma, the clock shifted its hands around its face in slow deliberate ticks and tocks.

Tick-tock. Tick-tock. Tick-tock.

An eternity seemed to stretch between the hours—no change in Wilma, still a raised temperature and unconscious. And no men.

'Where are the men?' Frau Biar asked.

'In the field with Myrtle—it's a difficult birth. Breech, they said.' Amie didn't know the word "breech" in German.

'Oh, yes—breech? What's that?'

'Bottom first.' Amie pointed at her backside.

'Oh.'

Another hour dragged by.

'What's happened to the men?' Frau Biar asked.

'Helping Myrtle calve—it's a difficult birth.'

'Oh.' Frau Biar wrung the cloth and dabbed Wilma's forehead. 'Why are they taking so long?'

'It's breech,' Amie said. 'They could be at it all night. I gather you don't have a vet.'

'A vet? What's that?'

'An animal-doctor.'

'We have one of those—a cow healer,' Frau said. 'Perhaps you could go out and call him. You know Doctor Zwar. He could help. He does animals too.'

Amie sighed and rested her hand on Frau Biar's. 'I couldn't do that. I couldn't leave you and Wilma—not with Boris out there on the loose.'

'Aber, Dr. Zwar is very good.'

'I won't go out at night. The men know what they're doing. Joseph grew up on a farm and knows all about cows and stuff.' Amie made up that last bit of information, but she imagined that if, Joseph lived in the hills, he might live on a dairy farm. 'Tell you what, if they're not back by lunchtime, I'll go and get Doctor Zwar. Is that alright?'

Frau Biar nodded.

Tick... Tock... Tick... Tock.

The night continued to drag. The gap between the hourly chimes seemed to grow longer and longer.

As the first sun split the horizon and cast the landscape in shades of pink, Amie stumbled down the stairs. Mother and daughter had curled up in the bed asleep. But Amie who must keep alert was stale and seedy.

Amie poured the last drops of boiling water from the kettle hung over the fireplace, into a teapot of dandelion leaves. She could do with a cup of strong black coffee—real coffee—brewed in a plunger or coffee machine—but she'd have to be satisfied with dandelion tea. Amie poured a jug of water into the kettle.

She heard voices. The crunching of boots on gravel. Her heart skipped a beat. Amie put the teapot on a brick by the fireplace and raced to the door.

She opened it and asked, 'Did you find—?'

Two men caked in mud and dried blood stood before her. They looked wretched and defeated as if they'd lost a fight with a Yeti— or more likely—Boris. They dragged their weary bodies through the door and hobbled to the fire. There they stood, like zombies, in homage to the flames. The stench of cow dung smothered the room.

'What happened?' Amie joined them by the fire. She poured two more cups of dandelion tea and handed each man a cup. 'Tea?' She made this verbal offering as an after-thought.

As if running on automatic, the men accepted the drinks and sipped while staring at the fire. They did not complain about their tea lukewarm and dandelion.

'So, how was it?' Amie persisted.

'How do you think?' Joseph mumbled.

'Not too good, I gather.'

'We got to the cave, but it was blocked,' Herr Biar said. 'And we find no Friedrich.'

'No,' Joseph said.

'Did you have a run-in with Boris? You look like you've been in the wars.' She noticed a cut on Joseph's cheek. 'That's a nasty cut— you need to get that cleaned up or it'll get infected.'

Joseph touched the cut. 'Oh, just a flesh wound where the cow kicked me.'

'Cow?'

'Yeah, one of the cows was calving—we would've been here hours ago but there she was when we were coming back...'

Herr Biar sighed. 'The cow was ready to calve.'

'She was in a lot of pain—breech birth,' Joseph said. 'I helped the calf into the world and,' he pointed at his cheek, 'this is the thanks I get.'

'Mother and child,' Amie gestured upstairs, 'are asleep, just so you know.'

Amie tended to the men's cuts and bruises with the warm water from the kettle, and then she ventured to the hen house to collect eggs for breakfast, so allowing the men privacy to wash and change their clothes.

Over a meal of scrambled eggs, the men discussed their next plan of action.

'We have to organise a town meeting,' Joseph whispered. 'Boris'll be back and we need to be ready when he returns.'

'Aber, it may be difficult. There's some who like Herr Roach. The teacher for one. Boris brought him in after he got the last one hanged as a witch. Strange fellow, the new one—not one of us.'

'But Herr Biar, you don't think Boris could already be gone—or dead?' Amie interrupted.

'No, not Boris, he's like a cockroach, no matter how hard you hit him, and I've tried. But he always comes back. He knows I don't like him. That's why he's giving me a hard time.'

'Have you tried to shoot him?' Joseph asked. 'Surely if he's in human form, a bullet from a rifle would do some damage.'

Herr Biar looked at Joseph. 'You have a rifle?'

'Yes, I brought it back with me from the cave. I left it behind there hidden under some rocks.'

'Boris made sure all the weapons were confiscated when we joined him on the trip here. Not that any of us had guns. We were just poor farmers. But there were a few young men who managed to get a gun or two to defend themselves when the Prussian War and uprisings began.'

Joseph clapped. 'I reckon a rifle might do the trick.'

'Like with the Cylons,' Amie said.

Both Joseph and Herr Biar looked at her with blank expressions.

'Oh, yeah, you don't watch T.V.'

Herr Biar continued to stare at her. 'Tee-Vee?'

'Television,' she mumbled. 'Oh, never mind.'

'So the plan is to have a town meeting,' Joseph said. 'And run this nasty creep out of town. Then I'll shoot him.'

'Not sure about shooting,' Herr Biar said. 'He's an intelligent being and it's a sin to murder.'

'Okay, if it gets desperate, I'll shoot as a last resort?'

'No, not even then.'

'Self-defence?'

'Maybe, but not before he tells us where our Friedrich is.' Herr Biar trod towards the stairs.

While the Wendish father crept upstairs to check on his wife and daughter, Joseph whispered to Amie, 'I'll hunt Boris down and with this gun pointed at his puny head, I'll force him to tell us where Friedrich is.'

'And how to get back home? So we can get proper medical help for Wilma?'

'Yeah, that too.' Joseph nodded. 'But, maybe, I should teach you to shoot. Now, that's an idea. He won't expect you to go 'round shooting cockroaches like him. Yeah, when we have the town meeting, I'll get you to hide behind the organ or something and then pop, you can finish him off when he least expects it.'

'But what about him telling us where Friedrich is? Or how to get back home?'

'Oh, yeah, of course, we'll make sure we have that information first.'

Herr Biar returned. He placed his fingers on Joseph's shoulder. 'Don't do anything rash, my son, it's not like shooting rabbits.'

***

'Come on, Amie, be brave. Anyway, there's nothing to it.'
Joseph cocked the rifle for a third time and thrust it into her
folded arms. 'You said you had a brother, surely you've used a gun
in your life.'

'I just don't see the point.' Amie resisted Joseph's suggestion to
take the weapon. 'I know Boris's mean 'nd all that. But I just can't
do it. It's wrong. We'll get in trouble.'

'Bull! The Wends will thank us. Do you think they are happy
under that man?'

'Yeah, but, isn't there another way? I just don't feel right about
it.' She edged away from the altar. 'I mean we are in a church. We
are breaking the commandments, if we kill Boris.'

'Yes, and what about all the people God struck down?'

'But that was different! God can do that sort of thing to evil
people. We can't. I could never kill anyone.'

'Not even if they are evil?'

'No.'

Without looking, Amie stepped sideways and bumped against
the pianoforte, causing it to wobble on the uneven floorboards.

'So you are going to let the Wends suffer. Let that man take
them to their deaths. Those good people.' Joseph examined the
rifle. He allowed silence to cause his words sink in.

Amie watched Joseph stroke the barrel. She gripped her arm
that begged to be released to grab the gun. Beads of sweat trickled
down her cheekbone. She dug nails into her forearm.

'Oh, well, maybe I'll do the job myself. I'll work out a way.'
Joseph scanned the hall. 'He's got to come in here some time—
soon. They said he's back—and the meeting's starting soon.'

'Who said, 'He's back'?'

'The doctor, Doctor Zwar, when I saw him. I returned the car,'
Joseph replied. 'He told me he'd seen him around.' Joseph
stopped pacing and then stared at the double doors at the end of
the aisle. 'Did you hear that?'

Footsteps. Crunching. Each crunch competing with Amie's
racing heartbeat. Her arm burst free from its captor and reached
for the rifle. 'Here, here. I'll hide behind the piano while you—as
you said.'

In the Morgue

Central Australia

A crack and a flash. Then everything went dark.

Friedrich was sure it was his fault. He was always getting smacks or the belt from his father—usually for not polishing his boots perfectly. Or for spilling milk on the floor. But when he saw the blue line in the air, the urge to escape, was too great. This was not the first time he'd ventured beyond the thin blue line under the outhouse. He just had to go through the light—for Wilma...

Then bang. Everything went black...

Friedrich put out his hands and shuffled forward. He groped for a wall, a surface, anything to orient himself.

He tripped over some bulk. He fell onto it. It groaned.

Friedrich scrambled to his feet. His mouth went dry. It was like his heart, lungs and guts were in his mouth. *Oh, no! I'm on an alien world without light and with groaning monsters.*

The thing at his feet moaned. It sounded like a man.

Friedrich gulped. He knelt down. He held out his shaking hand. He touched something soft and greasy. Was that hair under his fingertips?

'Who are you?' he asked in his Silesian language. 'What's your name?'

The man-thing with hair moaned again and then mumbled what sounded like forbidden words in another language. He'd heard Joseph use such words when angry.

'My name's Friedrich,' the boy said. 'And you?'

'Oh, the pain! The pain!' the man-thing said in that strange language. It did sound like the tongue Joseph and Amie used. They spoke using similar sounds when they were together.

Friedrich presumed the man spoke English. But he knew few English words, so he still hoped the man understood his native language. 'How are you?'

'Oh, the pain! My stomach! My head!'

Friedrich traced the head, the shoulders, arms and distended stomach. 'You're a man, aren't you?' He patted the spongy surface in the middle.

The man groaned and squirmed.

'You're a sick man,' Friedrich said using the word in his language "krank".

'Too right, I'm cranky!' the man straightened up. He grabbed Friedrich's wrist. 'And who the heck are you?'

'Huh?'

'What?'

'Huh? What?'

'What? Huh?'

Friedrich shook his hand free from the man. How was he to make sense of this man in the dark? How was he to make this man understand him? Joseph and Amie could speak his native tongue, Silesian, but this man couldn't, apparently. Friedrich rubbed his hand.

'Who are you?' the man asked. 'Where the frick are we?'

What was this man saying?

What did Joseph do when they met? He asked him if he spoke Deutsch—now he remembered. It was worth a try.

'Sprechen Sie Deutsch?' (Do you speak German?) Friedrich was unsure why Joseph used the word "Deutsch" but it was worth a try.

'Deutsch? Deutsch?' the man said. He squealed, then exclaimed, 'Geez! Why didn't you say you were German?'

'Huh?'

'I speak a little German.'

'Ah!'

'Guten tag—Wie geht es Dir?'

What a funny man. Now he's greeting me and asking how I am. Strange! I better be polite and reply. So, speaking his best in his native language, Friedrich replied, 'I am well, and you?'

'Not so good,' the man replied in Friedrich's language. He talked through his nose, his accent sounding similar to Amie's only thicker.

Friedrich held out his hand in front of him. In the dark he was not so sure where the man was. 'My name is Friedrich Biar. And you?'

'Walter, Walter Wenke.'

Walter's hand grasped his, a firm grip, and they shook hands. They continued to converse in simple German.

'Pleased to meet you, Mr. Walter Wenke.'

'Pleased to meet you, Friedrich Biar.'

'You're not going to hurt me, are you Friedrich?'

'No, why should I?'

'Good, the last thing I remember is some smelly man sticking a big needle into me and now my head hurts and so does my stomach. I feel like I've eaten a sack full of cockroaches.'

'Oh, if it's the smelly man I know, you may well have done,' Friedrich said. 'We had to do just that before I came through the light.' Acidic lumps the consistency of cockroaches crawled up his oesophagus. He forced them back down with a gulp.

'Where did you come from?' the man asked. 'Boy! It stinks down here. That's not you, is it?'

'I don't know—I came down under the outhouse. Perhaps it is you, no?'

'Me? It's you who came through an outhouse? Do you mean the toilet? I guess that'll explain the smell.'

'But this, it smells like dead animal. That is new to me,' Friedrich said. 'I climbed down into a room under our outhouse and I walked through a blue light. But I heard thunder crack, and all is dark now.'

'I get it, you're an alien from another world, or maybe that ghost the locals have been going on about,' the man said. 'You been here before?'

'I'm not sure, last time I went down here, I went out a door and into a village. There were black people,' Friedrich said. 'Mostly I go by the cave and into the wilderness. I met Joseph and Amie there at the waterhole.'

Friedrich heard shuffling and grating against the concrete floor.

'Joseph and Amie?' the man raised his voice. 'You met Joseph and Amie?'

'Yes.'

'Where?'

'At the rock hole.'

'No, where are they now?'

'They're on my world, the world with two suns. The world the smelly man Herr Roach, said was Australia. But I'm guessing it's

116

not Australia.' Friedrich leaned against a slab, the height of a table. It was cold and he shivered. 'Herr Roach smells like dead animal sometimes, and other times like a cockroach. And this place has the dead animal smell. Is he from Australia? Is that why it has that awful smell?'

'That's incredible! We've been abducted by aliens.'

'Our whole town was taken and it was by just one alien, I think. Herr Boris Roach.'

More shuffling. 'Any idea how we get out of here and into the light. I don't want to be hanging around waiting for this smelly Boris alien, do you?'

'No. No I don't know how to get out.'

'We need to do something. We need to get out of here before he comes again,' Walter said. Friedrich could hear Walter scraping his feet along the floor. 'Hurry, we must find a way out.'

Friedrich followed Walter's voice; the nasal twang fascinated him. Joseph had it. Amie had it. Did all Australians have it? Did they all speak through their noses? Even when speaking his language.

Friedrich touched the stone wall. It was freezing. He stepped forward, one foot in front of the other, tracing the line of the wall until he came to a corner. At the corner, he turned to his right and bumped into Walter.

'I think there's a door here,' Walter said. 'I can feel a dent that runs up and down. And it's wood.' His voice rose an octave and seemed more nasal and more excited. 'Yeah, and I think I see some light—well, less black than in here.'

Friedrich heard rattling. He jumped back. His heart pounded.

'Nah, the door's useless,' Walter continued. 'It's locked.'

Friedrich sighed. 'Oh, really. I thought someone was coming to save us, but it's just you. Do you know where we are?'

'Yes.'

'Where?'

'The Mission. I reckon the joker who clobbered me locked me up in the morgue in the Mission.'

'Mission?' Friedrich was confused. 'Where is this Mission?'

'Australia. The Mission is in Central Australia.'

'Central? Right in the middle?'

'More or less,' Walter said. 'Actually founded by your lot from Germany.'

'Germany?'

'Yeah, where you come from.'

'But I come from Silesia, the land of the Wends.'

'Huh?'

It was obvious to Friedrich that Walter had no idea what he was babbling on about. Maybe he spoke too fast for this foreigner.

'Never mind,' Friedrich said. 'If we thump and shout, someone in this mission town might hear us.' He began hitting the door and yelling in Silesian.

Walter joined in the banging on the door and shouting, through his nose in English.

They bellowed and banged for some time. Then Walter stopped. 'I hope whoever hears is not that Boris.'

'I hope so, too,' Friedrich replied and then pounded the door.

As they continued hitting the door, a disturbing thought crept into Friedrich's mind. *What if Walter is not who he says he is? What if he's Boris pretending to be Walter? It was his den I have been using. What if this man is just lulling me into a false sense of security and then—bam!* It stood to reason that Boris could be behind all this. He was a slippery character. One minute he was stranded by the bull horns, and the next, he'd sprouted wings and buzzed out the door and out of sight. Friedrich hoped Boris had been injured and had flown away to somewhere quiet to lick his wounds. He'd hoped he did and was glad he flew out the door and away from his family.

But where did the creature go? Friedrich assumed where he went, but he wasn't sure. Or maybe there were more creatures? Maybe Boris didn't work alone. Could Walter be another Boris-like being? *What's to say he's not working for him? Perhaps Boris got angry with him and locked him up.* Friedrich shrugged, *Never mind,* and resumed thumping the wall and hollering.

Again, Friedrich stopped hitting the door. He had to know. 'You sure you're not one of them? One of those smelly creatures? Boris or like him?'

Friedrich heard Walter exhaling. 'Do I look like it?'

'Don't know. Can't see.'

'Good point.'

'Well, are you?'

'Do you think I'd be hitting the door and making my fists sore if I had anything to do with that creep?'

'No, I suppose not,' Friedrich said. 'So, we better hit the door harder and shout louder. Maybe the villagers are asleep.'

***

Nathan sauntered down the main road. The full moon cast a silvery path over the gravel. The gums shimmered above the white sands of the dry riverbed. The SES search and rescue crew had given him a lift in their utility back to The Mission on their return to Alice Springs.

Nathan thrust his hands in his baggy trouser pockets and stared at the sand shifting beneath his bare feet. *Another day lost. It's hopeless. That desert has swallowed the children. Their souls lost. Lost in the never-never land of spirits.* He paused from strolling and gazed around him. Shadows hovered and shifted in the white walls of the historic church, teasing his eyes. *Was that mean fella, the cockroach Walter hiding behind the church?*

A dingo sprang out from the darkness and sauntered across the compound.

Nathan took a deep breath. *Just a dingo.*

He approached the back of Walter Wenke's house which was not far from the Historic Precinct. *Strange—the back gate is wide open—that's not like Walter Wenke. But then, Walter hasn't been himself lately.*

Nathan entered through the unlocked back door. That was normal. No one locked doors out here, except the Southerners when they were new to town. Walter got used to the Mission ways, but he still made a big fuss about the gate. *Keep us out.* Nathan chuckled. *If we really wanted to get in, how's a fence going to stop us?* Anyway, Nathan had special privileges. Walter had given Nathan a key to the padlock he put on the gate.

Nathan pushed open the back door and stepped into the laundry.

What's happening in Walter's house? Why are the lights off? Thought everyone would be there by now.

He ran his fingers along the door post and finding the tab, switched the light on. Light flooded the hallway. Nathan blinked, his eyes adjusting to the intensity of the hundred-watt globe.

He moved into the kitchen. He fumbled for the switch. Finding it, he flicked on the kitchen light.

Nothing.

The place was empty. No human life, only the essential pieces of furniture; a table and chairs standing guard for the next invasion of humans. *What's going on with this Walter? How did he grow those wings? How did his hand grow into a gun?*

Nathan slumped into a chair at the dining table. *Walter's not here. That's good. I can relax now.* Nathan gazed at the table surface decked with five teacups and a plate of half-eaten cake as the centrepiece.

Nathan liked cake. He cut a slice, peeled off the icing and dumped it on the table. Then he popped the rest into his mouth. The sweet crumbs melted in his mouth. With two gulps he swallowed the cake and commenced to cut another piece. He was hungry.

Just wait a minute. He stopped swallowing; the cake bunched in his mouth. *Five cups of tea?* He stood and circled the kitchen area. He studied every surface, tracking for clues. *Why did they go? Why didn't they finish drinking their tea? Did the helicopters find and rescue the children?*

Nathan stalked out to the backyard. There was Walter's utility truck. He strode around to the front. Dan's patrol car sat out the front. *Who did they go with? Where are the helicopters? No big chopper flying above on the road to town.*

Parrots squawked and chatted in nearby trees. They gathered and gawked like some crowd around a recent drama—a fight perhaps. *Strange, the birds like the Precinct at night. They don't like all the carry-on in town. It's quiet in the Precinct. They like the gum trees near the old church. Were the birds scared of spirit men visiting in the Precinct?*

Was the bad spirit man there? Was that Walter there? He's definitely changed—for the worse. He's turned into some evil spirit. He even smells like evil—like cockroaches with a hint of death.

Nathan crept into the historic town square. He stuck to the shadows. Another gate was left unlocked and ajar. *Was Walter a "min-min" man? Was he a demon?*

The dingo, a scrawny slip of a creature trotted across Nathan's path and disappeared behind the historic church.

Was that wailing and thumping? What's that bumping? Nathan stood still and searched for the sound on the breeze. He scanned the gleaming walls, the scraggly gardens, and the date palm, fronds swaying with the puffs of air. He peered through the eucalypts and then studied the café from afar hidden behind the bushes.

Where were the parrots?

The thumping stopped.

Walter and Friedrich slumped to the floor. They'd been hitting the door and yelling for what seemed an eternity, but no one had come to their rescue.

'I'm tired,' Friedrich said. 'I need a break.'

Walter massaged his hand. *This is going from bad to worse. Now I have a sore hand to join my aching head and stomach,* he thought but tried to reassure the boy. 'Perhaps it's night and no one can hear us. There's no one in the historic village at night.'

'Then why are we thumping? We're wasting our time. We must try and get the door open ourselves,' Friedrich said.

Walter heard rattling as Friedrich tugged at the handle. Then a thud.

Friedrich groaned. 'Ah! The handle slipped! Ouch, my back hurts.'

Walter sighed. 'I guess we better keep on trying. Maybe someone will come along and hear us. Come on.'

'Who will hear us? It is the middle of the night, so you say.'

'Young lovers.' *It's possible,* Walter mused. *In this town, anything's possible. Including being abducted by aliens and locked up in the morgue.* After all, the last thing he remembered was some over-sized cockroach stunning him with a hand shaped like a gun, and then dragging him into the old morgue at the back of the historic church in the Precinct.

'It's terrible!' Friedrich's voice was hoarse from all the shouting. 'I'm tired. I'm all sore. I can't do it anymore. You keep on if you feel like. I just want to sleep.'

'Very well.' Walter resumed hitting the door. 'Help! Anyone there?' He pounded the wood and repeated, 'Help! Is anyone there?'

***

Nathan drifted past the church to inspect the old schoolhouse. He chuckled. *I'll give these young lovers a fright.*

In his periphery vision he noticed a wild dog crouching low by the morgue and whining. The dog pawed at the door and scratched at it.

Lovers in the morgue, what next? Shaking his head in disapproval, Nathan changed direction and marched to the old morgue. *What are those young ones doing for thrills?* He imagined the antics on the slab inside. *No respect, no respect for those dead fellas.*

The dog whimpered and sniffed the door.

Nathan clicked his tongue. *I'll give those naughty children a thrashing when I catch them.*

The thudding grew louder. It was coming from within the morgue. The dog stood on hind legs and stretched himself against the door. He whimpered while softly pawing the wood panels.

'Not a safe place for you, dog,' Nathan said. Then he stopped and listened. *Was that a voice?*

Bump! Bump! Bump went the door. *Definitely people in there. What are they saying?*

The dog howled and clawed at the door.

'Shh!' he told the dog and pushed him away. He then placed his ear flush with the wood.

'Help! Is anyone there?'

'Yes,' Nathan replied with a knock. 'What are you doing in there?'

'Praise the Lord!' the voice sang, then, 'Blimey, you took your sweet fricking time!'

'Who are you? What are you doing in there?'

'One frickin' question at a time,' the voice snapped. 'Walter here. And a German boy called Friedrich. We're stuck in this fridge.'

'Walter?' Nathan stepped back. *Perhaps he better leave them in there.*

'Com' on mate! It's you, Nathan, isn't it? I can tell your voice. What'chya doing taking you're time? Get us outa here.'

'I don't know if I should.'

'Bitte, bitte, bitte,' the small voice of a boy pleaded.

'For f...'s sake get us out before that smelly cockroach comes back.'

'What cockroach? What do you mean?'

'The one what's locked us in here,' this Walter said. 'He might come back and finish me off. And the boy.'

The dingo circled the small building and continued to whimper.

Unlikely Band of Three

Central Australia

Nathan sniffed the night air. *He sounded like the Walter he used to know. And he didn't smell like the other Walter. Maybe this Walter, maybe he was telling the truth.* 'Okay, I get you out.'

Nathan braced. He clutched the handle and yanked it downwards. No joy. He wrenched it upwards. Still no success. He pushed it. And pulled it. 'It's locked. Who locked it?'

'Who do ya think? The stinker who put me in here,' Walter shrieked. 'Can't you ram it or something?'

'I'll try.'

'Oh, by the way, you're not him are you?'

'No, it's me, Nathan. Do you think I'd be ramming down the door to get you out if I had the key?'

'True, you have a point, mate. Stupid question. Been locked up here too long, ya know what I mean?' Walter said. 'Hurry up before the cretin comes lookin' for us.'

'All right then, stand clear!' Nathan paced back a few metres and then rushed at the door. He bumped against it, barely making it move. Rubbing his sore shoulder, he said, 'Hold on, I'll be back.'

Nathan raced to the workshop. He pulled the switch for the light. The shed glowed amber. He hunted for something heavy. A pole. A wooden beam. Anything. The expanse was so neat and tidy. *Typical, just like a museum.*

'There must be something,' Nathan muttered.

He studied every corner of the shed. Nothing. 'I'll get the ute and ram the whole building with that.' Nathan was desperate.

'Nothing here,' he muttered and turned to leave the shed. Leaning up on the wall behind the door, a pickaxe. Nathan smiled. *That'll do.*

He lifted the pickaxe lugged it back to the morgue.

He faced the door. With all his strength, he hoisted the tool to chest-level. 'Get back!' he warned.

Nathan charged at the door.

Crack! The door splintered.

Nathan paced back. He raced at the door again.

Crunch!

The lock splintered from its mounting and the door flung open. Nathan and the pickaxe charged through, hitting the slab with a clunk. There he collapsed over the concrete table gasping for breath and rubbing his shoulder.

'Hallelujah! You took your time.' Walter slapped Nathan on the back.

The boy held out his hand and rubbed his eye with the other. 'Danke schön! Danke schön!'

Nathan straightened up and with a blank expression, stared at the boy with white hair that glowed by the light of the full moon. 'Ghost boy!' he cried. 'The spirit boy of the Precinct.'

Walter hugged Nathan's arm. 'Come on, mate. Better get out before smelly pants gets back. Oh, did I mention I was abducted by an alien and he locked me in here?'

As they stepped out of the morgue and into the soft moonlight, Friedrich's eyes fixed on Walter. He recoiled.

'What's wrong?' Walter asked in German.

'You! You look like *him*—Boris!' Friedrich pointed at Walter. 'How do I know you're not Boris and you are just pretending to be a nice person?'

Nathan glanced at Walter who, even in the dim light, had a face that glowed pink. 'What's he jabbering on about?'

Walter shrugged. 'Thinks I'm some bloke called Boris.'

'Boris?' Nathan asked Friedrich.

Friedrich looked at Nathan, his mouth agape.

Walter translated for Nathan. 'Who exactly *is* Boris? Why do you think I look like him?'

'He's that evil cockroach man, you know, the one we were talking about in the—the dark smelly room. You know, the stinky one we are trying to escape because he locked us in there. I told you, the one who made me eat his cockroaches and gravy.'

'Oh, that one!' Nathan nodded and then leaned over and sniffed Walter. 'He doesn't smell. This Walter's not evil Boris cockroach man. He just looks like cockroach man. But he's not. Tell the boy you're not.' He was beginning to connect the dots in the whole messy picture. *So, this big-bad creature Boris must have taken on Walter's form and locked the real Walter away in the morgue.* He puffed out his chest like a rooster and grinned while Walter continued with the translation. Then his smile vanished, and he stared at Friedrich, who appeared to glow in the dark. 'Are you the ghost boy?'

'He thinks you're a ghost,' Walter said in German.

'Ghost? I'm real,' Friedrich held his hand out to Nathan. 'See, touch me. I'm real.'

'Touch 'im,' Walter said.

With a sidelong glance, Nathan nudged Friedrich's hand.

'Is he real enough for ya, mate?' Walter asked, and then explained, 'I think the bad man caught him too and locked him in the morgue like me.'

'Oh.'

'Well, at least that's one German tourist from that bus found,' Walter said.

'Right.' Nathan led Walter and Friedrich out the Precinct and to the main street. 'We need to find the others; Fleischer and the Smith family. They are lost too now.'

'The Fleischer's were here?' Walter smacked his head. 'Ouch! Crikey! How long was I gone?'

'You must be the real Walter,' Nathan said. 'They're all gone. That bad smelly man pretending to be you, has got'em. We must look for them.'

As they babbled, Friedrich trudged behind them until they reached Dan's patrol car. Behind them all, the dingo sniffed their trail and padded after them.

On the Bus

Central Australia

When Arthur woke up, one thought was on his thumping head. *Gotta get out. It's like an oven. It smells. Gotta get out.* He was crammed in a seat by an enormous man, his fat spilling over his side of the seat, pushing him over the edge and into the aisle.

Arthur grabbed the metal handle of the seat in front of him and pulled himself to standing. He began staggering down the aisle to the front. He had to get out.

The bus rocked and groaned with each step.

'Vat are you doing?' a voice behind him yelled. 'Get back!'

Arthur took another step.

The bus lurched forward, and the floor tipped on an angle. More orders, German flavoured, cascaded over him.

'Stop!'

'*You vill kill us all!*'

'*Ve vill fall over ze edge!*'

'*Get back—to ze back!*'

'*Get back!*'

'*Get back!*'

Arthur halted.

The bus creaked and tipped further. Silence from behind. The Germans held their breath.

Arthur grabbed a seat and dragged one foot back, then the other. He grasped the rail and swung himself around. 'What's going on?' he asked.

It was Jakob Smith who replied, 'We're on the bus on the edge of the cliff. What do you think is going on?'

'I get that,' Fleischer said. 'But how did we get here? And who are all these other people?'

'I don't know.'

Arthur swept his gaze over the dozen fair heads bobbing above the blue velvet. 'Who are you?'

'Vir the German tour group from Far Flung tours,' replied a wiry man closest to him.

Arthur glanced out the window. Cliffs shaped like giant stained teeth grinned back at him. Way below, tiny trees dotted the valley. Arthur estimated the bus was some one thousand metres above the valley. 'I guess when you booked this Far Flung tour, you never imagined you'd be sitting on a bus on the edge of a cliff.' He laughed nervously.

Twelve pairs of pale eyes glared at him.

'Hmm, no sense of humour,' Arthur muttered. 'What do you expect from a busload of German tourists?'

More harsh glares.

'Sorry,' Arthur said.

The bus groaned and lurched forward. Arthur's feet skidded from under him. He clung to the handle at the top of the seat.

'Get back! Get back!' The Germans emphasised the urgency, crying out and gesticulating.

Arthur dragged his legs up the slippery aisle. He reached his seat.

His heavy companion glowered at him and growled, 'Nein! Nein! Furder! Furder to ze back! Schnell!' Then he spread his generous proportions like jelly to envelope the two seats.

Arthur inched his body to the next row back.

Panting he gazed around the cabin. 'Hey, anyone seen my wife and son? And where's the copper, Dan, when we need him?'

Jakob Smith piped up. 'Down the back—with my wife. Still out of it, I think. Not happy about him being with my wife.'

There they were, Dan, Carol, Mrs. Smith and Adam, jumbled together like spaghetti. Loaded either side of them were mountains of cabin luggage. Arthur was still three rows away.

'At least they're sleeping,' Arthur said.

'Yeah, sleeping with my wife. That sounds good. Not.'

Fleischer pulled his body to the next seat. 'How the hell did we all get here?'

'Ich weiss nicht,' someone replied. They didn't know.

'They don't know,' Jakob said. 'They woke up and...'

'And no one's tried to get out of here?'

'The only exit is down the front.'

'Oh.'

'What about breaking a window?'

'Any movement and—'

'I get the picture,' Arthur said. He lurched to the next seat back. One row to go. 'Any idea how long we—they've been here?'

Jakob shrugged.

'A few hours, perhaps,' the fat man said. 'Before zis ve ver in a dark und cold place und floating sometimes.'

'Next you'll tell me little grey men probed you,' Arthur joked.

'Yah, dem also.'

Arthur shook his head. 'Unbelievable.' He then dragged himself towards the next row. Nearly there. The bus clonked, easing the gradient to almost level. 'Sure this isn't a dream?'

'I vish it vas,' said the fat man. 'I vish it vas.'

Arthur staggered the last few steps and crouched near his sleeping wife and son. Next to them, a dozing Dan held Jakob's wife, Heidi. Arthur stroked Carol's locks. He pondered. *Great! What are we going to do?*

***

'What are you going to do?' Walter asked Nathan.

'Track 'em,' Nathan said. 'We'll get in the truck and drive around lookin' for them lost ones.'

Nathan and Walter circled Dan's patrol car. The dog sniffed at the rear tyre and lifted his hind leg.

Friedrich watched at a distance. A smile flickered over his face as the dog marked his territory. *Same as der hund at home,* he mused.

Meanwhile, the men lapped the police car like sharks.

'How are you going to get in?' Walter asked.

Nathan peered in a window. 'Where's the keys?'

'You need keys or the siren goes off. You'll wake half the town.'

'They won't care. Sirens go off all the time.'

Walter nodded and laughed. 'Probably. Where's the keys? How are we going to find them anyway?'

'Keys must be inside. Dan must'a left keys in the house.'

'Or in his pocket,' Walter said. 'That'll look good you breaking into his patrol van if you can't find them.'

'Wouldn't be the first time.' Nathan chuckled and then turned. His grin vanished. He stared beyond Walter, into the darkness.

'What's up?' Walter followed his gaze.

A man, about Walter's height and build, emerged through the precinct gates. He drifted towards them.

'Boris!' the boy whispered.

The dog cowered beside Friedrich and whimpered.

'Oh, the bad Walter.' Nathan ducked behind the patrol car.

Walter stood at the side of the car facing his double. Barely moving his mouth, he said, 'Can't do us that much harm—if he's my dopple—dopple—whatever. He can't be so fit. I'm not...'

'He's the cockroach man,' Friedrich said in German.

'His hand's a gun,' Nathan whispered.

'He has a handgun?'

'No, a gun—hand.'

Walter's hands trembled. 'Whatever. He's armed, we're not.'

The figure trod toward them. His footsteps crunched on random stones. Slow deliberate crunches.

'He's seen us,' Nathan said. 'Hide.'

Walter remained frozen to the spot. *So, this was the man who knocked him out. This was the man who pumped stuff into his stomach and made him sick.* He willed his legs to move. But his legs were not taking orders. His stomach hurt. He murmured, 'Too late now.'

The figure loomed larger, closer.

'What are we going to do?' Walter's throat tightened.

'Run!' Nathan pulled Walter. He dragged him up the street.

Walter's feet woke up and connected with his mind and the dirt on the road. Walter and Nathan scampered up the street. They darted from bush to fence. They tried to stick to the shadows. They assumed that Friedrich and the dog were following them.

They rounded the block and then climbed through the fence. The trio landed on the soft sand of the dry riverbed. Moonbeams cast silvery ribbons through the forest of eucalypts. Brumbies grazed on the grassy banks and dozed in the fragile blue of dawn.

Walter leant against a trunk of a tree. He gulped air like a goldfish out of water and then gasped, 'Have we lost him?'

Nathan sidled up to him. 'I think so.'

They stood there panting, catching their breath.

Walter looked around the riverbed. 'You haven't seen where the lad went, have you?'

'He was behind us with the dog.'

'Not anymore.' A cold chill, as if someone had dropped ice down Walter's back, trickled through him. He glanced around hoping to see Friedrich crouching by a bush, or under a log. But the creek was still and silent, except for the horses neighing in the distance.

***

Friedrich flattened his small body against the concrete building behind the historic church. So far, so good. He pushed the door. It creaked and opened a crack. He slid through the gap. He gestured to the dog. 'Come here!'

The dog hung back.

Friedrich tried again. He urged his new friend to join him. But he refused to move. *Afraid of the ghost,* Friedrich thought.

In the morgue he hunted for that blue ray. Surely there must be one—it must appear from time to time. How else did that nasty Boris come so quick?

But all was black in there.

Friedrich ran his hand along the slab in the centre of the small room. He stepped gingerly to the back where the darkness was thickest. He stretched out his hands and shuffled into it. He touched the wall. Cold, wet stone and solid like ice.

Nothing. Was he stuck here? All this because he wanted to escape Boris...and because he wanted to find help in this world for Wilma? Maybe if he waited, the ray of light would appear. He had another plan. He'd block this outhouse passage and so free his world of that smelly Boris. That's what he'd do. Imagine how happy the townsfolk would be without that bully lording it over them and plaguing their world with bugs. *But, then, what about Wilma?*

'Well, well, well, what do we have here?'

Friedrich gasped. His hands gripped the stones on the wall. Slowly, he twisted his head.

He saw a glow, but it wasn't the ray of light he was hoping for. It was Boris' hand—his ray-gun hand.

'Here you are my little bunny rabbit, just where I want you.' He cackled.

The door clunked—shut.

Friedrich gasped. His mouth went dry.

Boris continued, 'You will do just nicely. I have just the Grey-girl for you to build my army of hybrids.' He scuttled towards him. 'I'm sure your friends will be here soon. They'll be looking for you.'

The glow hovered just above Friedrich.

Friedrich dodged it and moved sideways.

'Oh, come on! Don't be like that,' the creature said. 'I won't harm you. I'll give you anything you want. More than anything.'

'Anything?' Friedrich squeaked.

'Anything.'

'My sister—make her well.'

'That can be arranged…but, there will be a price. You understand?'

'I understand.' Friedrich sighed. *What choice do I have?*

'Now, come here—it won't so bad, you'll see.'

Friedrich sank to the floor. His heart became like lead as if he'd sold his soul to the devil—all to save his sister.

The Hand

Central Australia

Friedrich wiped his eyes. They were damp.

'Now, where are you?' A voice in the darkness said. The glow grew closer and closer. 'Ah, there you are.'

The line of light sparkled.

'Just follow me and do exactly as I say.'

Friedrich nodded.

A growl, a low menacing growl, filled the room. The red hand hung, suspended in the darkness. 'What?'

The hand switched left and right.

A pair of scarlet eyes flashed with it.

'Aghhh!'

The sound of ripping.

Zap! A ray of light hit the ceiling. Rocks and plaster showered over Friedrich. Then, the sound of scraping. A thin, blue strip peeled away the darkness.

A shadow blocked the dawn.

Thud! Bang! A bark. Then a growl. Eyes glowed. More zapping. Screams. Low growls like a predator eating its quarry.

Strong arms lifted Friedrich. As he was carried out of the morgue, Friedrich watched a bulk intersect the blue ray. Then the line of light faded.

***

On the World of the Wends

Boris swaggered into the church and crawled up the wall at the back of the hall. *Now let's see what these suckers are up to.* He nursed his stump. The new hand was already pushing its way into existence—like a shark's tooth; it merely replaced the one bitten off. Boris mused. *Serves the dog right for attacking me. Could be interesting what effect my hand will have on a wild dog. May give it a taste for human flesh—the folk better watch their babies. Hmmm, could be one way of keeping my "hand" in the affairs of that town while I'm away on business.* Boris chuckled.

The hall was crowded. Every pew filled and the folk flowed around the edges to standing.

Boris rubbed his hand and stump together. 'Ooh, I do like a good gathering.'

Herr Biar presided over the congregation.

Boris remained glued to the wall and unnoticed, while Biar railed against the evils of Boris.

'Typical. How could he, after all I've done to him. Will he never learn?' Boris tutted.

Some villagers hurled insults at Biar. Others cheered in response to Biar's words and then jeered at the doubters. Someone threw a rotten apple core into the air. It landed with a splat on the front of the pulpit.

'Now where's that boy and girl?' Boris scanned the congregation with his multiple but unseen eyes. He studied each corner of the church's interior and structure: the altar with simple wooden table white cloth placed on top, the rough-hewn cross hung on the wall behind it, the polished pine pulpit, the arched ceiling not quite egg shape and fragile; the slightest bump and it would probably collapse onto the mass (oh, Boris would like to see that), then the beams that kept the walls from falling in or out, and finally the organ tucked away in the rear of the hall. Surely the boy had to be somewhere, it's not possible that he followed Boris to Earth from the outhouse "porta-transwarp" station. The "transwarp" had briefly opened with the storm and just as quickly, shut down after the lightning bolt hit the lavatory.

Boris frowned. *Never liked the look of that young man, with that blonde wavy hair and ruddy complexion, he looks like that Joshua I ate all those thousands of years ago.*

Boris' blood-filled campaign began when a human called Joshua invaded his planet. Joshua defiled Boris' kingdom with goodness; just when Boris had his world just the way he liked it, rotting with evil and corruption. Then Mr. Goody-Two-Shoes pranced in on the violence and destruction and began converting his cohorts, including his wife, Maggie to purity and light. How Boris hated goodness. He couldn't allow this Joshua to undermine his empire of evil. He had to do something about it. Boris killed Joshua and feasted on him. Energised by his nemesis' dead flesh, Boris flew up to Joshua's spacecraft to conquer and consume his crew. But his attempt to invade Joshua's ship caused the vessel to explode like a red dwarf gone supernova annihilating Boris' planet and solar system. Ever since, Boris has roved the universe, consuming planetary systems and colonies, enslaving every sentient and non-sentient species, and building his forces with the intent of someday—soon—very soon—dominating the planet from which Joshua had come—Earth.

Boris eyed the lively brood of villagers. Humans, how he hated them. He clocked the doctor. Doctor Zwar lounged in the back corner, his feet raised up and resting on the pew in front. Boris purred. *Still they are useful. I like the way you can pit one against the other. So stupid...and yet, so useful. That guy with the funny moustache was like putty in my hands. Pity he got so cocky he thought he knew better and didn't listen to me. I told him not to invade the Russian-front in winter...I almost had Earth...now I'm back to square one.* Boris' antennae twitched. 'Now, where was I?'

The townsfolk jumped up and down and shook their fists. They argued against each other.
'We are in Australia.'
'No, we're not.'
'Do you not trust Herr Roach?'
'He has led us astray,' a woman said. 'It was him who killed my baby.'
Boris leaned forward. *Frau Neuman, you'd think she'd learnt her lesson having her baby killed. I guess some humans are just too dumb and never learn. I'll deal with her later.* Boris sighed. *Oh, well, I suppose I better keep my promise and heal Wilma. The brother's allegiance could come in handy...especially against that Joseph character. I'm sure Joseph's here somewhere. I can smell him.*
Boris detached one of his eyes and sent it on a mission. His eye flew over the crowd of Wends and hovered just behind the altar table.

Boris exclaimed, 'Gotcha!'

A beached whale of a woman turned around. She looked directly at him and screamed.

O-oh, I've been spotted. Boris buzzed out the double doors and hid behind some bushes. There he squatted, gritted his spiky teeth, clenched his three and a half hands and transformed. The eye returned like a homing-pigeon and buzzed around Boris' now human-form head. Boris swatted the eye. 'Get back in there! Find the girl!'

The eye-drone whirred back into church.

With his damaged hand in his trouser pocket, Boris strode back into the church hall and boldly down the aisle. All the Wends turned and watched him march up to the altar as though he were the Messiah.

'Joseph, come out from behind the altar—I can see you.' *Still can with my robotic nano-eye-drone.*

Herr Biar's face flushed. He patted the blonde mop behind him.

Boris hastened to the back of the pulpit and grabbed the lad. He hauled him into view. Then he pushed Joseph forward so that he stumbled on a step. He raised his voice like a preacher. 'This fellow is who you should be afraid of—not me. He is a devil.'

Gasps rippled through the congregation.

'No, he's not,' Herr Biar said.

'He is and I can prove it.'

'No, you can't,' Biar argued.

'Yes, I can.'

Boris groped Joseph's trouser pocket and pulled out a flat silver object. Bingo! But then Boris was confident that all Twenty-first century people can't live without their mobile phones, after all, he'd designed the technology that way. Boris glanced at the object. A camera. *Oh well, that'll do.*

Boris held up the camera. 'See this? It takes images of you.' He pressed a button and the camera flashed.

More gasps.

'These images, of you, are a curse. These images will make you die.'

The people howled.

Herr Biar shook his head.

'You don't believe me?' Boris pointed at Herr Biar. 'Just ask your burgher here. His daughter is dying—and it is this fellow here with his magic box that has done it.' While gripping Joseph's arm, Boris pressed the camera a few times and smiled. Just as he hoped, a photo of Wilma appeared on screen.

Boris passed the camera to the people in the front row. Each man held the object with the tips of his fingers and nodded, then passed it on.

After inspecting the sorcery, they glared at Joseph. 'Evil!' they screamed and hammered their fists in the air.

Joseph glanced from left to right. He searched for support. As the crowd grew more hostile, the colour drained from his face. *So far so good, all going to plan,* Boris observed and so gestured to the doctor who now stood at the rear of the church. He beckoned him to come to the front. He knew he could trust Doctor Zwar who waded through the thickening crowd towards the altar. More putty in his hands. But he had to get Joseph off his hands for the next cunning move. *Have to be the Messiah so they don't doubt me again.*

The doctor shouldered his way down the crowded aisle. When he reached the front, Boris thrust Joseph at him. 'Here, do to him as you see fit, Doctor.'

The men either side lurched at Joseph. They were in lynching mode.

Boris held up his hand, the whole one. 'Just wait a minute. I have something to show you. Then you can drown or burn or whatever you do to witches and devils.'

The men froze in their aggressive poses and looked at Boris.

Boris turned to Herr Biar and snapped his fingers. 'Herr Biar, go—get your wife and Wilma.'

The mayor stood there as if a monument.

'Move it!' Boris stamped his foot. 'Don't you want your child saved?'

Herr Biar looked at Boris and blinked. *Stupid humans, more brains in those cows of his,* Boris thought.

'We are waiting, Biar. Get your wife and child.'

Herr Biar climbed from the pulpit, plodded down the steps and then shuffled along the aisle, the people parting to make way for him.

Boris called after him. 'Hurry! We haven't got all day. We have a public execution to do before sundown.'

The double doors shut with a jarring clang as Biar left the building.

While Boris watched with the congregation, waiting for the mayor's return with wife and daughter, he decided he'd better be convincing. He picked up a pitcher of water left over from the recent and rather urgent baptism of Frau Neuman's babe. He licked his lips savouring the late infant's flavour. He filled the baptismal font. Then scooping the water with his fingers, he flicked droplets over the altar, the sacred table, the pulpit, and the worshippers. He uttered Latin-sounding incantations spellbinding the people with the meaningless words of religiosity. He was careful to create nothing too spectacular, as these Puritans weren't into signs and wonders. *But, they did believe in the Messiah. Surely raising Wilma from her deathbed wouldn't be too wonderous—just enough for them to believe he was good—oh, how he hated that word "good" and Joseph, the spitting image of Joshua. Oh, how satisfying to see him executed. I can't wait.*

Pity Friedrich wouldn't be there to see the destruction of his friend. What ever happened to him? Boris guessed the "trans-warp-porta-wormhole" just didn't last that long to allow him complete passage. *Maybe he got caught in the fabric of time and space. What a shame!* Boris mused. *Oh, well the price one has to pay. Or is he still stuck on Earth with that black man and that white wimp of one? Will deal with them—later. First things first...*

The doors opened. The afternoon sun streamed through. Bathed in a halo of mauve rays, Herr Biar carried his daughter down the aisle. His wife bent double in grief, trailed behind him.

The little family walked to the altar where they laid the girl on the sacred table. Frau Biar sobbed.

Boris raised his hands and uttered more Latin-sounding phrases. *They won't know, they're simple Wends. Must sound holy.* The attention of the congregation was upon him. He had to look good. *There's that horrible word again.*

Boris sang Gregorian chant-like, and then laid hands on the girl. The nanobots that restore the body parts that regularly go missing in battle from his body, the nanobots that help Boris transform from cockroach to human, entered Wilma's body. She appeared so white, so still.

'Wilma, I command you to arise!' Boris sang, his voice resonating throughout the sanctuary.

The girl's eyes fluttered. Boris grasped one hand and pulled her to sitting. *Works every time.*

Wilma rubbed her face and looked around. 'Mama what are all these people? Mama, I'm hungry.'

Boris paced from one end of the podium to the other. He raised his arms above his head. 'See, she who was almost dead—is alive. I have performed a miracle. She is alive. Who gives life? Who demands your worship and praise?'

***

Nathan carried Friedrich out the morgue.

'Did you get him?' Walter asked.

Nathan placed the boy on the sand and then shrugged. 'He's still in there. Never came out.'

The dog emerged, head shaking something in his mouth.

As the thing scraped against the ground, sparks flew. The dingo yelped and dropped his prey. The three fellows stared at the mangled crab-like creature writhing on the grainy surface. It spun and fizzed, a demented break-dancer.

'What is it?' Walter rubbed his hands as if one of his were missing.

Crouching, the dog eyed the beast and growled.

'It looks like a hand,' Nathan said.

Bang! Bang! Bang! The dingo skittered sideways as rays from the hand blasted holes in the plinth of the morgue.

The guys jumped back.

The dingo barked at it and then pounced.

Dodging the dog's aim, the hand scuttled towards Walter.

Walter raised a foot ready to stamp on it when it stopped moving. But it kept crawling around like a rogue tarantula.

'Don't touch it,' Nathan warned.

Walter placed down his stomping foot and sidestepped out of the hand's way. 'It's crazy. How does it do that?'

'It's Boris' hand. Told you he's dangerous,' Nathan said.

'I know that,' Walter replied. 'Perhaps we could crush it with the pick-axe over there.'

'Good thinking.' Nathan lifted the axe and slammed it on the hand.

With a crunch, the hand gurgled. From under the heavy metal of the tool, fingers fitted with spasms. The hand then became lifeless like any hand separated from its master.

The dog crept up to the crushed hand. He sniffed it and then nibbled the fingers.

Walter observed the dog gnawing at the digits. Something was not quite right about that. 'Should the dog be doing that?'

'Probably not, but the hand's dead now; just a bit o' meat.' Nathan seemed unconcerned. 'One less hungry dog to worry abou'.'

***

Back on World of the Wends

Amie remained crouched out of sight under the pipe organ. *Good thing Boris is so full of his own importance, he hasn't noticed me,* she thought.

A couple of times she considered shooting Boris.

She saw him, an over-sized cockroach plastered against the back wall. But too many heads in the way. Guns from the olden days weren't so accurate and neither was she.

Then, when Boris had morphed into human and was less than three metres away, she weighed up the situation and decided shooting Boris was not such a good idea.

She lifted the antique rifle to her shoulder, aimed and waited. Boris paraded about the stage as if he were an over-rated television-evangelist. *Can't these Wends see they're being taken for a ride? Obviously not. They ended up on this planet with two suns, didn't they? And what has possessed them to believe every word Boris says?* Amie feared for Joseph.

Boris slowed down. He was tiring of the charade. He stopped dancing and glorifying himself. *Bad sign. They'll jump on Joseph in seconds.* Boris placed his hands on his hips. Was that a stump of a right hand? What happened there?

At the foot of the pulpit, Herr and Frau Biar fussed over their daughter.

'See now who is good. Is it not I who healed the girl?' Boris pointed at Joseph who trembled in the doctor's hold. 'See—see the evil man—he's the one who made Wilma Biar ill to the point of death with his evil magic box. Justice must be done. We must scourge our town of this evil. Get him!'

The congregation rose as a mob and roared.

'Right! Now!' Amie muttered. She directed the rifle to the beams holding the roof of the church. Shoot. Make chunks of wood fall. Shock them.

The crowd surged to the back, to Joseph.

Amie pumped the trigger.

Gunpowder blasted, kicking her against the organ. She landed on the pedals. The organ boomed a dissonant chord. The beam exploded. It split in two. Splinters of wood showered on the crowd. Chaos. Screaming. Yelling. The structure groaned and swayed.

'Oops, I didn't expect that to happen.' Amie wrapped her arms over her head and curled into a ball as the roof collapsed.

Tiles pelted the floor and around her like a meteorite shower.

The crying, writhing mob scattered as God's house dumped its wrath on them.

Amie took shelter under the lap of the organ, the pedals dug into her thighs. Random chords wheezed into the fray. *All this from one shot,* she lamented.

Amie glanced up at the gap. Was that a whirring sound? Ah, the unmistakable buzz of Boris. Was Boris hunting her?

She looked up and noticed the gap in the roof. The sky for a moment was blotted out by a shiny black object. *Boris can't handle the heat,* Amie mused.

When all was quiet, Amie crawled out from her refuge. The Biar family huddled under the bench in the pulpit. She placed the rifle on what was left of the table.

Herr Biar emerged and dusted bits of plaster from his arms and head. He stared at a couple of people dusting off splinters from the roof collapse.

Biar frowned. 'I'm not sure I should congratulate you, Amie.'

Wilma shuffled on her bottom out of the pulpit. She gazed up at the gaping hole and then down at the people emerging from the shelter of the broken pews. 'Now how are we going to go to church on Sundays?'

Frau Biar appeared. She surveyed the damage and swayed her head. 'Now we have a church to repair as well as my kitchen.' She glared at Amie. 'I don't know who to believe. Ever since they came, it's been ganz schrecklich.'

Herr Biar rested his hand on his wife's arm. 'Jane, please, you must not be so harsh on the girl. We know Boris is evil. And we can't have people chasing Joseph as a devil. We know he isn't evil.'

Frau Biar nodded.

Herr Biar turned to Amie. 'Go now, before "it"—Boris returns. Go and find Joseph. Make sure you escape to the hills und hide there where it is safe.'

'What about Friedrich?' Amie asked.

'He might be in the mountains. He often went exploring there.'

'But what about you? How are you going to defend yourselves against Boris?'

'We have ways und means.' Herr Biar pointed at the rifle and then gave Amie a nudge. 'Now go! Schnell!'

Amie picked her way through the wreckage and raced out into the street.

***

Central Australia

The unlikely trio, Walter, Nathan and Friedrich slouched on stools at the table. Friedrich gaped at the assortment of dark-coloured people drifting in and out of this eating place. Some were like Nathan. Others were taller and their hair like sheep's wool glued to their scalps. The women who served were not white, but were tanned deep yellow, their eyes slanted.

Friedrich bit into his bread-meal that Walter named a "burger". He thought that was a strange name for bread buns with meat in the middle. His father was a "burgher", but here these people from the world of Australia called food, "burgers".

What a strange world where most people were brown and black and yellow, and bread and meat were townspeople.

They had embarked on the transport in a horseless carriage that made Friedrich ill to the point they had to stop on the side of the road several times for him to be sick, before they reached this town Walter called "Alice". He remembered before they left, Nathan had poked his head in the morgue. No Boris, he reported.

Friedrich sighed. Now he was stranded in this weird place called Australia in a town that had a girl's name. Was this the price he had to pay to save Wilma's life? The Wend boy ground the tasteless "burger" between his teeth. How would he survive without his mother's cooking? How would he cope being a white Wend in this vast land of colourful people? The novelty of visiting and exploring this strange land Australia had worn off...

The two men, one white, one black chomped through their burgers and jabbered in their Australian language. Friedrich had no idea what they said. He just hoped they were plotting to outsmart the cunning Boris.

Boiling

Central Australia

Using one hand, Dan rubbed his eyes and blinked. He looked at Heidi, Jakob's wife.

Her eyes widened, and she screamed.

Jakob glared at the two. 'Get away from my wife or I clobber you.'

Dan pulled his arm from her back. 'Sorry, I don't know how that happened.'

'A likely story.'

'What do'ya mean?'

'Hey maite, I saw what happened up there.'

'Please refresh my memory.'

'Yeah, you'd like that.' Jakob raised a fist. 'I know karate, you know.'

Officer Dan stroked the air in front of him. 'Now, calm down. I'm sure there's a simple explanation.'

'I hope so,' Jakob said. He shoved Dan into the baggage and then squeezed in the space next to his wife. There he sat hunched over wringing his hands.

'What's all this about?' Heidi patted her husband on the thigh. 'You seem to be over-reacting dear.'

'I'm not over-reacting!' Jakob barked.

Arthur leaned towards the couple. 'What exactly is going on?'

Jakob and Heidi snapped their attention to him. 'None of your business!' Jakob said. His mouth was quivering.

Heidi shrugged. 'He gets a bit emotional under the circumstances.'

'No, I mean, do you have any idea what we are doing here?' Fleischer locked eyes with Dan. 'Dan? What's going on? And how are we going to get out of this mess?'

The afternoon sun beat down on the bus. Its metal body radiated the heat to over fifty degrees Celsius inside. The windows seemed glued shut. No matter how hard some of the passengers tugged at their windows, they didn't budge.

The last of the water had almost dribbled away; rationed down the fifteen of the seventeen passenger's throats. Arthur's tongue stuck to his teeth. Each time he swallowed; it was like sawdust.

And he worried about his wife Carol and son Adam. They were still unconscious and seemed unresponsive to attempts to keep them hydrated.

Arthur moistened his handkerchief and dabbed their lips.

'Don't vast ze wasser!' Fat Tony, as Arthur had named him, just had to give his two Pfennigs worth.

Arthur snapped. 'I'm trying to keep them alive, for Chrissake!'

'Ve must wasser save.'

Arthur rolled his eyes and swayed his head. 'Any other bright ideas?'

Fat Tony shrugged.

'Fat lot of use you are. We can't just sit here and boil to death,' Arthur said.

'Calm down,' Dan said.

'Is that all you can say, Officer?' Arthur asked. 'Calm down?'

'Well...'

Fleischer waited for the policeman to finish his sentence. In the pause, he was aware of the laboured breathing and soft moans that filled the cabin. 'Well?' he goaded Dan. 'Well, what are we waiting for? Do you think some helicopter's going to fly over—?'

The bus listed forward. Arthur glanced out the window and surveyed the cliffs. One thousand metre cliffs...One thousand metre drop...the cliffs...purple...like teeth. His mind was ticking over and putting the pieces together. Then ding! Arthur clapped his hands. 'Hey, Dan! I think I know where we are.'

'Do you now?' Dan pressed against a sports bag with his arm and peered out the window. 'Sure we're not on some alien world?'

'What do you mean, alien world?'

'Last thing I remember I was on some ship being probed by grey-like creatures. It stands to reason this isn't earth,' Dan kept looking out the window and studying the cliffs. He took a sharp breath, then said, 'That and the bus being on top of a mountain on the edge of a cliff. How else would it get there?'

'Could still be Earth. In fact, I'm certain we're on top of a mountain in the Western MacDonnell Ranges. If I could just break a window and get out.' The cogs were turning so fast in Arthur's brain, they'd been sent into over-drive. 'Just wait a minute, you think we were abducted by aliens? You mean the Germans weren't joking?'

Dan nodded.

Heidi whimpered and shook.

'I'm sorry. I did over-react, my little cabbage.' Jakob stroked a stray curl on Heidi's forehead. 'What did they make you do?'

Fleischer looked at Jakob and then Dan. 'My daughter Amie—where's she? Jakob—Heidi—your son, Joseph—where's he?'

'And your point is?' Dan asked.

'My point is—if we've been abducted by aliens and ended up in a bus full of Germans on a mountain-top, isn't it possible Amie and Joseph were taken too?'

Carol moved. 'My baby girl—my baby girl,' she murmured.

Adam's eyes sprang open. 'I told you, it's Walter—he did this. He did all this. I kept telling you, but you wouldn't believe me.'

Arthur ground his teeth, then muttered, 'Walter! I knew it! I knew that man was trouble.' He hugged his wife and son and then looked each of them square in the face. 'Darling—my son—I have to go. I have to get out of this bus and find help before it's—too late.'

'Nein! Nein! Achtung!' Fat Tony again. 'If you go, you'll destroy de equilibrium—ve vill all fall to our deaths.'

'Stuff the equilibrium!' Arthur replied.

'Nooo!' Fat Tony shook his head making his double chin wobble.

'How are you going to get out?' Carol asked.

Fat Tony nodded. 'A good question.'

'I'll—I'll think of something,' Arthur said. 'For a start, you, yes, I'm talking to you, Fat Tony—'

'Mein name ist Antony Wurst.'

'Figures.' Arthur muttered and then raised his voice. 'You can get your body down here near the back seat—no, better still, everyone, get down the back. Now, there's your equilibrium.'

A volley of excuses rebounded.

'I'm sick,' started the Herr Wurst. *He did sound a little "worst" (sic) for wear*, Arthur thought.

'But if we move, the bus vill tip.'

'I'm too veak.'

'I'm too tirsty.'

Jakob echoed Arthurs command, but added that it was an order from the policeman sitting at the back.

One by one, the Germans moved, until all were crowded at the rear of the bus.

Arthur climbed over the luggage that had been piled on the backseat for that all-important equilibrium. With a wad of windcheater wrapped around his elbow, he beat the back window. His arm bounced off the glass. He hammered the pane with his fist.

'Ouch!' he cried and then rubbed his sore hand. 'It's as hard as steel!'

'Try your boot,' Jakob suggested.

'Alright.' Arthur reclined on the baggage, and clutching the handle of the seat in front, he kicked. The bus rocked.

Dan groaned, 'I think I'm going to barf.' He cupped his hand over his chin.

'Sorry, mate, try not to. Look, I have to get out and find help,' Arthur said. He wished Dan was well enough to accompany him. But for some reason, the so-called space travel had drained Dan's physical resources more than his own. He studied the rest of the travellers. They'd been stuck in this bus longer than he had and so were weaker from lack of food and water. It was up to him. Arthur kicked the window again. His foot slipped on the glass.

'What's this stuff made of?' Arthur grumbled. 'Think! Think! What can I use?' *Perhaps Dan had a gun.*

He glanced at the policeman. His skin appeared pale and beaded with perspiration. 'Do you have your pistol on you, Officer?'

Dan groped around his hips where his holster would be. He wriggled and squirmed in the midst of the crush. 'I don't know.' He frowned. 'They might've, I mean the aliens might've...' He patted his chest and ran his fingers down the outside of his trouser leg.

Arthur held his breath. Sweat like salty rivulets trickled down his cheek. 'You mean you think the aliens took it?'

Officer Dan Hooper continued to writhe in his confined space like a child in detention.

Arthur turned to the rest of the passengers. 'Anyone got a gun?'

Twelve heads bobbed left and right. No guns.

'Any heavy objects?'

Antony Wurst shifted uncomfortably in his seat. He looked guilty possessing two seats while the rest of the passengers crammed in the back few rows three people sharing two seats.

'Just wait a minute,' Dan said. 'I remember, now. I hid it from the cockroach man.'

'Who?'

'The alien that looked like an over-sized cockroach—up there,' Dan replied. 'I hid it from him.'

'Where?'

Dan squinted as he scanned the bus. 'I think, I was sitting where the rather large man is, now. I pushed it in between the cushions in the middle.'

'Hey, Fat Tony,' Arthur yelled, 'Can you feel anything in the crack?'

Antony Wurst ignored Arthur.

Adam giggled.

'I mean, Mister Wurst, can you put your hand down the crack—' Fleischer said.

Wurst bent over, the top of his track pants slipped half-way down his backside.

Adam snorted again and then held his mouth trying to control his laughter.

Arthur glared at his son, and then asked Wurst, 'Is there anything like a gun in the crack of your seat?'

Adam bent over. His shoulder blades shook as he muffled his mirth.

The dozen Germans narrowed their eyes.

'I'm sorry,' Arthur said, 'It must be that my son's heat-affected.'

Meanwhile, Antony Wurst pushed his hand into the split between the seats. 'Ah, sometink.' He pulled his hand out and attached to it was a standard issue police revolver. 'Is this it?'

'Yes!' Arthur reached over and grabbed the gun.

Fleischer turned the revolver over in his hands. 'Is it okay Dan, if I use this?'

'As long as you aim at the window and not us,' Dan replied.

Arthur knew Dan, despite feeling the effects of space sickness combined with heat-stress, was managing to display a sense of humour. 'Of course,' he said. 'Right, everyone down. Cover your heads with whatever you can to protect yourselves. This could be messy.'

Arthur cocked the revolver and aimed at the window. 'I hope it will be messy...for the window.'

Gulping, Arthur pressed the trigger.

Bang! Boof!

Dan raised his head. 'Did it work?'

'I don't know.' Arthur gazed at his reflection in the glass. His reflection was marred by a bullet frozen in the middle of his image. No mosaic of cracks. No shattering.

'Hit it, see what happens,' Jakob said.

'We'll see.' Arthur braced as he stabbed the pane with his elbow.

Nothing, but a sore elbow resulted.

'What have they done to this glass?' Arthur rubbed his elbow.

'I guess they made it space-proof,' Wurst contributed more Pfennigs worth of wisdom.

'I guess they did, Fat Tony,' Arthur said. 'I guess they did.'

'I vas just saying...'

Fleischer examined the glass or whatever compound it was. 'Now how are we going to get out?'

A woman with auburn hair wailed and then collapsed. The men around her fanned her face with sheets of newspaper.

'Schnell! Wasser!' a balding man, probably her partner, cradling her called.

A middle-aged man with a bulbous nose passed a flask.

The balding man tipped the flask over her lips. 'Nein! Nein!'

'It's all gone,' Jakob translated for the Australians benefit. He looked at Arthur. 'You better find a way out or we're all going to die.'

'But how?' Arthur scratched the top of his scalp. 'You'd think if they made the bus space-proof, they would've made it heat-proof.'

The woman began to fit. Her legs vibrated, and her arms thrashed. 'Is there nothing you can do?' her partner asked. He and the big-nosed man held her. Carol picked up a terry-towelling hat and fanned the poor woman's head.

'Get down!' Arthur said. He then punctured the pane with five more bullets.

And still the glass-like substance did not shatter or break.

Arthur locked the weapon and handed it to Dan. 'Useless,' he said. He stared at the scuffed floor. *Perhaps we're all going to die. I feel so useless.*

'Dad?' Adam's almost-broken voice pierced his father's sense of doom.

'What son?'

'Have you tried unlocking the window?'

'Unlocking? What do you mean?'

'There's a rubbery thing at the bottom of the window,' Adam said. 'Perhaps you have to lift that to unlock it.'

'What rubbery thing?'

Adam sighed. 'Dad! Sometimes you are so dense.'

Before Arthur had the mental space to respond, Adam had scrambled over the baggage and was fiddling with the base of the windowpane.

Fleischer peered over his son's shoulder. 'What are you doing?'

'I told you, unlocking the window.'

'I doubt a space-worthy vessel would have windows that lock and unlock.'

'Who said it's space-worthy? It's just bullet-proof, crack-proof glass. And this lock will open the window.' Adam tugged at the plastic lever.

'No, son. Bullet-crack-proof sealed glass shatters. No, this is definitely out-of-this-world technology.'

'How do you know?' Adam's fingers worked over-time trying to lift the lever.

'I've never seen bullets stick in glass like that.'

'You've never shot a bus window before, Dad.'

'Don't be smart, son.' Arthur moved to haul his son out of the way.

'But Dad, let me just try.' Adam pressed one side of the lever. There was a click. All the eyes of the people on the bus fixed on Adam as he dragged the window to the side.

'So that's how you do it,' Carol said. She reached over to the rear window opposite, unlatched it and pulled it open. A cool mountain breeze rushed into the cabin.

'There, Dad, what's stopping you?' Adam asked.

Carol hugged her husband. 'Go for it, Arthur, go rescue us.'

All the people on the bus cheered as Arthur climbed out the window.

Escape

World of the Wends

Amie hared down the main road. The glare of the two afternoon suns reflected off the pebbles dazzling her. Had it always been so bright? It seemed the recent rain had polished the stones making them shimmer like sunlight on snow. Amie's eyes ached with the glare.

But she kept on running. She could just make out the doctor's house at the end of the street. Had the doctor taken Joseph there?

Probably not.

Amie tried not to think of what the mob might be doing to Joseph right now. But the more she tried, the more frequent images of his torture—hanging from a tree—in stocks—thrown in a river—kept crowding her mind.

She forged onwards.

Then slowed her pace.

The road appeared empty as if she were jogging through a ghost town. *Not a good sign. Must be all out there crucifying Joseph.*

'There she is!'

'She's always with the boy.'

'She must be a witch too!'

The thunder of boots and hooves startled her.

'Get her!' they shouted.

Amie looked back. The angry horde rushed at her. Her heart jumped. Her legs moved. She turned and ran.

Time slowed...

For Amie. She was trapped in this bubble where everything crawled at snail's pace, like in a bad dream where you're trying to cross the road before being run down by a car and you hardly move.

Did God press the slow-motion button? Each step, Amie groaned and plodded like one of those old ladies inching across the bitumen. Even the thumps of blood through her veins seemed so slow it must be congealing. The shouts and cries deepened to agonised grunts and growls as if played at slow speed.

What's happening? Snap out of it!

Move legs. Faster. Faster! Don't stop!

They're gaining on me.

I can see their eyes. Bloodshot. Red. The veins in their cheeks popping. Fists raised hammering. In slow motion.

Amie pumped her legs harder.

The stones under her feet crunched.

Behind the cries pierced the air. She glanced back. Fingers stabbed the space above their heads.

'Get her!'

'Kill her!'

'Drown her!'

Amie turned and sprinted.

Then she stopped. She switched her head left and right and behind. She'd put some distance between the mob and her.

The doctor's house was on her right.

Worth a try.

She jumped the fence and climbed up the apple tree.

If they want to hang me, they'll have to catch me first, she reasoned.

The crowd surged past the doctor's house. They were blind with rage.

Amie launched from branch to the drainpipe and then shinnied up the pipe. As she reached the window-ledge to the second storey, she glanced down.

Well, I'll be.

Her pursuers had disappeared around the corner. She heard one of them yelling. 'Where did she go?'

Amie squatted on the window ledge and gripping the heart-shaped hole in the shutter, pulled it open. Then pulled open one of the glass panels.

She crawled in. Once inside, she closed the window and shutter behind her.

Amie stared at the bed covered in green and orange tapestry. She couldn't help thinking of the Sound of Music. With stiff legs, she walked towards the bed. She needed to sit and catch her breath for a while. And then decide what to do.

The door creaked open.

Amie froze.

Doctor Zwar appeared before her.

***

Central Australia

Arthur stumbled over the stones and weaved through the spinifex. He took no time to stop and admire the view. He'd been looking at it for too long, hours in fact, on the bus. He had to get down—fast—but not too fast...Not by the cliffs.

He reckoned if the mountains were the MacDonnell Ranges, one side would be sloping, and on the other, cliffs. He's seen the cliffs from The Spring and now he assumed from the summit.

He headed west along the saddle of the summit, only to be greeted with a fifty-metre drop. He'd need equipment to scale down there—he had no equipment; no ropes, or hooks for abseiling.

He hoped if he went east, he'd have more joy. He tried to picture the mountain in his mind as he'd seen it from The Spring. From there it had looked like a tooth jutting above the range in between. That tooth appeared to have jagged drops on all the sides he could see.

He had run north of the summit but faced more cliffs. But to the east...boulders blocked his way. Was he stuck on this God-forbidden pinnacle of the Northern Territory? Was there no way out?

Arthur sighed and stared at the cairn of stones. Yes, a pile of stones. True, someone had been here. Did they land by helicopter? Or use ropes and hooks? They had built the cairn, hadn't they?

Fleischer circled the cairn. A rusty can was jammed under a reddish stone. He lifted the stone and picked out the can. It rattled as he examined it. Gingerly, so as not to cut himself, he pulled back the sharp lid. A tea-stained paper fluttered inside like a trapped butterfly.

Arthur tipped the paper into his palm and unfolded it.

'Well worth the two-hour climb,' he read and then mumbled, 'So, someone got up here.' Arthur squinted and scanned a mountain to the south, and the ripples of desert like a red sea to the north. 'Yeah, okay, if you don't have your wife and son and a bus-load of German tourists to save,' he muttered.

Arthur read on. The ink had faded over the years this document had languished in the can. 'Ascended by the gully to the east end of the summit. Follow the pathway down through the boulders.'

Arthur studied the boulders. 'What path? Oh, yeah!' He detected a crevice between the boulders. He moved toward it, and then into it.

As if in some crazy Alice in Wonderland movie, he negotiated the tunnel of rocks until he came to a two-metre drop through a crag in a clutch of boulders.

Arthur lowered himself through the hollow and plopped into a patch of sand at the bottom.

He surveyed the gully to the north and nodded. 'That's do-able.' The breeze whistled through the alleyway between the peaks. 'Very do-able,' he said. 'Not exactly a stroll in the park.' He assessed the collateral damage of erosion, the wear and tear of the ancient mount. Huge rocks had chipped off the sides of the gully and scattered like ruins down the steep passage. 'But definitely do-able, all the same.'

After the initial obstacle course, the terrain splayed out like a skirt into hills and valleys and a gorge that seemed to wind its way onto the plain and the Indigenous settlement not too far away at the base—just out of sight.

'Why, there might even be some water.'

Arthur negotiated his way down the boulders. He was aware that his body maybe suffering some effects of dehydration after sitting in that oven of a bus, so he concentrated where he stepped, careful to hold, careful to balance. The previous climbers said it took them two hours to ascend, so, maybe he would take less than two hours to descend. But he had to be careful. He was his family's and the busload's only chance; that thought spurred him on—that and water. There had to be water he convinced himself. Water trapped in a bend in the gully. There's been recent rain—surely.

Arthur plodded downwards.

The scenery blurred before him. He halted. And squeezed his eyes shut. Then opened them. Now the land was swimming in an oily mirage. Or was it his eyes? His eyes dry from dehydration and the space travel? His head began to thump. He had to get water. He had to get down.

As if in a greasy fog, Arthur groped along the rocky walls. Stones rolled like marbles under his boots. He skidded; his legs slid from under him. And he thudded bottom-first on the one spinifex bush lurking on the path.

Arthur screamed. He jumped up and rubbed his rump.

The fog cleared, and all was sharp.

Spinifex needles stuck in his rear like pins in a pin-cushion—just another disaster he'd have to deal with, when he had time. With his bottom stinging from the needles, he hobbled down the gully to the slope.

At the base where the gully intersected the larger gorge, Arthur paused under a ghost gum. He perched on the root that coiled around a rock like a snake. As his tender buns did not appreciate any pressure from sitting, Arthur crouched, barely touching the seat of his pants with the otherwise perfect tree seat.

'Now, which way?' he asked.

Arthur Fleischer scanned the terrain. The gorge seemed to wind its way from the east of the range down through the foothills to the north. He decided to go east as the northern way seemed to require another climb. Besides, it appeared deeper and darker and more promising for a waterhole.

Even in mid-July, the heat of the Central Australian sun was punishing. Was it always so hot mid-winter? Or was this the effects of global warming? Arthur tried to ignore the steady beat of pain on his temples. The promise of water pushed him on.

He grabbed the trunk of the tree and hauled himself to standing. He heard a clattering, like metal hitting the stones. He looked down. Trapped in a net of rocks, an old mini billy can. Arthur scooped it up and examined the rusty but solid vessel. It was no bigger than a large five hundred millilitre cup. It looked like a metal travel mug, but old fashioned, perhaps sixty or seventy years old. Arthur transferred it from one hand to the other. With some effort he lifted the lid. The inside stank of rust. Arthur found a stick and poked inside. He didn't risk his fingers. Who knows, a spider might be lurking in there. But whatever was in there had long since deteriorated into a few small ashes at the base. No spiders. No holes.

He fitted the lid back again. 'Hmmm, could come in handy.'

So, with the small billy can dangling by his fingertips, Arthur advanced down the gorge.

Indeed, this ancient watercourse hid from sunlight. 'Must be water,' Arthur rasped. He relished the alleyway's icy coolness as he skipped over the dry creek-bed. At every bend, every corner, he anticipated a pool—at least a puddle—a basin-sized offering of water.

Deeper and deeper, he staggered down the gully. It twisted left and narrowed. *Surely something...if not water, the end soon.*

Fleischer seemed to have been walking this route for what seemed an eternity. How could it be so dry?

The gully narrowed into a canyon. A faint sound of rustling. Rushing what? A spring? Or the wind? There's enough vegetation. Green sprigs taunted him. They dotted the gully and jutted out of stone walls. On the floor were reeds, dry tufts of grass that crunched underfoot. And what's that? Small black balls, the size of marbles—euro (small kangaroo) droppings. Yes, there's animal life. There must be water.

Excited, Arthur scampered further down the gully. It must be just around the next corner.

Spanning the chasm, a spider web. In the middle lounging like the Jabber the Hut of spiders, one huge dude of a spider. Golly! That creature was as big as a small bird.

Arthur took two steps back. Maybe he *was* on an alien world. Since when were spiders as big as birds?

He gazed up at the thin strip of blue sky. Could he climb up the side of the gorge and go around the spider? He didn't fancy forging his way through the web. What if he got caught in it and eaten by the big spider? What if he angered the spider and it chased him? What if there were more bird-sized spiders?

But the walls of the canyon were high. The whole set up reminded Arthur of Stanley Chasm.

He turned and dragging his feet, tramped back up the gorge. 'Fine then, I'll go up and down the hills and dales and probably die of dehydration,' he mumbled.

As Arthur retraced his steps, he argued with himself. *It was just a spider. What am I afraid of? But I hate spiders. No, I'm terrified. What a goose! What's a spider doing there anyway? Probably guarding the water-supply. But I'm committed. Where's the settlement anyway? Perhaps I should get high enough to see where it is. Oh, gawd, I'm lost! Go back, kill the spider. How? I'm so stupid. They're probably all dead by now. Gotta keep going. High point—that's the best course of action. See where the settlement and the road is.*

But I'm tired. How am I going to climb? I don't want to climb. I need water.

I must—keep—on—going...

Arthur plodded up the gully. He laboured with each breath, gulping down air like a dying goldfish. Each step up was agony. He climbed the slope and staggered up the ridge.

The range's formations swam in a soup of golds, reds and oranges. The sun was fast sinking into the horizon. Arthur's heart sank into hopelessness. But he forced his legs to tramp higher up the slope. Perhaps...just perhaps he'll see some semblance of civilisation.

Something shimmered in the fading rays of the sun. Was that a land rover? Nah, he must be seeing things—his vision faded out and blurred. He rubbed his eyes. *Could it be real?* Was he imagining it? *It* appeared white and looked like a tiny oblong piece of Leggo placed on top of a sand hill—a sand ridge on the edge of a dry riverbed; the same riverbed that came out of the canyon he had been hiking down until the spider.

'Oh, what the heck. It must be a car. What have I got to lose?'

So, with the little white Leggo-looking truck his goal, Arthur raced down the slopes and scaled the rises. With each hill, the object grew larger and more detailed. Until black with specks appeared around its base. Tyres. Then the shape became more defined. A four-wheel drive Toyota, he assumed. And then he could see the logo, some community art Land Cruiser, and he detected dark figures drifting around a campfire.

Arthur scampered down the last hill like a crazy man. He waved his arms and hollered. 'Help! Please help us—'

On the plain near the creek, he lost view of the camp and the Toyota Land Cruiser. But he kept on running. He was so close. He could see the smoke. And he could smell it too.

He burst through a clutch of shrubs and entered the clearing.

'Help!' he rasped. 'I need help. I need water.'

Arthur slowed down. 'Hey, where is everybody?'

He staggered around the campsite. 'Where did they go?'

The small fire crackled, the few sticks disintegrating into coals. Bottles of cola lay scattered in the sand.

Arthur picked up a bottle and sculled the last few drops. They didn't even wet his throat. 'At least that's something, I suppose.'

Arthur stood over the fire, mesmerized. He absorbed the faint roar of an engine. The sky flared in shades of crimson and pink as the dying rays touched the cumulus clouds.

Tyre tracks digging into the sand caught Fleischer's attention. He decided to follow the tracks. *At least they'll lead to a road.*

Arthur knelt and traced the hollows of sand. Then he prayed, 'Please God, may these tracks lead to a road.' He lurched to standing. Then dragging one foot in front of the other, followed the tracks.

Das Auto

World of the Wends

The maiden, Amie's eyes grew as wide as dinner plates.

How did she get up here? The doctor pondered. *Perhaps Herr Roach was right. Perhaps. But witches? Nein, he didn't believe that. And using a little magic box that captured their image and then killed people? Definitely not. The first time he heard of a magic box doing such a thing. All superstition.*

Dr. Zwar recalled the travelling circus—they had a man with a magic box there. Cost a few Pfennigs, but he made pictures on the spot in his wagon. All Science. Chemicals reacting with light made the image, but not magic. *Did Roach think we are stupid primitives who believe in the supernatural?* The doctor was sure Boris' magic resulted from science too. *So many advancements had taken place since the Renaissance...and if these two young people came from a future time or place, what's to say the silver magic box wasn't just advanced science? And the girl standing here? What's to say she didn't use some advanced physical science to climb two storeys to gain entry?*

'Bitte! Bitte!' Amie pleaded. 'Please don't hurt me.'

Zwar raised his hand. 'I won't.'

She backed against the wardrobe.

'Believe me.' Naturally he wouldn't harm her. A pretty looking fraulein like her? If he was just ten years younger...then again what's age got to do with it? Widower Weiss wed a maiden twenty years his junior. When he was still a pastor, Zwar had married them. They looked happy—especially Weiss.

Zwar smiled. *Besides, I'm quite a catch, I'm a doctor, now, with a big house and an auto, after all. What more could a maiden want?*

He stepped toward Amie.

As if reading his thoughts, Amie slid sideways to the corner of the room.

'I won't hurt you,' the doctor said. 'I want to help you.'

She shook her head.

'Don't be afraid.' Zwar took another step.

Amie gestured, pointing, then clutching her neck.

Is she crazy?

The back of Zwar's neck prickled with heat. Warm air flowed down the top of his backbone. He switched his head around. 'What are you doing here still?'

Joseph towered above him. The young man's clothes clung to him, and his hair dripped water onto the Persian rug.

Doctor Zwar sighed. *Maybe he wouldn't have a chance with Amie, after all.*

***

Central Australia

Arthur picked his way along the riverbed. Night brought relief from the heat but not thirst. His mouth burned from dryness.

The drops of cola had done nothing to quench his thirst.

Through blurry vision he ascertained that the creek was the end result of the gorge he'd descended. The gorge blocked by the giant spider.

Yet the tyre tracks were fresh, very fresh. He knew the creeks around this area; not the easiest to drive through. Surely, the campers hadn't gone too far. Surely, the soft sand, roots and rocks would slow them down. He prayed one of their tyres would be staked. Then they'd have to stop. Then he'd catch up to them. And they would have to radio for help. Surely, they'd have a CB radio.

A roar. Cracking and crunching. Hope!

Arthur blinked and squinted.

Out of the twilight haze, a Toyota four-wheel drive rumbled towards him.

Joy surged through Arthur and he staggered to the mechanical beast. He waved his arms and yelled, 'Hey! Here! Help!'

The Toyota whined to a stop.

Six dark figures of various size and weight dropped from the vehicle's body.

'You lost?' an old woman, her body a round emu shape, asked. 'What'chya doing on our land?'

'I've come from a bus on the top of the mountain.' Arthur pointed up at the shadow of the mountain.

'What?'

Arthur realised not even *he* would believe that. 'I mean our helicopter crashed on the mountain. We need help. There's more people hurt—up there.'

'Oh,' Emu lady said.

The other women, five of them, hung back, eyes to the sand, yet observing every word and movement Arthur made. He knew he was on their land. He knew he was trespassing.

The Emu lady whom he presumed was the elder, waved at the younger observers and mumbled to them. Then she turned to Arthur. 'Who you with?'

'My family—I mean my son and daughter—and I came up with teacher, Walter Wenke and Nathan our guide.'

The elder nodded. 'Ooh. You belong to the girl got lost.'

'Yes, my daughter, Amie. We were searching for her in the helicopter.' *Just twist the truth to be more believable.* 'And it crashed.'

'Ooh.' The elder nodded. She didn't sound convinced. But she extended her hand to him. 'My name Daisy,' she said. She then introduced Arthur to the other women, all artists.

Finally, she asked the question he'd been waiting for. He knew it was custom not to make a direct request but to hint at it and wait.

'You thirsty? Like some water?' Daisy offered pointing to the Toyota.

Arthur nodded. 'Yes, please.'

'Mavis, get som' water for th' fella.' Daisy ordered.

A small rotund woman ambled over to the four-wheel drive and came back with a plastic bottle full of water.

The outside of the bottle was encrusted with red sand, but Arthur accepted it and drank. Water had never tasted so sweet.

Refreshed, Arthur could not resist asking, 'We need help. We need someone to come and rescue us. Do you have a radio?'

Daisy ignored his question. Arthur guessed that was always a possibility. Instead she chatted with her artist friends for what seemed ages and continued to act as if Arthur didn't exist.

While the women drifted around the four-wheel drive like ghosts in the dark, "yabbering" away, Arthur peered into the front cabin and then studied the dashboard. They had CB radio—a must in this remote part of the world. Why weren't they using it? Precious time was being wasted.

Daisy motioned to Arthur. At last! He thought.

As if speaking to the dry riverbed, she said, 'We take you to The Mission. Okay?'

Arthur's heart sank. He visualised his hopes buried in this soft sand. *Mission? That's hours away from here. How will my family and the others survive?* But he nodded again. 'Yes, thank you, that's okay.'

***

Nathan toyed with the patrol car's CB radio. He stabbed at the buttons, lifted the speaker to his lips and blew, and then switched the device on and then off.

Walter readjusted his grip on the steering wheel. 'You shouldn't be fiddling with that.'

'It should work.'

'You've done something wrong,' Walter said. 'Maybe you've broken it. Dan'll be pleased.'

'I use it all the time.'

'You're kidding me. Dan lets you use the Police Car Radio? I doubt it.'

'Yeah, why not?' Nathan looked at Walter. He smiled and tapped Wenke on the shoulder. 'So nice to have good Walter back.'

Walter rolled his eyes. 'Dan won't be happy you've broken his radio, bad Nathan.'

'It's not broke, it's just not working.'

Walter stared at the highway to The Mission. The sun dipped below the horizon touching the ranges, grass and trees in hues of gold, and tangerine. They passed the carcass of an unfortunate camel, its carcass splayed near a fence. Walter had to stay vigilant. Twilight and the wildlife emerged from their wilderness hideouts and took liberty in crossing the road.

Nathan and Walter discussed their plan.

Walter wasn't always a teacher. In a previous "life" he'd been a physicist. Then 2008 and the Global Financial Crisis (GFC) took its toll and with funding cuts, he'd been made redundant. It was then he moved into teaching to pay the mortgage on a house his ex-wife ended up owning. The position of teacher at The Mission his only success in winning a job. So here he was, at the coalface, and why no one questioned his driving the Police patrol car.

So, to Walter, two points in space joined by a wormhole was possible according to the theories expounded by some world-renown physicists, and not just a convenient construct of Science Fiction.

Walter tried to explain the physics behind the theory of wormholes to Nathan, but the Indigenous guide argued the morgue was merely a passage into the spirit world and proof of the Eden-like land from stories passed down from his ancestors.

Walter reasoned if this cockroach creature, the bad Walter, could shift between two worlds, so could he, the good Walter. And no, if bad Walter had come from this spirit world, Eden was not likely to exist there.

So, after escaping to Alice Springs for the day, research and a progress report on the lost Joseph and Amie (which proved fruitless), Walter and Nathan planned to return to The Mission and examine the morgue's interior. Walter hoped to boldly go where not too many humans had gone before and transport himself to this lost world.

But first, they'd send Friedrich through to test and prepare the way. He glanced to the back seat.

Friedrich slumped against the window, asleep.

***

Nathan, Walter and Friedrich arrived in The Mission just after dark.

The locals sauntering on the main road greeted Nathan with a dip of their heads. 'What's happening with the radio?' Nathan asked.

'Radio not working,' they replied.

'Though' so. Spirits have cut radio waves, I reckon.'

'Hmm, those spirits very busy lately.'

'Bad Walter, again!'

'Hmm, bad Walter.'

Of course, when he returned to the house and told good Walter, Walter said there had to be a scientific explanation. Several hours passed as they argued...

It was the same with the old morgue and transporting to another world. Why couldn't Walter see? It was clear as the big nose on Walter's face that this was spirit business. The morgue was the doorway to the spirit-world with min-min men and demons. He only had to look at the boy from that world, Friedrich—so white. He'd seen his ghost in the precinct from time to time over the past year. But bad Walter? The devil got into him and made him bad.

Nathan was convinced this world beyond the morgue was not a good place; not an Eden his people thought, after all. He tried to persuade Walter. But Walter would hear none of Nathan's concerns. Besides, Walter explained he'd been talking to Friedrich in his own language and Friedrich was sure the lost Amie and Joseph were there in Friedrich's world.

Nathan opened the precinct gate and Walter and Friedrich followed him to the building behind the old church. Nathan gripped his stomach. He was sure his insides were filled with a nest of cavorting snakes. He really didn't want to go there. But for the sake of Joseph and Amie, he would.

He prayed to the white-man's God. 'Help us pass through to the other world and get the children.'

'What are you doing?' Walter asked.

'I'm praying we get through.'

'Yeah, I guess asking God would help—but there's still a scientific explanation.'

Walter pushed open the door and crept in. He shone the torch at the walls and slab in the middle. 'There must be controls here, somewhere.'

Friedrich clutched the doorpost and refused to enter. Nathan continued mumbling his mantra and reciting the stories of passing from this world to the next.

Walter groped under the slab. He ran his fingers over the stone wall. His nails scraped at any cracks. 'Nothing!' he muttered. 'How did he do it?'

'Maybe your science doesn't understand about spirits,' Nathan said.

'It has to be here somewhere.' Walter crouched and then crawled on the floor.

Nathan knelt in the dust and prayed.

'Da! Da!' the boy pointed. 'Das blau licht!'

Both men lifted their heads and looked in the direction of Friedrich's pointed finger.

There by the back wall was a bluish laser-light.

Friedrich launched from the doorway and stumbled towards the light. Just before he reached it, he turned and waved. 'Alf Wiedersehen.' Then he stepped through the light and vanished into the wall.

'Yes!' Walter clapped. 'I don't know how, but it worked.'

'I prayed, Walter.'

'Yeah, well, whatever,' Walter replied. He rubbed his hands together. 'So, here goes.' Walter charged at the light and the wall absorbed him.

Nathan paced back and forth. Should he risk it? What if it was a trap and bad Walter was at the other side? No, he must. But first, he'd go and get his rifle he'd left by the laundry cupboard at Walter's.

He raced back to Walter's place and crept through the back door.

With the rifle in hand, he ran back to the Precinct. Glancing behind, he noticed a Toyota Land cruiser. In the dim light he scanned the logo on the car door— "Way Out West Community Artists"—just visible.

What are they doing here? He wondered. *Ah, well, I'll find out later...*

Nathan stepped into the morgue. He marched to the back. And through the light.

***

All the While on the World of the Wends

'Do something,' Amie yelled in English.

'What?' Joseph volleyed. 'Amie, what are you doing here?'

'Hiding from the mob, what d'ya think?' Her heart thumped so strong the beat echoed in her ears. 'Aren't you going to get the doctor? Tie him up?'

'No, why?'

'He's going to kill us.'

'Where did you get that idea?'

The doctor glanced from Amie to Joseph.

Joseph tapped Zwar on the back and spoke in German. 'Tell her you're on our side and going to help us.'

'But I did. She didn't believe me.'

'It's okay, Amie, the doctor's helping us.'

Dr Zwar bared his teeth and bobbed his head up and down. He turned to Joseph. 'Aber, why are you here still? I told you the way of escape. Swim through the river and run to the mountains, you must.'

'Some men blocked the way on the other side of the river,' Joseph replied.

'But didn't you stay underwater? Didn't you swim further down?'

Joseph shivered. 'They were everywhere.'

162

'So, there were men blocking the road out to the mountains,' Zwar said.

'Yes, I don't think they believed I was dead.'

'Hmmm.'

Amie raised her hand. 'Although, they may have been after me. I mean, I shot the church's ceiling down.'

'Hmmm, that is possible.'

'We have to find another way.' Joseph trembled and his teeth chattered.

Amie rushed to Joseph. 'First you need to get warm. You're getting hypothermia.'

'Come,' Dr Zwar said, 'take those clothes off and dry yourself, then warm by the fire in the living room. I have some spare clothes you can wear.'

Amie and Joseph, who both had changed into dry clothes, basked by the flames. Dr Zwar prepared a brew of coffee and made a supper of toast with blackberry jam.

They sipped the coffee and munched on the toast.

'You look like a homeless guy,' Amie laughed.

Joseph glanced down. 'Can't help if the doc's so short.'

'And fat.'

The trousers Joseph wore came a quarter way up his calves, and the cuffs failed to stretch past his wrists. The belt around his skinny waist bunched up the top of the trousers so indeed he looked like some homeless dude. *How embarrassing!* Joseph thought.

Outside, the crowd hammered metal tins.

Zwar drew the curtains and closed the shutters and suggested they hide in the attic for a few days until things settle down.

Joseph disagreed not wanting to cause trouble for the doctor.

'We can't stay here, how are we going to get out?' Amie stressed.

The men discussed in whispered tones possibilities. Each one useless and bound to go awry in Amie's opinion.

Amie spotted a beret on a hatstand by the door in the passage. 'Hey, I have an idea.'

Joseph and the doctor stopped and looked at her with dead pan expressions.

Amie pointed at the hat stand. 'Joseph, if you wear the doctor's beret, you may just fool the mob in the dark.'

'But in the car—'

'Was ist das?' Dr Zwar had no idea what Amie was saying.

'In das auto,' Joseph said with a sigh and roll of his eyes.

'Das Auto?' The doctor stroked his beard. 'Yah, that might work.'

'Are you serious?'

'Yah, und you could drive.'

'And I'll hide in the back under the seat or in the boot,' Amie said. 'They'll never keep up—even if they got on their horses. What a plan!'

'Have you seen the roads up to the mountains? Or should I say have you seen roads? You need a four-wheel drive.' Joseph couldn't resist putting a dampener on the whole idea.

'Got any other suggestions?' Amie said.

'It'll be fine. It's a Merc, no? Und what other choice do we have?'

'Yeah, Joseph.'

'Wait a minute while I fasten a scarf over my head und we can pretend I am Frau Biar who is helping me search for you two up in ze mountains.'

'They won't believe you.' Joseph again.

The yelling, screaming and kettling rose to fever-pitch; so loud the noise rang in Amie's ears.

'Where's the girl?' they cried.

'We want the girl.'

'She's a witch.'

'We want her to hang.'

'Throw her in the river.'

'Like the boy.'

They chanted: 'The girl...the girl...the girl!'

Amie paced the floor. 'What are we going to do? They know I'm here.'

'I'll tell them you're not. You've escaped to the mountains and that Frau Biar and I are driving the auto to the mountains to find you. That you trust Frau Biar and will come out of hiding for her.'

'What if they don't believe you?' Amie wiped her brow which was damp with perspiration. Her mouth went dry as she contemplated her fate of being set upon by the mob.

'Schnell,' the doctor said, 'to the auto by the back door while I deal with the people.'

Dr Zwar marched into the hallway, grabbed the beret and fitted it to his head as he approached the front door.

Knocking, rapid and urgent jarred Amie's senses.

Amie and Joseph crawled along the floor as if they were in a fire. They negotiated the lean-to kitchen, and when they reached the back door, they paused, their hearing set to hyper-sensitive, listening for any signs of life.

The pair crouched by the rear door.

'I don't like this,' Amie whispered. 'Sure there'll be some wise guy who goes around the back.'

'What about the window in the drawing room? It's on the side of the house where the car is.'

'But it's on the other side of the passage.'

'We'll keep low and in darkness so they won't see us. What choice do we have?'

Amie and Joseph shuffled to the passage.

Dr Zwar argued with the mob on the porch.

Joseph darted across the hallway. He pulled the door handle downwards. The door pushed open with a shudder.

Amie held her breath. She glanced at the front porch.

The doctor held the crowd's attention. 'She has fled to the mountains, I tell you,' he said. 'I will go with Frau Biar—'

Amie hunched over and scuttled across the passage. She pushed the door more open. Then she raced to the window. Joseph was already half out and beckoning her. 'No one's around. It's safe. Hurry!' he urged in hushed tones.

She poked her head out and looked left and right. The Merc's silver body gleamed in the reflected moonlight.

Joseph eased himself out of the window, then grasped Amie's hand and guided her to the shadows between the side of the car and geranium bushes.

The clamouring and shouting faded into silence.

'Quick!' Joseph said. 'In the boot.' He climbed in the driver's seat and pulled the lever.

Amie crawled in the storage trunk.

Voices. High pitched. Boots crunched on gravel. *Oh, no! Joseph!* The car rocked.

Amie curled up in a ball and prayed. 'Please God, save Joseph.'

The door squeaked. Then it slammed. The car swayed from side to side.

The rabble surrounded the car. Amie heard hollering and shrieking from every side.

The engine roared.

Amie heard the slow grind of gravel under rubber. The mob muttered and mumbled. Then they raised their voices which competed with the chugging of the engine.

The car jerked. Amie thudded against the inside of the trunk like a sack of potatoes. Someone screamed. The engine revved. Tyres screeched. A soft thud. More yelling. The car swung around. The sound of tyres spinning squealing in the dirt. The smell of burnt rubber. Then the car bolted forward.

In the dark all Amie could do was imagine the scene of the mob and roll around like a bag of loose groceries.

The irate voices faded until there was just the steady hum of the engine.

Then the car stopped. More stone crunching underfoot. Two men talking. Was that Joseph and the doctor talking? Door slammed and the car moved again.

This time Amie bounced and jiggled. The car revved and groaned as if in protest. Amie wished she'd thought to put padding in the trunk. Each thud sent shock waves through her prone body. Thump. Bump! Bang! Rattle and jerk! Amie hung onto any dents or holes in the floor of the trunk she could find.

The car bumped along. When was this blind roller coaster ride going to end? It seemed to be taking forever.

The car jolted and rumbled to a stop. The doors sighed and then clunked. A wheeze and Amie saw the night sky thick with stars. The moon was nowhere to be seen.

Amie climbed out of the trunk. She accepted the man with the beret's hand, and he drew her to himself.

The tang of tobacco hit her. 'Ugh! It's you!' She recoiled.

'At least you could say, thank you,' Doctor Zwar said.

'Not bad for a first try at country driving, doc.' Joseph's voice all falsetto sang out from the scarf-covered head.

Amie glanced from one man to the other half-dressed as a woman. 'What's going on? I thought...'

'It seemed the logical thing to do, once we got going and the mad crowd chasing us,' Joseph explained. 'Besides, I make a more convincing Frau Biar as I am tall and thin.' He laughed. 'And let's face it, Dr Zwar makes a pretty good rendition of himself.'

Dr Zwar chuckled as he surveyed the land formations; black outlines against the star-studded sky. He patted Joseph and then Amie on the arm. 'Go! Schnell! If they follow by horse, they won't take long to find us.' He pushed them. 'Schnell! To the mountains. Mach Schnell!'

Smoke Signals

Central Australia

Night fall on the summit of the mountain brought relief from the heat. Although the open windows on the bus cooled the broiling atmosphere, the passengers were still slowly cooking. The metal casing of the bus had heated up the people, dehydrating them as if they'd been stuck in a tin shed in the middle of summer. It would take some time to cool their body temperatures after dark.

The passengers gasped for air, gulping the pungent body odours as if fish out of water. The woman who had previously fitted, lay limp and ghost-white on the floor in the aisle. Dan had seen the signs in his job—especially up here in the Centre where death was so common, the gurney a permanent fixture at the entrance of the church. Ready to go. This woman, Dan observed, was near death. Her major organs were probably on the verge of shutting down.

'Anyone, if you have water, please, you need to share it, for everyone to survive,' Dan urged.

Jakob translated. His wife, sat by his side, meek and mouse-like, so different from up there in the spaceship or whatever it was. She put up a fight then, like a tiger, when the little grey men tried to probe her. Dan smiled. He was just trying to help...

Antony Wurst shifted in his seat. Dan had observed that guilty expression many a time in his profession as a police officer.

Dan leaned forward. The bus creaked. 'Is there something you'd like to share, Mr Wurst?'

Wurst cleared his throat. He then bent over (not a pretty sight with certain parts of his anatomy exposed as his trousers slipped with the bend), and he rifled through a bag at his feet. Dan mused if this Wurst fellow was a plumber back in his native Germany.

The bus tilted forward. Antony jumped back.

'Do you?' Dan asked.

Wurst pointed at the storage compartment above him. 'In dere, I have some, in dere.'

Dan looked up at Wurst's beige travel bag tucked in snug at the back of the recess. He shook his head. 'Great!' He figured they had no choice. They had to get out or risk going over the edge. 'Look, everyone, we need to get out of the bus. Or do something. We can't just sit here and wait for the bus to fall off the cliff.'

Protests volleyed back.

'We can't'

'How can we?'

'It's too dangerous.'

'We can't risk it.'

Then, 'Hey, Officer,' Adam said in a small voice, 'why don't a couple of us get out and put some rocks under the bus so it won't fall.'

'I don't know...' Dan said.

'Sure we can find some rocks. I'll climb out and find some.'

'No!' his mother, Carol cried.

'But mum!'

'You can't see. It's dark. You might fall off the cliff.'

'I won't.' Adam was resolute. 'My phone has a torch. And we have a full moon.'

'But, darling, I just want you to be safe. I don't want to lose you too.'

'I'll be fine. And the policeman can help me.'

Carol clutched Adam's arm. 'But you might fall.'

Adam shook her hold off. 'If we stay in this bus, we will fall. I have to do *something*.' He scrambled over the luggage piled on the back seat.

'No! Don't!' Carol hung onto his shirt.

'Let me go!' Adam grabbed her fingers and wrenched them away. 'Told you, we'll all be dead if we don't get out. You heard the policeman. Besides, when we make sure the bus won't fall, the fat man can get his water'n stuff.'

Dan knelt and placed a hand on the velvet-lined space beside Carol. 'It's okay, I'll look after him. But once we stabilise the bus, we should all remove ourselves from the bus.'

Carol dipped her head. A tear meandered down her cheek as she released her son.

Adam leapt out the window and for a moment disappeared. Then the rays of his phone torch hovered over the shrubs.

Dan wriggled like a worm over the baggage and then eased himself through the window. The bus rocked and scudded a few centimetres. Dan caught the window frame and held it. The ball of light, no larger than a table-tennis ball, bounced over the summit about ten metres distance. 'Keep from the edge,' Dan called.

The bus strained at his arm. He tried to stop the bus from moving. He wedged his foot against a rock to stem the flow of gravity. 'Is there a cairn? Get some rocks from that,' Dan yelled.

Adam's voice floated back. 'Okay.'

The bus groaned and scraped. Dan's arms ached as he pulled against it. The passengers inside were silent.

'Move to the rear!' Dan yelled. 'Especially Wurst—get him on the back seat.'

He looked at the tyre creeping over his foot. If the tyre were flat, would that cause more resistance? *Hmm, worth a try.* 'Hold on,' Dan warned. He removed his gun from his holster, and then pumped two bullets into the rubber. Whoosh! Dan pulled his foot away. The rim landed with a thud on the gravel. The bus listed on its side. It threatened to keel over on top of him.

Screams from the passengers descended on him. Dan held his breath and the side of the bus.

Carol hung out of the window. 'What happened?'

'I shot the tyre.'

'You idiot!' She forced a bag to tumble down, so he had to dodge. 'You trying to get us all killed?'

'I thought—'

'You thought?'

'Well, since I did it, the bus hasn't moved.'

Carol hopped out the window. She crouched and inspected the damage. Then she whipped up the bag and shoved it up against the pancake of a tyre. 'Better than nothing, I guess.' She stood up and scanned the surroundings. 'Where's my son? You said you'd look after him.'

Dan muttered, 'Sounds like my ex.'

'Here I am,' Adam sang out. He emerged from the darkness cradling a boulder the size of a newborn baby.

Carol sighed. 'You can put that under the tyre the policeman has kindly flattened with his gun.'

'Oh.' Adam approached the leaning tower of bus.

'Give it here!' Carol snatched the rock and wedged it under the tyre while Adam shone his little light on the operation.

'Shouldn't Dan do the other one, then the bus won't be leaning anymore.'

'Are you crazy?' Carol ranted.

Poor Arthur, no wonder he went on this trip without her, Dan mused.

'But mum—then there'll be less height and the bus won't lean over the edge anymore. And Mr. Wurst won't have so much trouble getting his bag with all his water and goodies.'

'What do you mean, goodies?'

'When Mr. Wenke first put us in this bus, I saw Mr. Wurst pigging out on all the food in that bag. I did, mum, honest. Made me hungry. Then Wenke grabbed the bag from him and shoved it right at the back in the over-head storage.'

'I see—well, that's something to look forward to. We won't starve, then.'

Carol followed Adam in the direction of the cairn. Meanwhile Dan pushed against the listing bus and kept an eye on the activity inside.

Mother and son returned with two more rocks which they planted against the rim.

'You could get off your butt and help us,' Carol said.

'I have to hold the bus from tipping, if you haven't noticed.'

'Rubbish, it won't.'

Dan moved his hands away from the vehicle. The bus groaned and tipped further. Dan pushed up and against the wall of metal.

'Told you it was a mistake to shoot the tyre,' Carol said.

'Too late now,' Dan said. 'See what can be done the other side.'

Carol and her son scrambled to the other side of the bus. She yelled, 'The tyre's lifted from the ground.'

Through the windows, Dan saw Adam's phone torch shining towards the front. 'The wheels of the bus are close to the edge,' Adam said.

Carol returned to Dan. She stood facing him, her hands on her hips. 'Great! Their fate depends on one flat wheel. That's just great!'

'They have no choice, mum, they have to get out now.' Adam stalked around the bus to Dan.

Jakob poked his head out the window. 'What are you going to do now? They're all asking.'

'Help you get out of this wreck,' Dan replied.

'How?'

'With much difficulty, I gather,' said Dan.

'How's Wurst going to get through?' Carol asked. 'And what about the weak and unconscious?'

'Start by getting as many as you can, sitting down the back on the other—high side as the bus is leaning over. Then we'll deal with the exit one by one.' The bus creaked. Then thudding and shuffling from inside the bus. Wurst grunted. Dan glanced inside. 'Get right to the back to the high side. I want people to leave the bus by the window, one at a time.'

Wurst inched his way to the back seat. The dozen or so passengers squeezed together to make room for him.

Carol and Adam joined Dan pushing against the tilting bus. One by one, those who were mobile and of sound mind, crawled through the window and jumped onto solid ground. Then the weak and less able were passed through the window. The unconscious woman was body-surfed to a prickle bush-free patch.

Finally, the only one who was left in the bus was Herr Wurst. He thrust his head through the window. 'I don't tink I can do it.'

Carol looked up at him. 'Nup, not possible.'

'Hey, Mum what about Wurst's bag?' Adam chirped like a hungry starling.

The bag, the bag, forgot about the bag. Carol cursed herself.

'Get the bag, Mr. Wurst,' Adam said.

'I don't tink I can. It is too far down. The bus may tip,' Wurst said.

'Try, we must—we need water.'

Wurst retracted his head. On the outside, the passengers watched as the shadowy blob moved to the second last row. The bus crunched and jolted sideways.

'Stop!' Dan yelled.

'Achtung!' Jakob cried.

The monolith inside the bus lumbered to the back seat. He looked out the window.

'Sorry,' he said.

Adam raised his hand and waved it around. 'I could go in and get it. I'm only fifty kilos and if Mr Wurst sits on the other side, where he was before down the back, I could be in and out in no time—with the bag.'

'No!' Adam's mum said.

Adam shone the torch on Carol. 'You want us to die of hunger and thirst just to keep me safe? Do you mum?'

'No, but...'

'Yes, but, it has to be done and I'm the only one who can do it.'

'He's right, Mrs. Fleischer,' Dan said. He surveyed the Germans scattered over the summit. 'Any other volunteers?'

All heads swayed from side to side.

'Go for it, Adam, but be careful,' Dan said, 'any movement, any sign of danger and get out, okay?'

'Okay.'

Dan hoisted Adam through the window. Adam shuffled and rustled, negotiating his way over the luggage, treading carefully down the aisle. The phone light, now faint as the battery was draining of power, bobbed over the rows of seats. It stopped and shone up at the ceiling. Carol wrapped her arms around her chest.

'I can't reach,' Adam said.

'Don't ask me to come und help you,' Wurst said.

'It's okay. I reckon I can climb up.'

The light wobbled as it gained height. The bus wobbled.

Adam's voice raised in triumph. 'Catch,' he said to Wurst.

A soft thud was heard as the carry-bag landed on the floor. Then scraping like rats in the ceiling.

Carol clenched her teeth. She prayed silently. *Please God, get Adam out safely.*

Adam appeared and said, 'Here!'

Dan and Jakob grasped the bag and hauled it to the ground. Adam scrambled down after the bag.

Mother Fleischer enveloped her son, hugging him. 'Thank God you're safe.'

Adam squirmed out of her arms. 'Mum! Stop embarrassing me. We've work to do.'

While Dan gathered sticks and commenced to light a fire with matches from one of the Germans, Jakob sorted the rations of water and food. He counted: two litres of spring water, five cans of fizzy drink, and food consisting of six packets of chips, blocks of chocolate and a box of six muesli bars.

Carol snapped up one of the spring water bottles and proceeded to dab the unconscious woman's lips with water. She moved and her eyes fluttered open.

Dan was concerned about Herr Wurst. He tapped on the window. 'Are you alright in there?'

Antony Wurst called from the bus. 'It is okay. I stay in the bus. I will sit at the back and it von't fall.'

'Here,' Dan said and tossed him a bottle of water.

So, as the moon drifted along with the canopy of stars, the group huddled around the fire, nibbling rations, sipping water and soft drink, hoping and waiting.

'This fire will make us visible for rescue,' Dan said. He rubbed his hands together. He hoped. He prayed that Arthur had made it down the mountain and had called for help. He gazed over the moon-lit landscape, south towards the silhouette of the southern range. Surely the helicopters will be coming soon—at least by daybreak.

***

In the light of the full moon, the brooding bulk of the northern mountain range jutted up into the sky like an under-bite of jagged teeth.

Nathan stepped out of the cave and examined his surroundings. 'The Spring,' he said.

A dingo howled in the distance.

Nathan glanced at Walter fossicking at the cave's entrance and then at the ghost boy who sat silent on a rock.

'What d'ya reckon, Walter?' Nathan asked.

'Crap! Absolute crap!' Walter hurled down a handful of sand. 'At least we could've gone to another country.'

'I don't know,' Nathan said. 'Usually takes me several hours to drive to this country. I'm impressed.'

'I s'pose, but another planet would've been nice, even if it were filled with evil Walters.'

'And what are you thinking of doing when you find this bad Walter?'

'Hunt 'im down and kill 'im.' Walter hunkered down near Friedrich. 'Sounds like quite a nasty character according to Fred, here. He's been killing their babies and their chooks lay cockroaches.'

'He sounds bad.' Nathan held up the rifle. 'You might need some help.'

Walter gazed at the gun. 'I was wondering what took you so long.'

'Yeah, went back 'n got it,' Nathan said. 'The ammo's in my pocket.'

Walter stood up. 'We better see what we can do to get the teleportation system or wormhole to work. See if we can find this bad Walter. I noticed some equipment right at the back of the cave. I think this character has set up a triangulation system—so the final point is the alien planet, I hope. We'll find those kids and bring them back.'

Nathan rolled his eyes, and watched Walter retreat into the cave, the torch in hand, darting left and right. Then he turned and joined Friedrich at the entrance.

They perched on the rock and waited. The desert cold seeped through Nathan's jacket and into his skin. He noticed Friedrich hug himself and shiver.

'I'll get fire going,' Nathan said.

The boy returned a blank look and then glance away.

Nathan rose and stalked to a ghost gum nearby. At the base of the tree, he gathered a few sticks for fuel.

As he straightened up and turned, a spark on the northern range caught his eye. It flickered, fading in and out of the darkness. Was it a star? Or a satellite? Or a helicopter crash and burn?

Nathan sauntered back to Friedrich and nudged him. 'Look.' He pointed at the mountain.

The boy glanced at the peak and shrugged.

Nathan sat on his haunches. He arranged the sticks and some spinifex. He held his lighter to the dry grass and then watched as the flames caught the grass and spread licking the sticks.

Soon fire glowed and crackled, its simple life providing warmth to Nathan and Friedrich who hovered over it, hands splayed to will the heat into them.

Every so often Nathan glanced at the summit of the mountain north of them. Was it a campfire? What would people be doing camping on that peak?

Walter strutted out of the cave. He jogged on the spot and clapped his hands. 'I've done it!' he announced. 'I've made the ray of light. I've succeeded!'

'Now we go?' Nathan asked.

'It was so simple. I don't know why no one's thought of it before. The secret is in the light and creating a stable mini black hole. Who would've thought?'

Nathan stared at the fire. 'Who would?'

'This is my lucky break,' Walter continued. 'If I can pull this off, I'm back as a scientist, a physicist. No more teaching for me. No sir-ree!'

'Are we going then?' Nathan rose to see this light Walter was raving about. 'We need to save those kids.'

Walter held up his hand. 'No, Freddie first. He's done it before. Let's check out that it goes to the right place.'

'Are you sure?'

'By golly, I'm sure,' Walter gestured for Nathan to come close. 'Freddie here will return and tell us. Okay? If it's not right, I think I can adjust it.'

'Hope you know what you're doing, mate.'

'Hey, I'm a physicist.'

'Whatever.' Nathan bit his lip. Was this a dream? Would they just end up in the morgue again? And what was that twinkling light on the summit of that mountain? And finally, was this venture a one-way trip to the spirit world?

Walter led Friedrich into the cave. Nathan abandoned the small fire to burn itself out and tracked behind them. The ray of light glittered in the darkness.

'Jah, whol!' Friedrich exclaimed and ran towards it. Then he was gone.

Nathan leaned on the cave wall. 'You sure he'll come back, mate?' He watched Walter in the circle of light from his torch which he had rested on the ledge above him. Walter fiddled with a box the size of an old computer. His fingers worked some knobs while he examined a screen. 'What happens if he doesn't?'

'Just stabilising, the ray seems to fluctuate,' Walter already seemed to be in the other world of his own making. He continued muttering, 'You can't see, Nathan, but um—I think from the readings, it's a success.'

'The boy's not coming back. What now?'

'Give him a few more minutes. I told him to come back—I'm sure he will.'

The two men stood, staring at the ray. Every so often, Walter nursed the box, touching a button or two.

He's not sure, Nathan thought.

Nathan broke the silence. 'There's a light on that mountain—'

'Shhh!' Walter cut him off.

Several more minutes passed. The ray fazed in and out.

'Oh, here he is!' Walter stepped towards the light.

But no Friedrich appeared.

'I don't think he's coming back,' Nathan said.

'Oh, what the heck, I can't wait any longer.' Walter rolled up his sleeves and bolted towards the ray. Just before he cut through it, he turned. 'You coming?'

'Why not?' Nathan said. He tapped his pockets. Bullets still there. Then he slung his rifle over his shoulder and together, Walter and Nathan strode through the ray.

Where the Grass is Greener

World of the Wends

Friedrich emerged from the cave and blinked. Mountains, shimmered blue and purple. Waves of pink and violet carpeted the hills leading up to the snow-covered peaks. Not like that dry dusty place he'd left which Walter insisted was the real Australia. Can't be. Didn't Boris promise a land of milk and honey? *Can't be the real earth, so barren. How could that be?*

The earth Friedrich came from, the Silesia he'd left with his Mutti, Papa, und his schwester was swamped in every shade of green. Boris promised a fertile land.

And that strange man who called himself Walter? That Walter looked like the Boris who promised such a land. How could he trust him? Sure, he said he was good Walter who wouldn't hurt him. That Walter said to trust him. Trust him? Friedrich would go along with him, but he wouldn't trust him. And he certainly didn't intend to go back. He preferred to stay with his family in the Australia with blue grass and two suns. He'd have to deal with Boris, which in that other Australia they called bad Walter. *Oh, now he was all confused getting.*

Friedrich glanced left and right, checking around the cave for any signs of Boris-bad Walter. Not that he expected any—he left Boris behind on the barren Australia. All clear. He stamped down the slope, kicking at stones and tufts of grass as he went.

The first sun peeped over the ranges to the east. Friedrich skipped. Bald birds that resembled parrots plucked of their feathers, swooped over the valley. He liked this Australia. He had to admit it did have some strange animals, but so did the other

"Australia". Animals that looked like deer but hopped on two hind feet, they were strange too. And then there was that tiny spikey lizard he once found on a former visit to that land. He smiled as he remembered the bulldog creature high in the trees that dropped loads of poop, as Joseph called that smelly stuff, and always when Friedrich walked in the woods. He'd have to watch them.

Home by lunchtime. Friedrich licked his lips and savoured in anticipation his mother's fried chicken. So much more appetising than those stale bread things they called "burgers" in the other "Australia". Ja, he was ready for some real food.

Someone called, 'Hey, it's Friedrich!'

He stopped and glanced about. Boulders sparkled, the specks of gems reflecting the sunlight. A nearby bush rustled. Who's that speaking?

'Friedrich!' the voice, a familiar male one, yelled. 'Over here!'

He looked at the rock. *Are the stones speaking to me?*

'Friedrich! Over here!'

The lad trod towards the rock.

'Here, silly!'

A hand jutted up above the rock and waved.

Friedrich raced towards the rock. 'Where are you?'

'Here, are you blind?' Amie popped her head above the rock.

Then Joseph bobbed up. 'Schnell, before Boris sees us.'

'Or the village folk,' Amie added.

Friedrich skirted the boulder and joined Amie and Joseph huddling in a small cave behind the rock. 'What are you doing here?' he asked.

'Hiding,' Amie said.

'Where have you been, Friedrich?' Joseph asked.

'Your family's been so worried about you,' Amie said.

'I to the other Australia travelled with the good Walter but he looks like Boris, and the man with brown skin, Nathan,' Friedrich said, 'and they are looking for you all.'

'How did you get there?' Joseph asked.

'I followed Boris down into the outhouse and through the blue light. There, I to a village like my own back in Silesia came, from another outhouse but they a morgue called it.'

'No wonder that morgue gave me the creeps,' Amie muttered.

Joseph gave Amie a gentle nudge. 'Hey, Amie, if the cave doesn't work, we can go through the outhouse.'

'Sure, if the villagers don't catch us and drown us in the river first.'

'What are you talking about?' Friedrich asked. Amie and Joseph had been talking in his language, but he couldn't understand why they were afraid of his people.

Amie clutched Friedrich's hands. 'Oh, Friedrich, you have to help us. You have to convince your people we're not evil. We're not witches.'

'They're after us.'

'Yeah, we saw a few of them climbing the mountain this morning just before dawn,' Amie said. 'We had to hide in this cave.'

'Why do they think that?' Friedrich asked.

'Boris,' Joseph replied, then hugged his knees and rocked.

'Oh, it was terrible!' Amie wiped her brow. 'Just when your father had almost convinced the townsfolk that Boris was bad, and they must rise up against him and drive him out, Boris turned up. He grabbed Joseph, and found his camera and took some photos, then said it was an evil thing and that the pictures captured their souls and would kill them.'

'If it wasn't for Doctor Zwar, we'd be dead!'

'A camera? Was is das?'

'A magic box,' Amie explained. 'It can take pictures of people, the land, animals—all sorts of things. But it doesn't harm anyone. Boris was lying.'

Friedrich's eyes widened. 'Is that why my sister got ill?'

'No!' Amie shook her head. 'No, that was the food Boris forced us to eat. You know Boris is bad.'

'And it sounds like he's doing bad things on our world, too,' Joseph said.

'Not so much,' Friedrich said. 'Although the food is bad. Boris, although he called himself Walter there, made me eat a bun called a burger and I felt sick in that carriage they call a car.'

'Walter?' Joseph asked.

'Told you Walter and Boris were one and the same. Now do you believe me?' Amie said.

Joseph thumped the only small patch of earth available. 'Time this Walter, I mean Boris gets his just desserts.'

'How are we going to do that?' Amie asked.

'I don't know, I'll think of something,' Joseph replied.

Amie peeped around the rock. 'Hmmm!'

'I know, I know,' Friedrich said. 'The men, this Walter and Nathan are going to come through the cave if I go back.'

'How are we going to fight them? We've got nothing,' Amie said.

'Could we block up the cave up there, and then they'd have to come through the outhouse?' Joseph said. 'Then perhaps with Herr Biar's gun and mad cows and bulls and stuff, we could fight them.'

Amie stroked Joseph's back. 'Somehow, I think, even if we had an army and weapons of mass destruction, that Boris character would find a way to survive.'

Joseph looked at Amie. 'Why do you say that?'

'I saw him—it. He wasn't human. It was alien. An over-sized cockroach. And they say cockroaches survive anything, even nuclear bombs.'

Joseph hunched over and sighed. 'Great! We're stuffed.'

Joseph, Amie and Friedrich stared at the large stone in front of them. The stone glittered as if flecked with fine grains of gold.

'Any idea what kills cockroaches?' Amie muttered.

Joseph shrugged and shook his head.

'I'm hungry,' Friedrich said.

Joseph's eyes brightened. It was as if a light bulb turned on above his head. 'I have an idea.'

'What?' Amie asked.

'Borax.'

'Borax?'

'Yeah, borax,' Joseph clapped. 'Told you I'd think of something.'

'But borax? What the heck is borax?'

'Ja, was ist das Borax?' Friedrich echoed.

'You know my parents are into all things natural,' Joseph began. 'Well, what they do to kill cockroaches is put out borax mixed with a little sugar to kill them. Their insides don't take the borax very well and they die.'

'Yeah, and how exactly, are we going to get a hold of Borax to kill Boris?' Amie locked her gaze onto Joseph.

Joseph shifted the weight on his bottom and glanced around. 'Well?'

'Perhaps the doctor, Doctor Zwar, might know,' Joseph said. A long shot, but out of all the villagers, Zwar seemed to be the most likely to have the information and resources. 'Um, after all, he's the village doctor...'

'Only because Boris made him so.'

'Yeah, well, better than nothing, I guess.'

'And how are we going to return to the village to get this poison?' Amie challenged.

Why did she have to ask so many questions?

Friedrich piped up. 'I'm hungry. Can I go now?'

Amie gazed at the boy. 'He could go for us, I s'pose.'
'Sounds like a plan,' Joseph said.

With specific instructions for Friedrich to locate the doctor and request some Borax, they sent him off down the valley to the town. Friedrich's stomach grumbled as he galloped down the slope. He'd have some lunch first. Then he'd go to Doctor Zwar and ask him for some Borax—whatever that was.

Voices. Rang in the valley. The hills seemed alive with the sound of people yelling and shouting.

'There he is!'

'It's him!'

'Get him!'

Friedrich hunted for a place to hide. But on the ridge of the slope, there was nowhere. Just short tufts of grass, stumpy bushes and loose pebbles. Friedrich froze.

The mob charged up the hill towards him. Their fists hammered the air. Their faces flushed almost deep purple with rage.

Friedrich's heart thumped as if a deer was trapped in his rib cage.

The group thundered up to him and then halted.

'Just wait a minute, it's not the demon fellow,' they said.

Kranz the banker dropped the aim of his gun from Friedrich to the ground. 'Oh, it is the Biar boy.'

'The Biar boy is found,' Frau Schultz sang from the back of the group.

The horde of twenty split in half. Boris strode through the gap as if Moses who parted the waters. 'Friedrich Biar, we've been looking for you.' He sniffed the alpine air. 'You haven't seen those other two, what are their names? Joseph, and Amie?'

Friedrich remained a statue, stone cold like an avalanche of snow had been dumped on him. He tried to move his jaw to answer but the words turned to ice in his mouth. How did Boris-Walter get here so fast? He was sure he left him back on the hot dry Australia waiting for his return.

'I think you know where the others are, don't you Friedrich,' Boris said.

Friedrich tried to shake his head but the muscles in his neck had seized up. He stared straight ahead at this man's pot belly.

Boris leered at him. 'You must understand those friends of yours are very bad.'

The crowd behind him roared. They waved their axes, pitch forks and rifles above their heads.

Boris nodded. 'That's why I had to discipline your family, you see. Those friends of yours are the rotten apples that spoil the whole lot.'

More grunts of agreement.

'You don't want to associate with them.'

Friedrich bit his lip.

'Tell us where they are.' Boris narrowed the gap between them. 'Remember, you have a promise to keep. I have healed your sister, Wilma, just as you requested.'

The mob cheered and surged forward.

Boris held up his hand. The crowd stopped.

'Now come boy,' Boris said, 'show us where they are.'

Friedrich refused to move.

'I'm warning you, my boy, if you don't tell us, we'll have to assume you're on their side and we'll have to kill you too.'

Although his muscles failed to budge, the cogs in his mind were slowly rotating. *He speaks my language very well in this Australia. How come he can't in the other Australia? Maybe there's a good Walter after all. And maybe this Walter, this Boris is the bad Walter.*

Friedrich took a deep breath and willed the words to flow from his tongue. 'Aber, Herr Roach, the two young people you are looking for are not up here. When I followed you to your secret place, I found them there.'

'Not possible! They were here.'

'Ja, the girl destroyed the church! What sacrilege!' the banker hollered.

'And the doctor and Frau Biar chased them with the horseless carriage up these mountains,' Frau Schultz added. 'So, they can't be back in the village.'

'But...' Friedrich had to think fast. 'But, they came not straight away. I was a whole day in the other land from where Herr Roach comes, before I saw them. You must go back to the doorway where they went, to find them. Herr Roach knows all about them, because they come from the same place he does, you see.'

Boris pursed his lips. 'Well, I'd rather go up to my doorway in the mountain, if it's all the same to you. They lead to the same place, after all. Then, if you are mistaken and they are hiding in the mountains, we'll catch them.'

'But, Herr Roach, I forgot to mention...' Friedrich recalled the warring and unrest in Prussia before his family left the homeland in the 1840's. *Surely Boris can't argue with the idea that soldiers with guns would be after him.* '...that because they are afraid of you, they've called up an army to fight you. The troops are coming through as I speak.'

Boris rolled his beady little eyes. 'Spare me days, as if I'd believe that! The cave is out in the desert, my boy.'

Friedrich remembered good Walter pointing out the American Defence Base just outside of Alice Springs. The absurdity of soldiers from the Americas being stuck out in the desert had impressed Friedrich. 'But, it is true, Herr Roach, they're coming from the American Defence Base in the Centre of Australia because they consider your presence in that land a threat to the kingdom, and um, the Americas.'

Boris bent his head and fondled under his mouth where his chin, if it were not so receding, should have been.

'And, when Joseph and Amie came through the doorway into that other land which you claim is yours, they jumped into one of those fast-horseless carriages and went straight there and told the soldiers all about you.' Friedrich nodded and tried to make his eyes wide and truthful looking. 'That's why I came back through the doorway, back here to warn you, Herr Roach. Honest.'

Boris patted Friedrich on the head. 'Very well, then, we will go down to the doorway in the village.' Under his breath he said, 'Your family's outhouse.'

Boris gestured to the mob to turn around, then he paused. 'But just to be on the safe side, I'll send some scouts up to the mountain cave.' He pointed to the baker, the fishmonger and Kranz the banker. 'You three, go up the mountain, over the river and you'll come to an outcrop of rocks. There, keep your eyes open for the pair, and this army the boy is on about. Just in case.'

'What do we do if we meet them?' Kranz asked.

'If you find the boy Joseph and the girl Amie, you know what to do. Eliminate them.'

'And the army?'

'Tell them I'm not here, and that they are trespassing in the World of the Wends and that they must turn back and go the way they came.' With a dismissive wave of his hand, Boris led the rest of the group down the mountain.

As they tramped downwards, Friedrich said, 'Herr Roach, thank you for saving my sister. And as a special show of gratitude, I will ask my mother to make you some of her cakes, just for you.'

'How kind,' Boris said. 'How kind.'

Friedrich raced ahead of the group. He was hungry and eager to meet with Dr Zwar. *Must get that special ingredient, from the doctor, just for Boris.*

***

Meanwhile, back in Central Australia...

'Might just be in time for cake,' Daisy announced as their Toyota Hiace van chugged up the road leading to the church. 'You hungry for cake, Arthur?'

'Sure am,' Arthur replied. He was so famished he could've eaten the dead horse on the side of the road just past The Range. But cake would have to do for now.

Earlier that evening, when they first arrived, and the sun had just sunk below the horizon, Arthur glanced out the window and caught a glimpse of a white man near Walter Wenke's home. He'd been hungry then. However, he'd put off eating, just to hop out of the van, and catch up with the creep. Every cell in his emaciated body wanted to punch some sense into the guy who drove away their best tracker, sleazed after his children, then deserted them and then, the icing on the proverbial cake, turned into a giant cockroach and abducted them to suffer torment and probing at the greasy hands of little Grey beings. He had to resist that urge. Besides, just the sight of Walter made what meagre food remained in his bowels turn to liquid. So, he sat in the van and waited. Can't rush the rightful owners of this land.

Arthur napped in the van while the group dropped by Mavis' cousin's place—for several hours. Precious time. He hoped the busload of tourists and his family were surviving. Must be so cold on that mountain. Hope they hadn't broiled to death first, though.

Then the van of artists crawled to the church. The women yakked and laughed. Arthur didn't understand a word. He hoped they understood the urgency of the lost bus of tourists' plight.

Finally, stiff from sitting scrunched up in the back of the van for more than seven hours, Arthur emerged from the vehicle and, after visiting the Men's Room, entered the church. The cake was all gone. Typical! Limp lettuce and soggy tomatoes languished on a plastic plate on a trestle table at the side of the hall. Arthur rescued the unwanted salad and made a beeline for the bright orange of the emergency workers. *Now, how was he going to explain the busload of tourists on the mountain summit?*

He caught the eye of a worker with dark bushy hair and a beard to match. 'I came across the German tourists,' he said.

The worker spat out his tea. 'What? Are they still alive?'

'They were when I left them.'

'Where?'

'Long story.' Arthur cleared his throat trying to dislodge the lettuce of truth. 'It seems they went for a dodgy flight way out west and crashed on the summit of a mountain way out west.'

'Strewth!'

'Yeah, just come from them. The, er, ladies,' Arthur chucked a thumb in the direction of the nattering artists, 'picked me up when I reached the base of the mountain. They'd been there camping and painting. And they took me back here to get some help, bless'em.'

'What were you doing there?'

'Um, searching for my lost daughter and the boy. Got a lift with Constable Dan Hooper,' Arthur continued with the charade. 'When we were around the Spring, we noticed something odd, like something reflected off the summit and Dan having heard that the tourists were missing decided to investigate.'

'Ye-es.'

'This we did. My wife and son climbed up with us. Dan stayed with the group. Somehow they all survived the crash.' Arthur hoped the rescue workers didn't ask too many questions of the group. Might get a bit embarrassing for Mrs Smith and the policeman. Still once they see for themselves, he guessed the whole deal would remain top secret.

The emergency worker nodded. 'We'll get onto it right away. But can't make any promises. It's very dangerous flying the copter at night. Might need to wait until first light in the morning and pray they survive.'

Arthur grasped the worker's sleeve. 'Thanks mate!'

The Cream on the Kuchen

On the World of the Wends

Once more Boris lounged at the table with the Biar's. But this time they sat around Dr Zwar's cedar table decked with polished silver. The doctor had shown Boris the "burnt effigies" of Amie and Joseph, and he appeared satisfied.

Glad he didn't check too closely, Friedrich mused, *or Boris might have seen the burnt sacrifices were of the schwein (pig) variety.*

The reunited Biar family and Dr Zwar held their breath and thoughts as Boris circled the tree of the hung and blackened corpses. He was rather pleased with himself. He rubbed his hands together and repeated: 'Well done, my subjects! Well done!' Then he patted Dr Zwar on the back. 'I knew you wouldn't let me down, my friend.'

Friedrich swore he witnessed Zwar almost choking. He disguised his discomfort with a coughing fit and a lame excuse. 'I hate the smell of burnt flesh.'

'You should get used to it,' Boris replied.

'I'm so sorry,' Frau Biar wiped her hands on her pinafore, 'I would've loved to have you at our place, but, my dear husband here, made such a mess of the kitchen, when he didn't secure the cows properly during the thunderstorm.'

'So kind of Doctor Zwar to put us up in his humble abode.' Boris raised his hairy mono-brow. 'I guess your husband has learnt his lesson.'

'We really do apologise for the trouble it caused you, Herr Roach,' Hans Biar said.

Friedrich sat next to Wilma and watched the charade. He hoped Boris was convinced. He suspected that Boris could read their thoughts, or at least sense when someone wasn't telling the truth. *Was it those antennae Boris displayed when no one was looking?* Nathan said he was a giant cockroach. Was that right? *He certainly acted like one*, Friedrich thought. He stopped his musing. *Boris must not suspect.*

Friedrich concentrated on the joy of anticipation of his slice of apple kuchen. Fresh from the oven and home-made by his mutti. So much better than those "burgers" from the town with a girl's name. He imagined scooping up a chunk with his fork and sliding it into his mouth. So smooth, the apples still warm and creamy. And the strudel on top would melt in his mouth.

Wilma thumped her fork on the table. 'I want my cake! I want my cake!' She'd certainly recovered and back to her hungry self— especially when it came to kuchen. Mutti would sometimes have to demand Wilma stop stuffing her sweet face with biscuits and cake. "Too much sweetness is not good for you," she'd say.

Friedrich heard "click-click-click" from the kitchen. Dr Zwar appeared at the doorway, stirring a bowl of cream. He caught Friedrich's eye and winked. 'Cream! I'm whipping the cream for ze cake. You must have cream with ze cake.'

Boris purred. 'Hmmm! Cream!'

'Oh, yes, Herr Roach,' Zwar said, 'you most of all must have lots of cream. After all you've done for us, you are most deserving.'

'Oh, you spoil me.'

'Not at all, Herr Roach!' Friedrich's mutti said. 'After all, it was you who saved my dear sweet Wilma, and brought back my beautiful son. It's the least I can do to thank you.'

Any more lashings of sweet creamy comments and I might be sick, Friedrich thought.

'You flatter me, sweet Frau,' Boris said.

'Almost ready!' Dr Zwar sang from the kitchen. 'A special treat, just for you, Herr Roach, our honoured guest.'

Friedrich stifled a snigger pretending to clear phlegm from his throat. *A special treat, that is true!*

Hans Biar drummed his fingers on the table. 'I can hardly wait. Hurry!'

***

Nathan and Walter stumbled over the button grass and loose rocks.

'I told you he wouldn't wait,' Walter said.

'No, mate,' Nathan said, 'I told you. The boy couldn't get away fast enough.'

'No wonder, you probably scared him off.'

'Don't be stupid, he was sh-t-scared of you.'

'Mind your language, Nathan.'

'Since when have you been bothered about my language?' Nathan stopped and surveyed the alpine vista. 'You know what, I think you've done it.'

Walter screwed up his nose. 'Yeah, right. Probably just hopped over to the Austrian Alps or some such thing.'

Nathan shaded his eyes and swept his gaze over the sky. One sun, then another peeped through the clouds. 'Hey, mate, Austrian Alps has two suns, does it?'

Walter looked up. 'Nah, what'chya talking about? I can only see one sun.'

'I saw two.'

'Yeah, sure.'

'I did.'

'Sure you don't need glasses?'

'Nup, my eyes are perfect,' Nathan said. 'I'm a crack shot with the rifle, ya know.'

'Look, what you saw was a reflection of ice-particles in the stratosphere,' Walter replied. 'After all, I'm the expert when it comes to Science.'

'Oh, for a minute there, I thought we were on another planet.' Nathan tramped downhill. He looked back to check on Walter.

Walter glanced up at the clouds. Nathan gazed up too. Two suns blazed down upon them.

Walter pointed. 'Just wait a minute,' he said breathlessly, 'there *are* two suns.' He raced to Nathan and hugged him. 'There *are* two suns! We did it! We did it!'

Nathan stared down the valley as Walter embraced him. Two specks emerged from the lush green slopes, human forms bobbing up and down over the shrubs. One carried a rifle.

Nathan froze.

Walter cleared his throat and then pulled away. 'Sorry about that, I was overcome in the moment.' He backed away. 'I hope you don't think—'

Nathan opened and shut his mouth. He made no sound. His voice seemed to have escaped and gone back to earth. He raised his hand towards the advancing men.

'What's wrong? Cat got your tongue?' Walter asked. 'I'm sorry, I didn't think you had an issue about—'

Nathan forced the words through his clenched teeth. 'Shut up, would you? Those men, they don't look friendly.' One man raised his rifle.

Walter spun around. 'What?'

A shot rang out. It echoed in the valley.

'Gawdblimey!' Walter fell onto his knees.

Nathan crouched and glanced about. He hunted for cover—a rock pile, a bush—anything. The mountain was bare. They were exposed to the elements and bullets.

Another shot.

'Run!' Nathan said.

'Where?'

'The cave.'

'What? Up the hill?'

'You got any better suggestion?'

They turned and scrambled up the slope.

A bullet pinged behind them.

Nathan zigged to the left. Walter zagged to the right.

A stone sparked and exploded in front of them. Dogs yelped. Men shouted.

Nathan and Walter weaved up the hill.

Bangs and shots peppered the path ahead.

Nathan spied an outcrop of rocks and yelled, 'Walter!'

Walter crouched behind a spindly bush. 'What?'

Nathan pointed to the pile of boulders.

Walter nodded and together they dashed up to the rocks, and then ducked behind them.

Several shots bounced off the stone.

Nathan panted to catch his breath. He swiped the .303 rifle from his back and peered around the rock.

Ping! Another bullet hit the rock.

Walter flinched. 'Shoot! That was close!'

'Shut up!' Nathan hissed. He took aim. A dog padded up the slope, sniffing at every blade of grass and bush. Nathan followed the dog in his scope; the dog's head in the circle with the cross. Walter's wheezing disturbed him. 'Can you shut up!'

'What do you want me to do?' Walter said. 'Stop breathing? I'm trying to catch my breath here.'

'Oh, go away! I'm trying to concentrate,' Nathan muttered.

'I'll just crawl into this hole, then.' Walter shuffled through a narrow gap in the rocks.

Nathan readjusted his focus on the dog. So much closer. *Not much left of it if I shoot it, now.* He squeezed the trigger and braced for the kick-back. Bang!

The force made the animal fly in the air and smash to ground.

A man wearing a straw hat stormed up the slope—twenty paces away. With his baggy trousers held up by braces, he looked like a character from history.

Nathan pumped a bullet over his head. He didn't want to kill him unless forced to.

Ignoring the warning, the man marched up to the dog carcass and inspected it with the tip of his rifle.

Are they stupid, or just plain deaf, dumb and blind? Nathan couldn't believe that the man didn't hide or take cover.

Nathan targeted a grassy stump near the man's feet and tugged the trigger. Thud! Puff! The man hopped on the spot.

Ha! Doing the dance of the two-sun planet! Nathan chuckled. S*tupid man.*

Boof! The rock under Nathan's elbow exploded into powder, and he toppled forward.

He slammed gun-first on the gravel. Twang! The rifle jarred in his arms sending a missile straight ahead.

'Ach—tung!' The man in the straw hat flailed on the ground clutching his knee. His baggy trousers soaked in blood.

'Oops!' Nathan heard blathering behind him. He twisted his head around. A barrel of a gun in his face.

The other man with a bushy beard stood over Nathan. He glared at Nathan with narrow eyes. The man shouted at him in some strange language.

Nathan pushed the gun from his face. 'Sorry about your mate, mate.' He gritted his teeth and forced a smile.

The man's cheeks flushed bright red. He spat more words out and insisted the rifle target Nathan's face. Behind him the other man moaned. This enraged the bearded man even more and he stroked the trigger.

Nathan gulped. He dared not move. His .303 was just out of reach. If he turned to grab it, he knew he'd be history. He raised his hands above his head. 'Please don't shoot. I'm innocent.'

Beard-man ranted. He stamped his feet. He waved the gun above his head like a demented middle eastern warrior. It was almost funny. 'Vo! Vo! Vo!' he cried.

Nathan took this opportunity of insanity to creep backwards. He touched the .303 with his fingertips. Perhaps he could scare him. He really didn't want to hurt some crazy native of this planet.

The man continued to rage.

Nathan shuffled back centimetre by centimetre. The .303 dislodged and tumbled down the slope. *Damn!*

The man stopped. He glared at Nathan. 'Nein,' he said. Then he lifted the gun and levelled it at Nathan.

'So, this is it,' Nathan said as he locked eyes with the crazy hairy man.

The sound of a thud came out of nowhere. The man keeled sideways, his head crunching on the rocks.

'Did I get him?' a girl's voice rang in the still air.

Nathan looked in every direction. 'Where? How?'

'Hey, silly, up here!' a young man's voice said.

Nathan looked up. He saw nothing but sky and a few cotton woolly clouds.

'No, wrong way.' Was that Walter?

Nathan spun around and looked up at the top of the rocky outcrop. There they sat, like the three monkeys—Walter, Amie, and the lad with the blonde curly top, Joseph, he guessed.

Amie climbed to the edge and jumped. She landed softly like a cat a metre from Nathan. 'Come on, we better hurry.' She glanced at the furry lump of a man motionless on the ground. 'Who knows, he might wake up any time now.'

Nathan knelt over the man and touched his neck. 'You're going to leave him here? Like this?'

Joseph scrambled down from the boulders. 'Get away from him.' He glanced at the prone figure. 'It's just a flesh-wound. He's after us!'

'Boris has the whole town after them,' Walter said. He pulled Nathan upright, dragged him past the other man groaning with the shot knee. They then scrambled up the hill.

'Come on,' Amie called back to the men, 'I'll show you the way to the cave.'

'Are you sure it's safe?' Joseph asked. 'What about Boris? Surely he's sent the rest of them to the cave.'

'Nah, I told you,' Walter said, 'there was no one there when we arrived just a few minutes ago. It'll be fine. We'll be in and out in no time. And back home all safe 'n sound.'

***

Boris tucked the napkin into the collar of his shirt. He licked his lips and picked up his silver fork. The apple strudel steamed still warm from the oven. Lashings of cream curled over the side of it like a foaming wave over a rock. Now, where should he start? Crumble? Cream? Or Cake? Cream, cake and crumble. He'd have all three at once. He loved dessert after gorging on another baby. He dug the fork into the sweet and with it laden with crumble, cream and cake, he slipped it into his mouth and savoured the decadent combination.

Dr Zwar with the Biar family watched on while Boris swallowed. Zwar imagined the pure bliss sliding down Boris' throat. Or perhaps, not so *pure* bliss; the added extras, namely Borax, that had been included in this cream recipe. They stared at him like an audience of one of those foody shows he'd seen on a visit to Earth. He'd gone there with Boris to select the Mercedes.

Boris gestured to them. 'Go on, it's delicious, eat up.'

Wilma hoed into her cake without cream. She didn't want cream, she'd informed her mother.

Frau Biar smiled a saccharine smile. 'It's fine, you go ahead.' She cut into the smallest of slices of her cake, avoiding the serving of cream, and dipped it into her mouth.

Herr Biar's plate was empty. 'I have to diet.' He patted his portly stomach.

'I'm not hungry,' Friedrich pushed his dessert away. 'I think I'm still suffering from the food I had in the other Australia—and the horseless carriage ride.'

Boris took another mouthful and caught Dr Zwar's eye. Boris lifted a piece of cake and cream to Zwar. The doctor raised his hand and shook his head.

'Am I the only one here eating cream? Why are you all watching me?' Boris glared at the group. 'Okay, what's going on?'

Boris stood up. He pushed his seat back, smacking it against the wall.

'Nothing,' Frau Biar said.

'The "nothing" that means "everything",' Boris scowled. 'What— are you up to?'

The doctor's stomach churned. *This is not going to plan*, he thought.

Boris lurched. He bent over. Then shrieked. He clutched Biar and growled, 'What have you done?' Boris then groaned as his legs buckled under him.

Zwar held his breath. *So far so good*. Then, his eyes widened at the unfolding scene of horror. That ugly little man, Boris, strained and pushed. Skin peeled into black scales. Four black pointy limbs poked out from his abdomen. Mouth transformed to a beak. And antennae swayed menacingly on his tiny head covered in beady eyes. Zwar raised his hands and covered his eyes from this sight.

The over-sized cockroach shrieked, 'You have made this Boris very unhappy—and you will pay!'

Then he aimed his gun-hand at Dr Zwar. Zwar gasped, his limbs refused to move, and his mind froze, trapped in the spotlight.

'Traitor!' Boris cried.

The cockroach's hand flashed. Then, *Boof!*

The blast hit Zwar square in the chest, the force knocked him to the floor.

Strange, Zwar reflected, *no pain...*The room around him turned grey and foggy...

He watched the action in slow motion, as if in some dream. Tired...so...tired.

Boris waved his gun at each member of the Biar family. 'Any one next?' He staggered towards the Biars huddled in the corner of the dining room by the display cabinet. 'Have I got a special treat for you.' He herded them together and shoved them to the door. 'I hate being tricked. You should see what "treat" I gave the families of those two kids, Amie and Joseph, who you seemed to have liked so much.' He pushed Hans, Jane, Friedrich and Wilma through the door. 'Right, you traitors, to the outhouse!'

'Wait for me!' Zwar rasped. 'Don't leave me to...'

***

'What about the boy, Friedrich?' Nathan asked.

Amie shrugged. 'He belongs here.'

'With that nut you call Boris?'

Joseph looked Walter up and down. 'Are you sure *he's* not Boris?'

'I'm not!' Walter pouted. 'I told you when I first saw you two back there, Boris impersonated me. The creep!'

Nathan tapped Walter on the back. 'Yep, he's the good, the real Walter. You can trust me.'

The hike up to the cave was steep. Amie, Joseph and Nathan climbed each level like mountain goats, but Walter strained with each upward step. Every few minutes they rested with Walter who puffed and wheezed.

Amie watched Walter bend over and grip his thighs. 'We're almost there.'

'Just five more minutes,' Joseph encouraged. And then aside to Amie he muttered, 'Definitely not Boris.'

'No,' Amie whispered, 'Boris would've sprouted wings and flown.'

They crawled at the speed of snails on a European holiday up to the cave. The suns sped across the sky as if on steroids. They reached the tundra that yawned ahead of them.

'I don't remember this,' Walter remarked in between wheezy breaths.

'We may be going a little bit of a different way,' Amie said.

'Just a slight detour,' Joseph added. 'Just in case we meet some unfriendly Wends.'

'Or Boris,' Amie snorted.

They crossed the alpine plain and then battled the rapids. Nathan hauled Walter's dripping body out of the stream.

'I don't remember crossing a raging river,' Walter complained

'Told you, the locals won't come this way,' Amie said.

'Just hope Boris doesn't, Amie' Joseph sighed.

'Oh, Jo, don't be so negative! By now the cockroach will be in the death throes from the Borax the doctor or whoever would've fed it to him.'

'I hope so.'

They schlepped over the last of the humps that were covered in freshly fallen snow.

'I don't remember the snow.' Walter shivered. 'Are you sure it's the right cave?'

Amie rolled her eyes. 'The weather changes in an instant. The snow's just fallen. If we don't hurry, we might get caught in a blizzard. We better keep on moving or we might suffer frostbite.'

Joseph stumped up the hill. 'Come on, it's just over there!'

Amie and Nathan chased after him. 'Careful!' Amie said.

Joseph halted and turned around. 'Now, who's going to climb up here in a blizzard?'

An olive-coloured flying creature, the size of an eagle but webbed like a bat, weaved in and out of the clouds and shrieked at their presence.

Nathan glanced back and gestured to Walter who lumbered up the hill way below them. 'Hurry, mate!' He patted his .303 and paced to Amie and Joseph. There they stood waiting for the struggling Walter.

When Walter was only a few steps away, they turned around and completed the journey to the cave. They were high enough so the clouds were below them, sinking into the valley and shrouding it with mist.

The first sun dipped behind the mountains. An icy gasp of air chilled Nathan through his bones penetrating his kidneys. He'd be glad to return to the oven-like heat of Australia.

Amie and Joseph edged towards the cave entrance. Amie looked at Nathan and gestured for him to enter.

'Me?' Nathan queried.

'You have the gun,' Amie whispered. 'Just in case.'

Nathan cocked his rifle and crept in.

For the second time that day, a barrel of a rifle greeted him.

'Stay out!' Nathan yelled. 'I think he's not friendly.' What could he do? If he shot this man with the mutton chop whiskers, in the cave at such close range, he might ruin their chances of returning to Earth through the portal. So, he backed out, "Mutton Chops" with his rifle pointed at his nose matching his retreat all the way.

Walter puffed as he stood behind Nathan. 'You didn't tell me we had company.'

Oh, the Joy!

Meanwhile, back in Central Australia...

The sound of faint juddering jerked Dan awake. The sun cracked through the clouds low on the horizon bathing in tangerine the mountain's grassy summit and the spine of the MacDonnell Ranges to the east. The campfire had dwindled to a few smouldering coals.

Dan hugged his bare arms and shivered. The bus was still there—caked in white. Was it frost? Or ice? Some Germans, like Lucie now revived, and her husband had crawled back in the vehicle—not satisfied with the level warmth afforded by the fire. Dan stared at them all bunched up on the back seat of the bus and shook his head. He couldn't stop them. The rest rugged up with whatever clothing Wurst found for them in the baggage and they huddled together by the flames which Dan nursed. Carol Fleischer and son were wrapped together in a large coat, probably Wurst's. It was certainly large enough. Jakob and his wife snuggled under a pink parka near the campfire. They must've sorted out their differences, Dan mused.

The hammering sound grew louder. Dan jogged along the summit in search of more firewood. More fire, more visibility. He hoped or made the assumption that the juddering was a helicopter. He squinted and surveyed the horizon, east—west—south—north. Nothing...but the "dja-dja-dja" continued, becoming louder and louder.

With a handful of twigs Dan sauntered back to the group. He dumped the sticks on the fire. Pathetic, really. The smouldering coals would eat them up in no time. Did Arthur make it? Did he call for rescue?

Dja-dja-dja! Dja-dja-dja!

Adam sat up and rubbed his eyes. 'Are they here yet?'

Dan shrugged.

'You need more firewood, Officer,' Adam said.

'Yeah, I know.'

Adam unwound himself from his mother. 'Mum, I'll go and get some more wood.' He then strode along the path between the spinifex.

'Be careful, my son.'

Adam disappeared into the scrub. Dan squatted by the miserable fire and held his hands over the feeble flames.

Dja-dja-dja! Dja-dja-dja!

Dan glanced at the sky; no longer salmon coloured but clear blue. No dots. Just the juddering. He sighed. *Hurry up!*

Adam bolted through the grass. 'It's here! It's here!' he cried and then stopped at the campfire. He waved his arms. 'It's here! We're saved!'

Carol, his mum yawned and stretched. 'Calm down dear, don't get your hopes up.'

'But it's here!'

'I can't see anything.'

'Look!' Adam pointed at the ranges to the east shrouded in the glare of the risen sun.

'Can't you see it?'

'What?' Jakob stared to the east. He stroked his wife's back. 'I don't see anything.'

'Can't you see it? The helicopter? Are you blind?'

'Manners, Adam,' his mum snapped. 'Show a bit of respect.'

'Yes, mum. But it's there, coming up from the clouds to rescue us.'

Dan shaded his eyes and examined the clouds lined golden with sun. *Dja-dja-dja! Dja-dja-dja!* If he concentrated, he could just make out a tiny dot hovering like a mosquito, tracing the spine of the mountains, searching.

Yes!

The policeman jumped up and down and waved. Joy had never been so pure...

***

Back on the World of the Wends

A man-size cockroach scuttled from the cave. "Mutton Chops" glanced at the creature. He screamed and darted out of its way.

Walter sighed. 'Oh, crud! Not that creep again!'

'Yep,' Nathan said. 'Afraid so. Boris.' He raised his rifle while stepping away from the big bug.

'Thanks for the compliment,' Walter said. 'It doesn't look anything like me.'

'It did, believe me.'

'Now you're making me depressed.'

The creature, Boris, stood like a statue at the cave's entrance, its antennae twitching. It raised a claw and aimed it at Nathan.

Nathan dropped to the ground and then commando-style scrambled behind a bush. Walter ducked behind the nearest boulder. He heard his heart pounding—*boom-boom-boom.*

Boris' antennae quivered. His armour vibrated. A high-pitched scream pierced the frozen air. 'I'll get you!' Walter sensed he was saying in his alien language. Boris' extended claw shook.

Walter gasped. 'Oh, no!'

Behind this creature, the boy Friedrich and his family huddled in the shadows of the cave.

The scream escalated higher and more irritating than a burglar alarm. Walter blocked his ears. The siren had no regard for fingers in ears; it penetrated every pore of his skin. Making it crawl. The claw glowed bright red.

'No!' Walter murmured.

A shot rang out. Then a ping!

Boris used another claw to brush the bullet from his shell. No harm. Then he pointed his claw at the bush where Nathan hid.

More screaming. More vibrating. More shaking.

Then...

The claw sparked. Poof! The claw exploded in a cloud of smoke. Boris inspected the stub that was his weapon. He then pointed another claw.

A crack. Walter looked above Boris.

There, small heads poked over a teetering rock. Joseph held a finger to his mouth.

Boris resumed his screaming, shaking and vibrating.

Another shot punctuated the tension. One of Boris' antenna wobbled like on a spring. Boris stamped his feet and waggled his tiny head.

The rock slightly larger than Boris, toppled over the edge and hammered the roach to the sand. The creature's six limbs that had been splayed by the rock, jerked and twitched. Amie and Joseph leapt from the low cliff. They gestured to Walter to join them and the Biar family in the cave.

Walter gingerly skirted past the squashed roach. This time Walter pinched his nose. The stink over-powered him with the urge to retch. Then he had to hold his mouth in case he did.

Nathan crept up to the splattered beast. He walked around the rock while twirling his beard.

'You coming?' Walter asked as he gulped down some rising acid.

'Nah, you go first. Get 'em back to the village safely,' Nathan said. 'I make sure he won't hurt no one.'

'Bah! He's dead,' Walter said. 'Isn't he?'

'Cockroaches, don't die—not that one, anyway.' Nathan flicked his hands at Walter, urging him to follow Amie and Joseph and the Biar family to the laser line. 'Get 'em home. I'll get "Mutton Chops" to help me.'

Walter nodded and proceeded to the light.

Then Nathan yelled. 'Walter!'

'What?'

'Can you set the thingy way out there in space for the cockroach here?'

'I'll try—but I better get through first and fiddle on the other side,' Walter answered. 'See you back in Australia.'

Walter watched Amie and Joseph and the Biars slip through the ray destined for the outhouse, then he darted through too.

    ***

This Walter ran from panel to instrument like a boy in a Hahndorf sweet shop. Amie struggled to get her head around how different this Walter was. He looked like the creepy Walter her Dad introduced her to back in her world, but this Walter wasn't creepy, just dorky and nerdy. This Walter was more interested in machines than people. If she hadn't seen Boris who looked like Walter turn into a big fat cockroach, maybe she wouldn't have believed that this Walter was good.

Then, she remembered the doctor.

'What about Doctor Zwar?' she asked.

The Biars stood around Amie and Joseph. They folded their hands in front of them and looked at the pair as if children waiting for their teacher to tell them what to do next.

'The doctor?' Joseph asked. 'He's dead, isn't he?'

'Maybe, maybe not,' Amie said. 'I reckon Boris' fire-power was weakened because of the Borax.'

'It's a possibility.'

'We should check.' Amie turned to the Herr Biar. 'We're going to see what's happened to Dr Zwar.'

Herr Biar nodded. Then he ushered his family up the ladder.

Amie and Joseph tagged after them.

They left the Biar home and then raced along the road to the large house on the corner. The sun dipped behind the mountains, the buildings turning mauve and the clouds tinted pink. The road was empty resembling a ghost town. Amie mused that some of the town folk would've witnessed Boris' transformation from weakling, almost nerdy-man-Walter to cockroach and were afraid.

Joseph caught Amie's hand and squeezed it. 'We did it.'

'Just hope this good Walter and Nathan can pull it off.'

'Sure they will,' Joseph replied. 'When we get back to the dunny, it'll all be over, and we can go home.'

'I hope so.'

They entered the house by the front door still ajar from the Biar's dramatic and Boris-driven departure. At the time the family had seen what happened to Dr Zwar and didn't want to be shot too.

Amie and Joseph trod into the dining room. Dr Zwar lay where he fell. A feeble groan threaded through the room.

Amie rushed up to the doctor and touched his neck. She looked up at Joseph who hovered over her and the doctor. 'He's alive, he has a weak pulse.'

'He's very pale though,' Joseph said. 'He may have internal damage.'

'We need to get him to a real doctor.'

'Like on Earth?'

'Well, yeah.'

'We need to get him to the car.' Joseph bent to lift the patient. 'Let's lift him to his feet and help him to the car.'

'Just one question, does the car have fuel?'

'Questions!' Joseph huffed. 'Sure, the tank's full. Not like the doctor goes anywhere.'

'But, where does he get it?'

'Does it matter? Let's just deal with the doctor first.'

Joseph dug his arm under the man's arm and Amie put her hand under his other arm. They encouraged the groggy man to stand.

'He's heavy,' Amie grunted as she strained to keep her side of Zwar upright.

'Use your arm up to your elbow,' Joseph said.

Amie followed Joseph's instructions. Slowly they helped Dr Zwar to the Mercedes. Joseph was glad he'd given the doctor a few driving lessons. The Mercedes with a few inevitable dents and covered in mud from the foray half-way up the foot of the mountain, sat at the side of the house.

Joseph tried to negotiate laying the doctor on the back seat. He moaned as the lad pushed him in and from the other side Amie pulled him though. Finally, he lay stretched across the back seat, but his feet stuck out one end.

'Turn him on his side,' Amie said.

Joseph leaned over the doctor. 'Doctor, roll over, your feet are sticking out.'

Dr Zwar groaned.

Amie huffed and puffed and then grabbed his right arm and leg. She bent the leg and then hauled him over. Dr Zwar screamed, but the manoeuvre worked. He curled into a foetal position and Joseph shut the door.

Make sure I drive this time. Amie jumped in the right side and Joseph slid into the left-hand seat. Amie raised her hands to grab the steering wheel and clutched at air. 'Hey, where's the—' she looked over to Joseph who grinned at her. 'Trust you to get in the driver's seat.'

'Left hand drive—right side of the road, Amie, it's European.' Joseph's smile spread from ear to ear as he turned the key. The car roared. He engaged reverse and with his foot flat to the floor, swished the car back and around to face the Biar's home. Then swiftly moving through the gears, Joseph sped the car like an ambulance the few hundred metres up the road, crashed through the fence, rolled along the grass and braked doing a one-hundred-and-eighty-degree spin splattering the outhouse with mud.

'I think you need to hone your driving skills,' Amie muttered as she glanced to see how the doctor fared. Dr Zwar had fallen off the bench seat and lay crumpled on the floor. 'What have you done? He'll really need a doctor now.'

Joseph took a quick look. 'Woops, I didn't think, I sort of lost control. I was just trying to get here as fast as I could.'

'Better a little late than dead on arrival,' Amie snapped, then moved to the back door, opened it and checked the doctor. He was breathing and cursing in his native language. 'Anyway, he's alright. I think the drive woke him up.'

Joseph managed to coax the doctor, who was now more alert after the ride of his life, out of the car. With Hans Biar's help they carried him down to the basement of the outhouse.

As Amie landed on the mud-packed floor, she looked around. Where just a few minutes ago, Walter had been tinkering with the machines, the place was empty. The men completed their mission of carrying the doctor ready to be delivered to earth.

Joseph turned around, examining each square metre of the room. 'Where's Wally?'

'You mean, Walter Wenke?' Herr Biar asked.

'Yeah, him.'

'Don't you know, he went back through there. He said he needed to help his friend finish Boris off.'

Amie's anxiety rose within her. 'Then how are we going to get home? How are we going to help the doctor?'

Dr Zwar looked up briefly and then his head flopped onto his chest. Joseph who was holding him in sitting position patted his cheeks. 'Stay awake. Don't go to sleep.'

'Well, how long is he going to be?' Amie asked.

'You're welcome to stay with us while you wait,' Herr Biar said.

'Thank you for the offer.' Amie paced the small room. She wrung her hands. 'We really need to get help for the doctor.'

Joseph spoke to Dr Zwar, 'It won't be long, help is on its way.'

Friedrich poked his head through the trapdoor. 'Oh, he is alive.'

Joseph nodded. 'Just.'

Friedrich retreated and a few minutes later returned with his mother and sister. Frau Biar carried a black bottle.

'I have here, bitter wine, it is a medicine from the old country,' Frau Biar said.

She soaked a handkerchief with the brew and dabbed the doctor's mouth with it.

The power of the placebo, Amie thought. She hoped it would do no harm.

But Dr Zwar's will to remain conscious was slipping. His lids drooped. His eyeballs rolled so only the whites of his eyes showed. His breathing became shallow. Frau Biar squeezed a few more drops onto his lips.

'He needs proper medical care,' Joseph muttered to Amie.

'I know,' Amie returned. 'I wish Walter would hurry.'

All who were in the small underground room stared at the blue ray. Amie knew a watched pot, or in this case ray, never does what it's supposed to, but she kept on watching, hoping. Her eyes glazed over.

Frau Biar turned to her patient and drip-fed him some more bitter wine.

Wilma turned to her father. 'Papa, when's the man coming back?'

'Soon, my daughter.'

Joseph glanced at his fingers.

Walter appeared as if by magic before them. 'I'm back,' he said. ' "Mutton Chops" and his mate are helping their wounded friend. They're walking him down the hill. But I don't know what happened to Nathan. We sent Boris off to a distant part of the galaxy, so he won't bother you anymore. Problem was, Nathan went in after him. I waited for Nathan to return, but he didn't.'

'Could he have gone straight to Earth—Australia?' Amie asked.

'It's possible,' Walter replied.

Amie glanced at the doctor. 'We better hurry—he may not last.'

While Walter fiddled with the controls, Amie and Joseph hugged each of the Biars, thanking them and saying their farewells. The ray pulsated in readiness as Walter who had finished his calibrations, shook hands with each of the Biars and told them how glad he was to meet them.

'Are you sure you don't want to join us?' Amie asked the Biars.

'Thank you for the offer,' Frau Biar said, 'but now that we seem to be rid of Boris, I think we shall do very well living here.'

Then one by one, the visitors from Australia, Earth, Joseph helping the doctor, stepped through the ray leaving the Lost World of the Wends behind.

So Far...

...In Central Australia

Dan Hooper waved.

The helicopter wheeled to the south.

Hooper grabbed the parka from the Smiths and hurled it in great circles above his head.

The helicopter continued in a straight line along the ranges to the south.

He jumped up and down and shook the pink parka in the air. Carol and Adam Fleischer, Jakob and Heidi Smith joined him signalling with their arms. The Germans waved whatever they grabbed first, bags, chip packets and drink bottles. All of them in a row looking like an aerobics session on the mountain summit.

But the helicopter seemed to come no closer.

Dan dropped his arms to his side. 'Surely they can see us. Why are they going there?'

'I don't know,' Adam said still waving, 'but perhaps it has something to do with the column of smoke over that hill over there.'

'What?' Dan peered at the range in the distance. The helicopter certainly was making a beeline for it. 'Do you think they are still searching for Amie and Joseph?' The smoke rose in plumes. Undeniable, obvious.

'It's possible, I guess,' Adam said. 'Maybe they're there and got a fire going.'

'Nah, we scoured the area. We had trackers. They weren't there.'

'Then, what's the fire?'

'Just that, a bushfire.'

'We could do that,' Carol said.

Dan glared at Mrs Fleischer. 'Create a bushfire on the summit? Risk our lives?'

'No, I just mean, if we make more smoke with our fire, we can be seen?'

Dan nodded. 'Of course, it's worth a try.' He gazed at the helicopter. It hovered above the crest of the range to the south, just over the cloud of smoke. He gestured to the Germans. 'Come on, get as much green plant material, let's make ours bigger than that one over there.' He pointed at the pyre of smoke on the peak of that southern range.

The helicopter stayed hovering over that distant mountain. Dan's heart sank.

***

Amie barked, deep racking coughs as she stepped into the haze.

'Get low and crawl!' Joseph wheezed from the darkness behind her.

'Oh, gawd!' Walter whined from somewhere through the smoke ahead of her. 'It's a bushfire!'

The doctor groaned.

Amie flopped on her stomach and wriggled like a snake towards the light filtering through the ashen clouds. She coughed and coughed and coughed. Any worse and she was sure she'd spew up her lungs. Inching forward. Coughing. Lungs filled with phlegm. Making her dizzy. Crawl. Arm over elbow. *Who was the fire bug? No! Where are we?* Roaring in the ears. *Is that the bush fire?* Stars pixelated replacing the smoke.

Bright light made Amie's eyes ache. She clamped her lids shut.

'Come on, Amie, wake up!' someone with Joseph's voice said. He shook her. 'We're out of danger.'

Her lids fluttered open. She winced at the stabbing pain from the sunlight. She blinked. The over-exposed blur sharpened and darkened, and she became aware of hands on her shoulder blades. Joseph leaned over her, holding her.

The urge to cough. She twisted out of his hands, heaved and coughed. Coughing possessed her. *When would she be free? Would she always be staring at that stupid rock and barking at it?*

***

'That's not the mountain,' Arthur said. Confused, he pointed at the cliffs in the distance and raised his voice above the whirr of the helicopter blades. 'We crashed on that mountain over there, not this one.'

The fire turned out to be nothing but an over-sized campfire at the mouth of a cave—large, extinguished, but still smoking.

Jim the pilot, seemed to ignore Arthur. Easy to do with earmuffs clamped to his ears. He insisted on hovering above, inspecting the smoky remains of a fire.

'They're over there!' Arthur ranted. He leaned forward and fanned his hand in the pilot's face.

Jim pursed his lips and pushed Arthur's hand out of his face.

Arthur shook his head and muttered. 'What is wrong with the guy?'

'I think I see some people down there!' Jim, the pilot groped in the recess near his seat. He plucked up a pair of binoculars and passed them to Arthur. 'Here, have a look.'

'What?'

'People! Down there! In the pound.'

'What?'

'Look in the pound! In the creek.' Jim pointed at some tiny specks. 'Use the binoculars.'

'Probably just some unfortunate wallabies,' Arthur mumbled as he lifted the binoculars to his spectacles and adjusted the focus. 'At best, some locals doing a burn off.'

As the helicopter continued to fan the trees lining a shallow creek bed, Arthur scanned the terrain for the people the pilot believed were there. For a few moments all Arthur could see were a mess of iron tinted rocks, broken branches and tufts of grass. He followed the crooked trail of the dry creek bed.

Then, under the scant shade of a ghost gum, he saw them—a man dressed in old fashioned garb, baggy trousers held up with braces, and a white puffy shirt. He reclined against a rock under the tree. Beside him hovered a familiar figure, from the bald patch on his head, the slightly stooped back to the whiskers of his ginger moustache—Walter!

'Why that dirty little creep!' Arthur snarled. 'So, he's been hiding in the Pound.'

'What?' Jim yelled.

'Forget about them!' Arthur yelled back. 'It's just Mr Wenke with some guy in a costume.'

'Who?'

'Just a couple of blokes, I don't think they need saving,' Arthur said and then to himself, 'Especially Walter Wenke, the cockroach.'

Jim turned to Arthur. 'Two men? I'm sure I saw four people down there.'

'Four?' *Probably some other victims of Wenke.*

'Yeh, just see if you can sight the other two.'

Arthur sighed and surveyed the pound with the binoculars.

The chopper lowered into the pound. The blast of the blades flattened bushes and branches in its wake.

Fleischer tracked the dry creek bed. He inspected each slab of stone, each stump of tree, and each windblown blade of grass. A foot...he spotted a hiking boot...and then another boot...a pair of boots attached to legs. He revisited the boots. They looked familiar. He followed the legs up to the jeans, the mauve tee shirt and then...the face. He dropped the binoculars from his gaze and looked at Jim. 'It's Amie! She's alive!'

Before Jim responded, Arthur lifted the binoculars to his eyes and inspected the scene. He had difficulty as the glass in the eyepiece kept fogging up. Arthur blinked and wiped his eyes wet with tears, and then rubbed the eyepiece. He looked again. A young man, hair like a bird's nest of dreadlocks cradled Amie in his arms. 'Um,' Arthur asked, 'what does the lost boy look like?'

'What?'

Arthur held up four fingers. 'I think we've found them.'

Jim took the helicopter lower. Without the binoculars, the people were visible, as stick figures. One, the one Arthur assumed was Walter stood up. He waved something like a red cloth.

'We'll pick up these people,' Jim said straining his voice. 'I'll radio help for the lot, I mean, the ones on the mountain to our north.' He continued hovering. 'Now, where can I land?'

Arthur gritted his teeth. *Just wait! Just wait till I get my hands on that cockroach, Wenke.* Then he started to recall the not so magical mystery-out-of-space-tour Wenke took his family, the Smiths and the bus load of Germans on not so long ago. 'You might need a gun, though with Wenke.'

'Pardon?'

'Wenke's dangerous,' Arthur shouted so loud he made his voice hoarse.

'What you say?'

'It was Wenke who made us crash. He's a nutter,' Arthur said. 'You need police or the army to catch him.'

Too late. Jim had found the only clear and flat patch of ground to land and settled the helicopter in the pound of the small range.

Arthur glanced at the higher range to the north, just visible over the lip of the pound, and smiled. A plume of smoke rose from above the cliffs.

Then his smile vanished, and Arthur trembled. 'Oh, no, watch that Walter…he's dangerous.' Sweat dripped from his temples and he cried, 'Oh, no, the probes, those little grey men…the probes…I don't want them to probe me.'

Jim squinted at Arthur. 'What?'

***

Amie took a deep breath and shuddered. She took several slugs of water from her water-bottle. The water was warm from having languished unattended in her backpack for several days, but Amie didn't mind. It was water, and she needed it to stop coughing.

Joseph wrapped his arms around her chest and gently drew her closer.

The young lovers gazed at the cave two hundred metres up the hill. The rising smoke obscured its entrance. A hundred metres to their left a helicopter descended to landing. The dry creek's steep bank blocked their view of it as the chopper descended.

'Who's idea was it to let a fire burn out of control up there?' Amie asked.

Joseph shrugged. 'Dunno.'

'Bet it was Wenke's,' Amie said. 'No common sense that guy.'

'Absent-minded professor.'

'Yeah.'

'Speak of the devil,' Amie muttered.

'Not exactly,' Joseph said, 'he's the good Walter, remember? The bad one, Boris, by another name, is in deep space and unable to harm us—or the Wends.'

'We hope.'

Walter Wenke, puffing like a steam engine, jogged up to them. He stopped in front of them and mopped sweat from his temple with a red spotted handkerchief. Then he stood there panting.

'Where's the doctor?' Amie asked.

Wenke pointed down the creek and bobbled his head.

'You shouldn't leave him,' Joseph said, 'he's not well.'

Walter Wenke gulped. 'He's walking around.'

'Great! First you set fire to the cave and nearly destroy all the transporter equipment,' Amie snipped, 'and then you abandon a

Wendish doctor in the middle of—' she looked around to confirm her location, '—Central Australia.'

Walter put his hands on his hips. 'For a start, I did not start a bushfire—that was Nathan or Friedrich. And secondly, I told the doctor not to move from the tree I sat him under. And, thirdly, I came to get you. Our taxi has arrived.' Walter stomped around the small creek, he kicked at some loose stones. 'Besides, I think Nathan had good intentions. He left the fire going so the helicopters could see us. And it worked.'

Amie rolled her eyes. 'Whatever!'

Joseph stood and then catching her hand pulled Amie up. 'Come on, our ride awaits.'

They followed Walter to the tree under which the doctor rested.

Dr Zwar, his eyes wide, studied the brilliant blue sky, and the parched landscape striped in sienna, yellow ochre, and khaki. He spoke in his native Silesian tongue. 'So, this is the real Australia.' He nodded. 'I think I prefer the fake one.'

Walter replied in his textbook German. 'It's not all like this. Australia is a big land. This is just the Centre.'

'Maybe so, but the other Australia is home now.'

'No harm in visiting us for a time,' Walter said. 'You'll even get a ride in a helicopter.'

'And when you want to go home, we'll send you back,' Joseph added. 'Won't you Mr Wenke.'

'Yeah, yeah.' Walter sighed. Amie guessed he'd prefer Dr Zwar remained on Earth with him as his newest best friend. 'Anyway, let's go and meet our rescuers,' Walter said.

A crack of a branch and then pebbles and clay showered the bank near Amie and Joseph.

Amie glanced up the slope to see her Dad stumbling down. He appeared paler than when she stomped off and left him all those days ago. His eyes possessed a look of terror and were as round as saucers. He had shaved off his beard, but a five-o'clock shadow had crept over his chin and upper lip.

'Dad!' Amie cried as she raced to meet him. As he landed on the stone floor, she wrapped her whole body around her father and clung to him. 'I'm so sorry for getting angry and running off.'

Her Dad patted her back. 'It's okay, dear.' He sounded exhausted. He then pulled his head back and surveyed the others over her shoulder.

Amie looked around. 'What Dad?'

'Where's that Walter Wenke?' Amie's Dad ground his teeth.

'Walter? Why do you want Walter?' It didn't occur to Amie that her father might have encountered bad Walter, alias Boris, in her absence.

Walter loped up to them, his hand extended. 'Arthur, am I glad to see you.'

Arthur tore himself from Amie. 'I'm not.'

'You'll never guess what happened—'

Amie watched in the horror of slow motion as her father punched Walter on the nose. 'I've been waiting to do that all week,' he said nursing his fist.

'Dad!' Amie screamed, 'What did you do that for?'

'Yeah, why?' Walter reeled from his friend. Blood streamed from his nostrils and he covered his freshly crooked nose with the reddening handkerchief.

Arthur, his fist shaking, again lurched at Walter. 'He's dangerous, my daughter. Did he hurt you?'

Walter cowered away from him. 'I did nothing of the sort.'

'Liar!' Arthur raised his voice. 'Jim, come here, quick! Arrest the cockroach!'

Jim, in all his bright orange safety gear burst through the tee tree bushes. At the same time, Joseph jumped between Arthur and Walter. 'No one's touching good Walter.'

'Oh, yes I am.' Arthur reached for Joseph. 'He's evil. He needs to be locked up.'

Jim stood back, legs astride. 'Looks pretty 'armless to me.' He waved at Walter. 'Hi there, Walter, would you mind telling me what this is all about?'

A light bulb moment finally went off in Amie's smoke-affected brain. 'Dad!' She leapt in front of her father and pushed him back. Then she met his wild eyes. 'Dad, this is good Walter. Not bad Walter. I met the bad Walter. All of us,' she swept a hand at Joseph, and Mr Wenke, 'did on the other world. The bad Walter is a cockroach, called Boris. Boris is an alien over-sized cockroach who eats babies and does all sorts of nasty things. But,' she pointed at Walter, 'this Walter is not him. This Walter helped us. He helped us send the bad Walter, Boris, deep in space to a galaxy far, far away...'

'Well, actually, the other side of this galaxy, which when you think about it, is far, far away,' Walter said in the background, 'and Nathan helped him get there.'

'Who?' Arthur asked.

'Nathan, our Indigenous friend,' Walter replied. 'By the way, where is he? He hasn't come back.'

'Who?' Jim asked.

'Nathan, he helped us fight the bad Walter,' Joseph said.

'Can't say I'm convinced,' Arthur said.

'But Dad, if it wasn't for good Walter, we would've been stuck on the Lost World of the Wends,' Amie said.

'Not such a bad thing,' Joseph muttered.

'Except for Boris and his cockroaches,' Amie said. 'He made us eat them. Oh, it was awful and then he turned the town against us.'

'Except the doctor and the Biars.' Joseph glanced around and pointed at the doctor leaning against a ghost gum. 'Speaking of the doctor, he needs a hospital.'

Jim and Walter helped the doctor hobble to the helicopter, while Amie, Joseph and a dubious and subdued Arthur followed them. Jim kept his promise and flew the stranded five in the Pound over the mountains back to safety of civilisation at the Mission.

Arthur insisted his daughter sit in the front with the pilot. He'd had seen enough of bird's eye views of the Central Australian wilderness and mountains, and he wanted to treat his daughter to such a visual feast.

Arthur watched his precious daughter gaze at the google expanse bathed in crimson, violet and gold of the late afternoon and the sun sinking into storm clouds.

'What you said back, down there,' Jim shouted, 'that's all a joke, isn't it?'

Amie shook her head. 'No,' she yelled in return.

'You serious?' Jim said.

Amie nodded.

Arthur realized he had some explaining to do. Some explaining that would shed new light on similar mysterious disappearances that had occurred around the world over the last few years. 'Well, actually,' he leaned toward Jim and spoke close to his earmuff, 'there's something you should know about the crashed craft on the mountain.'

'Erm, what?'

'It's a bus.'

'Right,' Jim said. 'I think there's a special force that deals with that. I'll let them know and be calling for back-up.'

'I see.'

'Tell no one.'

'I see.'

'I mean it.'

'Yeah, but look!' Arthur's heart skipped a beat as he pointed at the gathering of people around a campfire on the northern mountain summit. 'I see them! There they are!'

Jim swooped the helicopter in as close safely possible—close enough that the people rose from their fire-sitting and waved at them. Close enough that Arthur saw Carol's face beaming as she recognised Amie and Amie squealing with joy to see her mum and brother. But Joseph sank into the shadows of the copter and pretended he was still lost.

Jim circled the helicopter around the summit while radioing for help to lift those stranded on the peak. He spoke into his com in code, summoning, Arthur assumed, those special forces. Somehow Arthur had always suspected aliens existed and that someone somewhere on the Earth knew about them and kept such knowledge a secret from the general human population. After his unfortunate encounter with Boris, he was certain.

'Now, as I said,' Jim turned and then yelled to Arthur, 'best you forget this ever happened to you. Once your statements have been taken, I mean.'

Arthur shrugged. 'Who'd believe us?'

After all the excitement, the trip back to The Mission was a blur. Amie watched her father doze and snore. Never had the sound of snoring been so sweet.

At The Mission, special delegates from the IGSF (Intergalactic Space Fleet) who seemed to know all about Boris and his antics, interviewed Amie and her family, Joseph and his mother and father and the German tourists. All separately. The interviews dragged on throughout the night, yet having someone listen to her story, energised Amie. She couldn't sleep and reckoned not even a long drawn-out Russian movie would send her to sleep.

Morning, as the sun peeped over the nearby hills, Amie strolled past the empty basketball courts in search of Joseph. They'd arranged to meet there after their respective interviews.

A figure, a silhouette against the pastel rays leaned against a pole. Amie's heart pounded. She ran to the figure. 'Joseph!'

She stopped short.

Adam walked towards her. He grinned; his mouth stretched from ear to ear.

Amie raked her hair, matted and dry from a severe lack of showers and shampoo. *Just like Adam to butt in and ruin things*.

'He's not here,' Adam seemed to take pleasure in her pain.

'He'll come, though.'

Adam shook his curly mop. 'No, he won't'

'What d'ya mean?'

'They're gone, and that included your lover boy.' Adam giggled.

'But...he—they wouldn't.' Amie thumped the pole. The galvanized iron canopy rumbled.

'Couldn't get away fast enough.' More titters.

'How do you know?'

'Saw 'em go.' Adam sounded convincing, but Amie refused to be convinced.

'Liar!'

'No, true, I'm serious.' Adam looked straight at Amie. He tried his best to contort his mouth into a serious expression. 'I came out from the interview, and there they were, the Von Smith Family, piling into the Community Artists' van with a couple of those artists who helped Dad, and then driving off into the distance with a cloud of dust behind them.'

'I don't believe you!' Amie stormed off to Walter Wenke's cottage.

At the kitchen table, her father and Walter had patched up their differences over a souvenir mini mug of Tawney.

'Is it true that the Smiths have gone?' Amie demanded.

Dad nodded.

Her mum clattered away washing the breakfast dishes. *God! That sound annoyed her.*

'Mum!' Amie screamed. 'Did they leave? Did they?'

'Yes, dear.'

'*It'snot* fair!' Amie stormed to her designated room at the end of the hallway. She shoved open the door, then slammed it behind her, and then pounced on her bag. As she rifled through her bag in search of her mobile phone, she muttered like a mantra, 'I will search—Myface—Titter—I'll do what it takes to find him.'

In the background, her mother's voice rang loud and clear. 'She'll get over him.'

'No, I won't,' Amie sobbed. 'No, I won't!'

***

As the Fleischer family returned to Adelaide and ordinary life, the extraordinary faded into the background but never completely left them. And although Amie moved on with her life, after failing in her attempts to find Joseph, she never forgot him nor the Lost World of the Wends.

Some Years Later...

...in Central Australia

Amie scooped up a forkful of apple kuchen. The spiced cooked apples blended with the crumbly biscuit topping and cream melted in her mouth. *Divine! Absolutely divine!* On a neighbouring table of the Precinct Café, a handful of German tourists struggled to praise the same perfect dish. Amie had it on good authority from her friends who owned a bakehouse in Hahndorf that the German tourists were the most challenging to please. *Still, it never ceases to amaze me why Germans would want to visit a German town when touring. Bit like me going to Germany to see kangaroos and koalas in a zoo. No wonder they're picky.*

The Germans continued to bicker over imaginary faults in the dish, the weather—couldn't fault that either; a perfect July day, sunny and twenty-three degrees—and then the atmosphere—*what do they expect? Disneyland?* Amie smiled and then savoured another spoonful of heaven.

Dan, now a detective inspector with the South Australian Police Force, returned from his mission to the counter, armed with a tray laden with a pot of tea and several cups. He placed them on the outdoor table. 'It's serve yourself,' he said.

'Thanks Dan,' Arthur said.

'You're welcome.' Dan delivered a cup to Amie, her father, and then took one of the two remaining for himself.

'You've got too many there,' Amie observed. She had come up to The Mission with her father. She'd finished an Arts degree at University the previous year and jobs being scarce for Arts graduates back in Adelaide, she had leapt at the opportunity to work in the Centre at the local mission store for a few months. Her Dad, of course, couldn't resist another pilgrimage to the Centre. And what do you know, he could not resist informing her, Walter Wenke had taken a break from his busy schedule as a leading Physicist to also revisit his favourite town, as he called it. Dad was bursting with enthusiasm the whole two-day road trip up to the Centre. *Not just sad,* Amie thought, *but tragic.* 'You have four cups and there's only three of us.'

'I know,' Dan Hooper said and then pursed his lips.

Arthur rubbed his hands together. 'Oh, a reunion! Just like old times!'

'Mr Wenke will be joining us,' Amie sighed, 'I guess.'

'Maybe,' Dan Hooper said.

Both men leant forward in their seats, faces aglow as if they were excited schoolboys sitting on spinifex bushes. Amie didn't know if she could take much more of this suspense. She checked her Myface status, still single and unemployed, and disappointed she didn't have a load of messages from well-wishers in her new adventure. After all, she'd spent two days blogging and The Mission had amazing internet coverage. *What are they waiting for? Oh, well, change the subject...*

Amie poured herself a cup of tea. 'So, D. I. Hooper, whatever happened to the fat guy on the bus? Adam said there was a man on the bus too big to fit through the window.'

Dan blushed.

'My brother reckoned he wasn't a man but a woman and that she had a baby. Then in the morning, she and the baby were helped out of the bus.'

'After it was anchored by the State Emergency Services (SES) so it wouldn't fall off the cliff,' D. I. Hooper said and then coughed.

'So, you're saying it's true?' Amie asked.

Her father's eyes widened. 'Really? He, um, she looked like a man to me.'

Dan rubbed his nose. 'I never said that. Your brother's got a fertile imagination.'

'Well? How did he get out?'

'Somehow, I don't know—jaws-of-life—bolt-cutters—crash diet—but he got out.' Dan shifted in his seat like his rear was being troubled by extra spikey spinifex. Amie guessed he'd be changing the subject in the next second or so.

A woman in a long grey dress and white pinafore approached them. With a thick German accent, she asked, 'Would you like some more of our special Apple Cake?'

'Yes, please!' Amie pushed her plate forward before looking up to see her properly.

'It's the reason our dear son Friedrich preferred to stay in the wonderful world of the Wends and why Mr Wenke—'

Amie gasped. 'Frau Biar? What are you doing here?'

'Oh, I come from time to time and help out,' Frau Biar said. 'It makes the place more authentic and they like my apple kuchen.'

'Oh, I love it!' Amie said.

'You are too kind,' Frau Biar replied with a courtesy.

They caught up in German about the Biar family and the Wend village. The community was thriving under the care of the IGSF. The Biar's farm had been blessed with abundant crops. The cows over-flowed with milk. And Herr Biar had his hands full running the farm with the help of his wife, Wilma and Friedrich. The Biars had been blessed too with a baby brother, Nathaniel for Wilma and Friedrich. 'Little Nat is three now,' Frau Biar said.

Walter waddled out of the entrance. On his rounded belly rested a tray filled with more apple kuchen. Since Amie had seen him last, just a few months ago when her father had invited him for a nostalgic slide-show night, Walter had grown around the girth another ten centimetres. *He better not get stuck in a bus on the edge of a cliff...*Amie lifted a hand to her mouth to mask a giggle.

'You're not goin' to eat that all yourself, are you Wenke?' Arthur said.

'Oh, no!' Walter replied. 'I'll be sharing it with the doctor. He insists on Kaffe und Kuchen three o'clock sharp, every day while he visits. You know, Dr Zwar? He's been helping me with my family history and details on the Wends.'

Amie glanced from Frau Biar to Mr Wenke. 'How is that possible?' She was sure the IGSF disabled both trans-warp devices to prevent Boris from returning like the terminator and announcing, "I'm back!" before wreaking havoc with baby killing and eating and his plagues of cockroaches.

Mr Wenke lowered his massive tray to the table and tapped his nose. 'That's why I'm now senior world-renown Physicist.' He puffed up his chest, picked up the tray of kuchen and strutted along the garden path, over the sandy common area and out of the Precinct.

When he had disappeared, and Amie was sure he couldn't hear them, she muttered, 'Heaven help us!'

Her Dad patted her hand. 'But he's the good Walter. And besides, he's assured us there is no way Boris can get anywhere near Earth in a hurry or any time in the next millennia.'

'I hope so, because if Boris does return, he'd make a beeline for Walter,' Amie said. 'He likes a bit of meat on his victims.'

'Well, then, I guess that's why you and that old boyfriend of yours were safe,' her father said.

'Dad!'

Her father smirked. 'I wonder whatever happened to him?'

'I don't know, he seemed to fall off the face of the Earth,' Amie said with a stab of pain in the pit of her stomach. She stirred her tea and pretended to be cool about the non-event of her love-life.

'Now, dear, just because someone is not on Myface or Tatter or whatever in the computer world, doesn't mean they don't exist,' her Dad said.

'Might as well.' Amie bit her lip before taking a deep breath and saying. 'Anyway, I'm getting on with my life.'

D. I. Hooper snorted. Pretty rude of him, Amie thought.

Frau Biar stood there like a Madam Torsades wax replica of a German Frau although if she grinned any harder cracks at the side of her face might appear. *What is going on?*

Amie lifted her cup of Earl Grey to her lips. Gingerly she took a sip and swirled the hot liquid in her mouth. Tea, nothing like it! Refreshing on a hot day, warming on a cool day, and just perfect on a perfect day...what better way to wash down heavenly kuchen and the strange antics of one's elders. In the pregnant pause of her elders' grins and sniggers, Amie gulped the tea down and took another sip. *What is wrong with them?*

Dan Hooper nudged the air near Amie's face. 'We have a surprise for you, Amie.'

'Oh, Amie!' Frau Biar said.

'What?' *Belated twenty first birthday? The appearance of the lead singer of her favourite band? Boris' head on a plate? What?*

'There you are! What's taken you so long?' Dan stood up.

'Been a lot to do, mate since you deserted me for the big smoke down south,' the young man said. His voice sounded familiar.

Amie twisted around to see this man.

Who was he? This man, with a muscular build, in the uniform of the territory, cropped hair in line with the thin blue of the profession. For a moment the heat of anger rose. *How dare they! Match-make!*

'Hi Amie,' he said. 'Remember me?'

***

A week later, Joseph drove Amie in his Toyota Hilux which was shrouded with the obligatory red dust, to The Spring. They climbed hand in hand to the cave.

Joseph explained that after his parents were rescued and he unwillingly reunited with them, his father insisted they escape the Centre, and flee as far from it as humanly possible. His parents ended up in Strahan, Tasmania—a compromise—as his mother didn't want to go to ends of the earth like Siberia. He had intended to find Amie and contact her, but soon after the IGSF interviewed him, they called him up to serve in a mission to fight against Boris' army which threatened to destroy the Wends on their World. This required some travelling through inter-stellar wormholes and travelling at the speed of light so while years passed on earth, only a few months progressed for him.

'I'm so thankful to Mr Wenke, Dan Hooper and Frau Biar who have made it possible to see you again,' Joseph said as they reached the cave.

Amie hugged him. 'So am I.'

Joseph brushed his nose against Amie's face. 'I love you, Amie,' he said.

'I love you, too.' Amie tingled all over as she closed her eyes and positioned her lips to be kissed by Joseph.

'I like him, too,' a man said.

Amie froze. Her eyes sprang open. 'What?'

Joseph twisted his head around. 'Nathan! I told you to wait!'

Amie peered over Joseph's shoulder. 'Nathan? You're alive!'

'Why wouln'I be?'

'Yeah, well,' Joseph said, 'now you know who I've been working with.'

'In that special space thingy?' Amie said.

Joseph placed a finger to her lips. 'Shhh! And here, he's my assistant, so to speak.'

'I mind the cave 'n make sure no nasty cockroaches come out.' Nathan leaned back against the white tree trunk. 'I like it here. I like the view of the Pound. My country.'

'He plays an important role keeping Earth and the World of the Wends safe,' Joseph said.

Nathan nodded. 'For the here 'n now.' He nodded again. 'We wait. That big cockroach never dies. That Boris could have a son and daughter.' He swept his hand tracing the sky. 'We safe now. But we wait and watch.'

The End...or is it?

ABOUT THE AUTHOR

Lee-Anne Marie Kling graduated from Adelaide University with a Bachelor of Arts majoring in English and Japanese. She also trained as a high school teacher and taught junior high school and primary school in Melbourne, Victoria. Lee-Anne worked as a Research Officer publishing three research reports of youth needs in towns in Victoria and southern New South Wales. She lives in Adelaide, South Australia with her husband and is mother of two adult sons. She is also an artist and enjoys travelling, especially exploring the Australian outback. She has travelled overseas to Japan and Europe. Her experiences teaching, travelling, and raising her sons have provided inspiration for her writing.

Other Works (Available on Amazon):

Science Fiction

> *The Hitch-hiker*
> *Mission of the Unwilling*

Travel/Memoir

Trekking With the T-Team: Central Australian Safari 1981

www.ingramcontent.com/pod-product-compliance
Lightning Source LLC
Chambersburg PA
CBHW072053170626

46813CB00004B/1329